Impending

A Genealogical Mystery

by

Richard Davidson

Imp Mysteries Volume 4

Books by Richard Davidson:
Self-help:
DECISION TIME! Better Decisions for a Better Life

Mysteries:
The Lord's Prayer Mystery Series
Lead Us Not into Temptation
Give Us this Day Our Daily Bread
Forgive Us Our Trespasses
Thy Will Be Done
Deliver Us from Evil

Imp Mysteries:
Implications
Impulses
Impostor
Impending

Anthology: (Editor)
Overcoming: An Anthology by the Writers of OCWW

This book is a work of historical fiction. Any resemblance of foreground characters and created story scenes to actual events or persons, living or dead, is entirely coincidental. Background events and characters are drawn from historical records.

"Impending," by Richard Davidson
ISBN 978-0-9976381-2-7
A Genealogical Mystery

Published 2017 by RADMAR Publishing Group, P.O. Box 425, Northbrook, IL 60065, U.S.A.
Manufactured in the United States of America

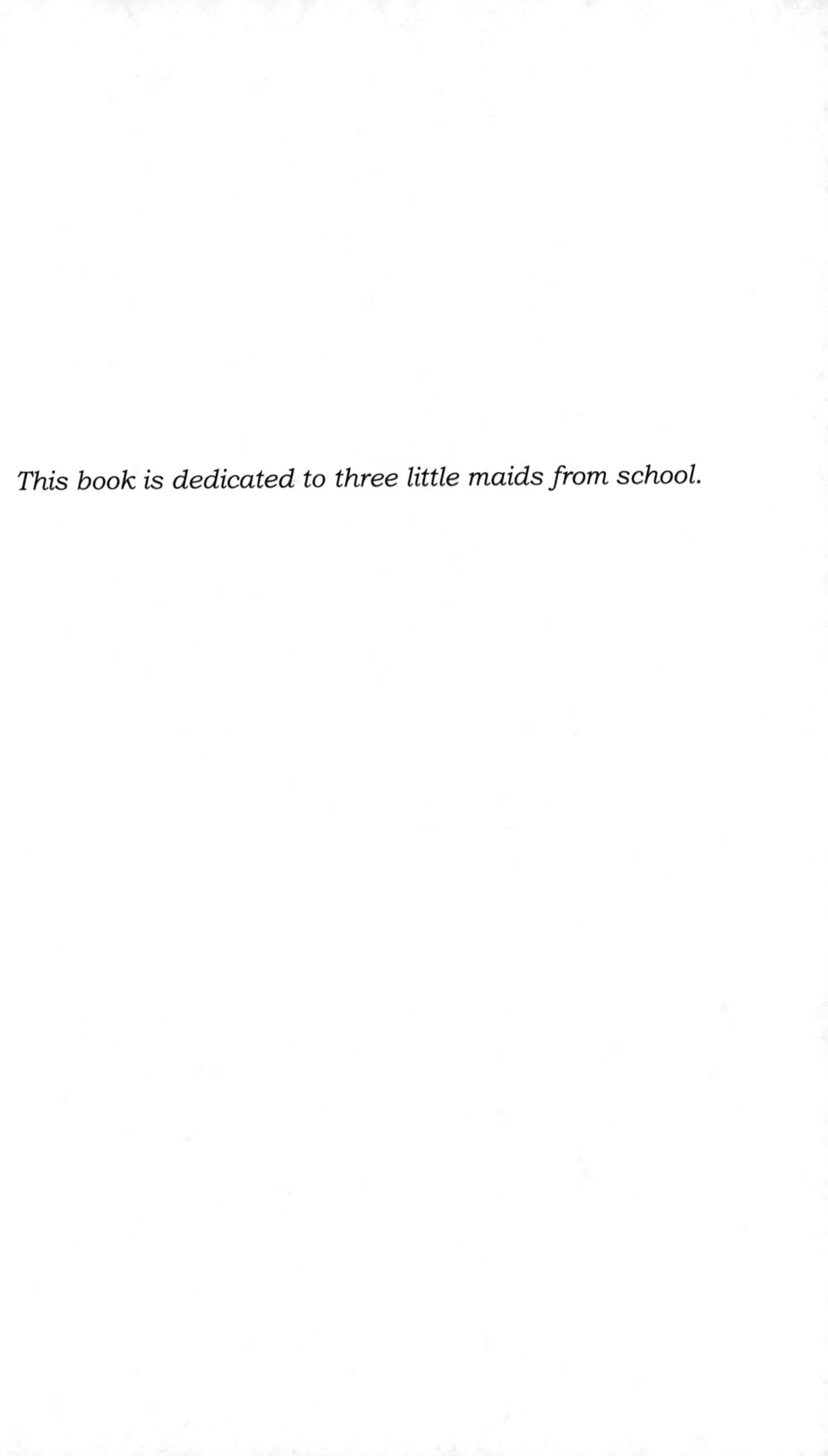

This book is dedicated to three little maids from school.

CHAPTER 1 – CONTACT

As the telephone rang for the third time, Debbie Hadley hurried through the front door of the apartment. It was home but also served as headquarters for the detective agency that she and her husband Jeremy operated. She dropped her grocery bags on the couch, grabbed pen and paper, and ran to the telephone. They needed a new case to investigate, and this might be it.

She lifted the handset from its desktop cradle and inserted a smile into her voice as she pushed some errant hair away from her right eye. "Sandley Agency – Debbie Hadley speaking; may I help you?"

"Hi, Debbie; it's Jeremy. Your grandmother called. It was the first time I talked to Marie, because we didn't include her in our rushed wedding. I left my note about the conversation on my desk rather than near the phone, so I thought I'd better call to make sure you found it. She said it was urgent."

"Clue me in. What's bothering her?"

"She said that there's a problem with the Danforth family secret. Marie wants us to visit her right away to discuss it. She says she'll need our detective skills."

"I don't know about any Danforth family secret. Are you sure that's what she said, Jeremy? And why are you calling her Marie instead of Grandma?"

"She said she would feel younger if I called her Marie. She gave me the impression that this secret was a big deal, but she wouldn't say any more. I thought you'd know about it. Call her if you need more info."

"Honestly, Jeremy, I never heard about a secret. I'll call her now."

Debbie disconnected from Jeremy and keyed in the familiar number for her father's mother. "Hi, Grandma; I'm sorry that our wedding was so small and spur-of-the-moment that you weren't able to be there."

"Don't fret about that; we'll make up for it. Jeremy sounds like a movie star, but I can't remember which one. Anyway, I told him to call me Marie, so you probably should too. It will make me feel younger and on an equal footing with you when we work on our project together."

"It will seem strange to hear myself saying Marie, but if that's your wish, I'll adapt. Now, what's this project you mentioned?"

"I need you to come help me solve a major problem concerning our family secret."

"What family secret, Gran ... Marie? There's nothing unusual about the Danforth family beyond our zest for solving both our own and other people's problems."

"I hope you and Jeremy are available to visit and assist me. I don't discuss secrets on the telephone."

"We'll leave for your place tomorrow morning. From here in Parkville, Illinois to your place in Stevens Point, Wisconsin should take about three hours. That should get us there by the early afternoon. Is this a new or an old secret? I never heard even a whisper about such a thing during my growing-up years."

"Our family secret is very old indeed, but we'll have no more discussion of that subject until you arrive here. I'll see you tomorrow."

CHAPTER 2 - MARIE

Marie replaced the telephone handset onto its wall-mounted cradle and sat at the kitchen table. She stared at the walls and cabinets around her. *Yes, the family secret dates back many years, as does this farmhouse, and for that matter, as do I.*

The pine doors on the cabinets had long since lost their protective finish, and the old red and black linoleum floor showed cracks and worn spots, but this kitchen was her favorite room in this most wonderful of homes. She and Gregory had built it with very little outside help. As Marie looked at herself in the mirror on the wall by the back door, she tried to overlook the recent increase in the roundness of her figure. Instead, she thought back to when her reflected image had been young and trim. This same kitchen had hosted many tender moments, like the time when her son Max, Debbie's father, as a youth had brought home a young fox with a broken leg. She had helped him set and splint it, thinking as she did that he might be on his way to becoming a veterinarian. Instead, he had opted to care for human patients and had applied his eventual medical training to missionary medicine. He had taken his portable medical practice to many areas of the rural United States and the islands of the Caribbean, growing ever more dependent on an air taxi pilot named Trish whom he inevitably married. Now Marie was summoning her granddaughter, Debbie, the offspring of that union and a missionary to others in her own way, to aid their proud family with its problem.

Marie had joined the Danforth family after having met her late husband Greg at the Appalachian Mountain

Club's hut at the peak of New Hampshire's Mount Washington. They had verbally fenced with witty conversational thrusts, slashes, and parries while working together on the early morning sandwich assembly and packaging line. Later, they disentangled themselves from their respective climbing groups in favor of descending from the summit together. Several frenetic months later, Marie O'Hara gave her enthusiastic consent to becoming Marie Danforth. Not only had Marie received a warm welcome into the family, but she also found herself gradually becoming the primary gatekeeper for interactions among the various Danforths. Whenever someone wanted to organize a group activity or family gathering he or she would seek Marie's approval before pursuing the matter further. When Marie later shepherded her son Max through Cub Scouts, she realized that she had become a Den Mother in both the scouting and family senses of the term. All the Danforths gravitated to her when they had confidential matters to discuss. She appreciated their trust, but felt increasingly burdened by it, especially when she was privy to secrets from both sides in a marital conflict.

The confidences had grown into dependencies, to the point where, at one difficult point in Marie and Greg's marriage, his siblings and parents had dissuaded Greg from a threatened divorce because they needed Marie to guide them and mediate their disputes. The Danforth family needed Marie, and she needed them, because she had found inner peace by becoming important to others.

CHAPTER 3 – ARRIVAL

After parking in the driveway, Jeremy took three steps toward the front door before Debbie stopped him.

"Not that way; Grandma always entertains visitors in her kitchen. Follow me down the flagstone path to the back door."

Jeremy let Debbie take the lead while he scanned the bushes, casual plantings and backyard garden, appreciating their neatness of layout, while also observing the rich mixtures of plants that screamed deliberate haphazardness. *You can learn a lot about people from their gardens and bookshelves. Marie contributed to Debbie's development. They both appreciate simple structures but have unexpectedly diverse interests.*

Debbie gave the familiar shave-and-a-haircut knock on the kitchen door. Jeremy heard two answering knocks against the inside of the door before it was thrown open to reveal a short smiling woman with dark curly hair wearing a flowered apron over blue jeans and a black blouse.

"Come on in, you two. I didn't expect you for a while, so I started to make some cookies. I'll finish them later." She greeted both of them with hugs. "Good to finally meet you, Jeremy. You're a bit taller than I imagined, but not quite out of my hugging range. Debbie, you're as fit and unique as ever. You positively hurdled those three steps to the back porch before you did your favorite knock. I watched you from the window over the sink. You make me want to be back in my twenties again. It's great to see you both."

Debbie laughed as she examined her grandmother's outfit. "Most women wear an apron to protect a favorite dress, but jeans have always been the preferred garment you'd want to shield."

"I'll bet you don't even own an apron. You're too sophisticated for old-fashioned country styles."

Jeremy joined the banter. "She does own one, Marie, but it's a denim shop type that she wears while working on technical and craft projects in our back room."

Marie raised her right eyebrow in a questioning manner. "I assume that you have some luggage and will stay here for a day or two while we discuss the family problem. Jeremy, why don't you bring whatever you have into the house while I have a brief chat with Debbie? Then we'll get you folks settled in the guest room."

Jeremy took his cue and went out to the car.

Debbie sat at the oval-shaped kitchen table across from Marie. "I could ask you about the increased size of the kitchen and the new island counter in the middle of it, but you sounded as though you wanted some one-on-one time with me."

"I'm glad you spotted the changes. I hardly ever used the dining room during the seven years since your grandfather died, so I put some of our savings into tearing out the dividing wall and making the kitchen spacious and more welcoming. I hope you like it."

"I do. It has more of your *let's get down to business* style. Speaking of that, what has to be between just us girls?"

Marie checked that Jeremy was not about to come back through the kitchen door. "I want Jeremy to see our family as welcoming and enthusiastic about all matters, but several relationships have soured. We now have four family factions that rarely communicate with each other. Three of them are here in Wisconsin, and one group of families has moved to Jacksonville, Florida."

"Are those divisions and conflicts due to what you called the family secret?"

"To some extent, but some of it is due to indiscretions among marital partners during multi-couple vacation trips. Frustrations and temptations don't mix well."

Debbie stood, looked out the window, and then stared down at her seated grandmother. "Jeremy's on his way back. I want to stress that he and I have no secrets from each other. You don't have to shield him from family squabbles, because I'll tell him anyway. We have a detective agency business, and we couldn't do a good job at it without sharing all of our information. He's new to you, but he's not an outsider. He's as much family as I am."

Jeremy opened the door. "Is it safe to come back now? I don't want to intrude on your catching up with personal matters."

Marie stood and waved him in. "Jeremy, please excuse my excess of caution. I didn't know enough about your relationship with Debbie, so I had to find out for myself. Your wife declared that you have no secrets from each other, so after Debbie leads you to the guest room and the two of you take some time to freshen up, come back here, and I'll continue the discussion of family matters among the three of us."

A short while later, Debbie and Jeremy returned to find Marie reading a newspaper while seated in a black wooden rocking chair with gold trim accents.

Debbie said, "I didn't see that rocking chair in here when we first came in. Did you just move it into the kitchen?"

Marie folded the newspaper and dropped it into a magazine rack. "Your mind is as sharp as ever. If I were to stand up, you would see that there is a crest with the name Danforth underneath it on the chair back. Several members of the family bought this for me a few years ago.

They called it a token of their respect, which I appreciated. I sit on the rocker whenever I conduct family meetings."

Jeremy sat at the kitchen table and gestured for Debbie to sit next to him. "I take it from that statement that we are about to have an official family meeting of some sort."

"We are about to have a discussion that may determine the destiny of the Danforth family."

CHAPTER 4 – ROOTS AND BRANCHES

Marie leaned back in her rocking chair. "To begin with, our family name was not always Danforth. Before our people came to America, it was Dernford in early England. We have an old family, and it's rather loosely connected. One of the earliest to head to America from England was Nicholas Danforth of Framlingham, England whose family settled in Massachusetts shortly after the Pilgrims arrived there. Others settled in Georgia, North Carolina, and Kentucky. One early settler of interest was Asa Danforth who served in the Revolutionary War under his father, Colonel Keyes Danforth, and fought at the Battles of Lexington, Bunker Hill, and Saratoga. Asa and his family later settled in the state of New York where they lived in close contact with the Onondaga and Oneida Indians. Other Danforths in that same area a little later included David Danforth who married Paulina Richmond who was descended from Thomas Rogers, a *Mayflower* Pilgrim. They gave birth to Jonathan Richmond Danforth in 1809, and he, moved to Portage, Wisconsin in the 1850s, where his wife Phoebe died in 1857. Jonathan joined the Wisconsin 18th Infantry Regiment during the Civil War and died at Grand Junction in Tennessee of disease in November of 1862.

"Many of the other Danforths followed Jonathan's pattern of moving from New York and other eastern states to Wisconsin during the first half of the nineteenth century, so that by the beginning of the Civil War, there were many Danforths living in our state. Some of them included members of the Oneida Indian tribe either through intermarriage in New York State or through later

Wisconsin marriages. After the war, Danforth veterans and widows throughout the state and among the Oneidas received average pensions of eight dollars per month."

As Marie paused for a breath, Debbie interrupted her. "This family background is all very interesting, but does it have anything to do with this family secret you mentioned in entreating us to visit you?"

"Indeed it does, granddaughter, so be a good young person and listen to Marie for just a little while longer."

"May I get a drink to improve my attention span?"

"Help yourselves to iced tea or soda pop in the refrigerator."

Debbie and Jeremy poured drinks and returned to their seats.

Marie leaned forward on her chair. "I'll skip the details on the Wisconsin Danforths and jump ahead to events that led to our family secret. It all started at Gettysburg.

...

CHAPTER 5 - GETTYSBURG

Debbie and Jeremy found themselves leaning forward on their chairs to be sure they didn't miss any of Marie's softly-intoned narrative.

Rain, mud, and blood marked the takeover of the Spangler farm on Blacksmith Shop Road in Gettysburg, Pennsylvania on July 1, 1863 as the battling Union and Confederate forces surging back and forth left many mangled bodies in their wake. George Spangler's farm became the main battlefield hospital, although every farm quartered some of the wounded. During the course of the three-day Battle of Gettysburg, more than 1800 Union soldiers and 100 Confederates would be treated at the Spangler farm. Because of heavy rains the basements of those buildings that had them were flooded. Many of the wounded faced treatments and operations outside under the eaves of Spangler's massive barn, with rainwater splashing them as it cascaded from the roof. Seven Union surgeons under the direction of Dr. Daniel G. Brinton of Chester, Pennsylvania tried desperately to keep up with the incoming wounded. Most serious limb wounds led to amputations using the same tools and cloths on multiple patients without any form of sanitizing between operations. Cries of anguish both inside and outside the barn were so frequent that they had become commonplace and partially overlooked by both medical staff and post-surgery patients. Those with major head and body trauma were deemed mortally wounded and given only pain-killer treatments to ease their inevitable transition to death. This is the story of one such patient. We look in on him inside the barn on July 3rd two days after he was shot during the first round of fighting. Doctors and assistants rush back and forth, trying to cope with the screams and chaos around them. Our patient, an officer, talks with a private he has had brought to his bedside following that enlisted man's lower leg amputation.

"Danforth, I've discovered an intriguing aspect of this process of dying; and the surgeon assures me that I have no hope of eluding death. My epiphany is that I am now living in the past, present and future, all at the same time. To be precise, I am in quite present agony because of the minié ball that pierced my left side and shattered to slice up my bowels. The doctor managed to clamp off the bleeding, but I'm oozing other fluids into my gut and none of my internal plumbing works anymore. I'm living in the past, because in distant time periods I actually am seeing various segments of my life as I prepare for death. In the recent past, I'm wondering how a Confederate soldier could have shot me in the left side as I stood behind the center of our ranks urging the men forward into a stand of trees during the very first volley of this battle. One of our own men must have shot me, either accidentally or on purpose. The how and why don't really matter at this point. I'm afraid that in death I'll have a kinship with that graycoat, Stonewall Jackson, who was also shot by his own people at Chancellorsville a couple of months ago. He held off death for eight days. I doubt that I'll last that long. The battle here at Gettysburg is still raging, and I don't expect to outlive its hostilities by more than a day or two."

"Hey, Doc, it hurts pretty badly. Could you conjure up another one of those opium pills? ... Better make it two ... and I think Danforth, here, could use one too after his amputation. Thanks."

"Getting back to my living in other times, I feel as though I'm in the future, because while I'm closed up here in Spangler's barn, my mind sees many acres covered with bodies of men and horses, plus gravestones everywhere. They're going to write books about the thousands on both sides who died here at Gettysburg, and I refuse to be one of their anonymous numbers. I'm drafting you to document that I've had a good life, Private Danforth. Your job will be to tell my story to others so that I won't be completely forgotten. I reckon that the closest thing people have to life after death is someone remembering them.

"Yes, I realize that you have your own wound to worry about, but you'll get over that amputation below your left knee. They'll give you a wooden leg, and you'll go back to civilian life. I wish you the very best of futures. I'm picking on you to be the keeper of my memories because I've seen you writing long letters home. That tells me that you know how to handle the language and that you have caring people to share stories with. Both of those things suit my goals and portend a thriving life for you. Don't get me wrong; I'll see that you're paid for passing along my story. My brother Charlie is here with the Wisconsin Sharpshooters, and I'll ask him to take care of your needs. Your first name is Cyrus, isn't it?"

"It is, sir."

"As I said earlier, people are going to think of those dying here at Gettysburg as faceless entries in record books. You're going to remind them that I was a human being with a damned interesting life. Here we go; you should start writing now.

"My full name is George Henry Stevens, although I'm known to most as George H. Stevens. I doubt that many know my middle name ... I'm rambling a bit. Between the pain and those pills, it's a little hard to think straight.

"I guess I was one of the lucky ones, being born into a family of some means in New York City and later educated in private schools there. My birth date was December 8, 1831, just about thirty-one-and-a-half years ago. My parents were socially active, due to my father, John, being a shipping merchant. He and my mother, Lucy, were well regarded, both for their personalities and for Dad's ability to import hard-to-obtain commodities for the upper class folks. I was the fourth of five children and the only one who left New York looking for adventure and opportunity at an early age. Actually, my adventures started in New York City, following the Astor Place riot in 1849. I joined the 7th Regiment of the National Guard after seeing how well the militia handled the angry mob. Their acts of courage convinced me that there was something special about a military life, at least for a while. Without additional riots to put down, I became bored as a member of the Guard, and in 1852, at twenty-one years of age, I drew upon my father's shipping connections to secure a passage to Australia. I had always considered that a special place with great challenges and opportunities for young people.

"Unfortunately, the real Australia didn't match my fantasies. Most of the country was completely undeveloped, and there were far too few women to satisfy the number of men there. I tried several business ventures in Australia, but most of them were a waste of time. Romances weren't successful either. I finally gave up and returned to the States and New York in the summer of 1855. Fortunately, my old friends and contacts pointed me toward an opportunity in Milwaukee, going into the retail business with a local man named V. V. Livingston."

"Hey, Doc, that pill's wearing off. Get me another one when you get a chance."

"As I was saying, I ended up working a business in Milwaukee, and in my spare time I took another crack at the military by joining the Second Company Light Guard. It was more of a fraternal group than a regiment, and I won a prize medal as the best drilled member. I was a sergeant then. The combination of military and merchant work led me to move to Fox Lake, Wisconsin in the fall of 1858, where I opened a grocery store and sent for my brother Charlie to help me run it."

"Double thanks, Doc; I won't take the second pill until I really need it. I have to keep my head clear while I tell Danforth my story. He's a good listener and writes well too."

"Things get slow in Fox Lake during the winter months, so I organized a voluntary military unit I called the Citizens Guard. It kept me interested in something beyond business. ... I shouldn't say that. I was involved at the Congregational Church, even though my parents had raised me Episcopalian. Through church contacts, I met Harriet Purdy and married her in 1859 on March 23rd. If she were here, she'd be pleased that I remember our wedding date.

"Harriet and I had some good times together, despite the separations caused by my military obligations and the war. Our son Walter was born in February of 1860, and she's carrying a second child right now. I won't be around for him or her, but I hope Harriet raises that child to think well of me. You'll have to greet that new child for me, Danforth.

"Anyway, in April of 1861, When President Lincoln called for more troops to put down the rebellion, they gave me a commission as a captain and instructed me to reorganize my Citizens Guard unit and recruit more men for it. We met our requirement right away and marched to Camp Randall in Madison. There, we were renamed Company "A" of the Second Regiment Wisconsin Volunteer Infantry, and were the first unit to change our enlistment from three months to three years. They transported our regiment to Washington, D.C., and we saw our first action at the First Battle of Bull Run.

"Following Bull Run, there were a whole string of battles, some with the 2nd Wisconsin acting alone, and later as part of the Iron Brigade, which included the 2nd, 6th, and 7th Wisconsin regiments plus regiments from Indiana and Michigan. At Second Bull Run, I ended up in command of the 2nd Wisconsin as a captain because of the loss of the colonel and the wounding of the lieutenant colonel. I missed the Antietam battle because of illness. – There was so much of that among the troops everywhere. I was a major, serving under Burnside at Fredericksburg, and a lieutenant colonel under Hooker at the Second Battle of Fredericksburg. We had an intense skirmish with the enemy at Fitz-Hugh Crossing just prior to the Chancellorsville combat, but we weren't involved in the main event there.

"Hold it for a minute, Danforth, while I take my reserve opium pill."

"You've been through so much, sir. I didn't join the Second Wisconsin until just after Second Fredericksburg. I was with you at that skirmish before Chancellorsville, and then got hit with you the day before yesterday."

"Yes, July first was the capper, in several ways. You're done with soldiering and will go home to be with your family. I'm on my way out and will go home to God. I'll soon find out what He thinks of soldiers and our killing each other.... I started to say *old soldiers*, but I won't live to see my thirty-second birthday. The worst damn thing about July first isn't that we got hit during the first full-scale volley of this battle, but that the 2nd Wisconsin lost so many men. Doc told me that only 34 men were present for roll call on Cemetery Hill at the end of that day. We started the day with 306 men, 278 of whom were combatants. That's the number that fought in the morning to keep the Confederates, under Archer, from breaking through from McPherson Ridge to the heights on Cemetery Hill. We held them back, but due to the way we recruit units made up of neighbors, there are going to be many villages in Wisconsin without any young men left.

"Believe it or not, Danforth, you're one of the lucky ones. These surgeons and self-trained medical people can save those wounded in their limbs by means of amputations, but a snowball in hell has a better chance of surviving than those of us who were hit in the head or the gut. Then there are all those who die from diseases before the battles even start. I wonder if men on the two sides of this war will ever be friends again.... God, this gut of mine hurts. The pills don't nearly free me from pain."

"I've taken seven pages of notes, sir. I think that's enough for now. You try to rest. As soon as there's a lull in the fighting, I'll send one of the medical assistants to fetch your brother, Charlie. Sharpshooters don't fight after the sun sets, not that there is much sun getting through the battle smoke and frequent rainstorms. We'll get him here in time. I promise."

Lieutenant Colonel George H. Stevens succumbed on July 5, 1863, two days after the fighting at Gettysburg ceased. His remains were buried at Evergreen Cemetery in Gettysburg, with his family stating that they planned to take him back to Wisconsin after the war ended. Thanks to the dedication of a new National Cemetery adjacent to Evergreen on November 19, 1863, marked by Lincoln's Gettysburg Address, the Stevens family decided that he should permanently rest there. He is buried in a grave immediately behind and to the left of a large marker that reads WISCONSIN 73 BODIES.

Marie Danforth continued her tale. "Death didn't end the story of George H. Stevens' connection to our family. Before he died, he had a second confidential meeting with Private Cyrus Danforth, uninterrupted by the busy surgeons. During that session they reached the agreement that constitutes our family secret."

CHAPTER 6 – THE SECRET

Lieutenant Colonel George Stevens leaned toward Private Cyrus Danforth. "Listen carefully, because I don't want anyone else to hear this, and I won't have the strength to talk very long. They won't think it unusual that a dying man is talking softly with a friend. You are my friend, you know. You're going to tell the world about me and together we are going to do our best to make things right for a lot of people. If you were going to continue soldiering, I'd give you a battlefield commission. You deserve recognition, but you won't see a battle again."

"I'm more than willing to help, sir, but I don't see how we could be carrying out a mission together. I don't mean to be unkind, but you are expecting to die soon."

"I'm going to give you an assignment plus the resources for carrying it out. Those resources are my half of this partnership."

"What's the assignment, sir?"

"The 2nd Regiment Wisconsin Volunteer Infantry grew out of the Citizens Guard unit I organized in Fox Lake. Because of that, I feel responsible for all the families that have had men wounded or killed here at Gettysburg and elsewhere. We did a great job keeping the rebels from gaining the Cemetery Hill high ground, but we paid a hell of a price, only 34 out of 306 men still able on the day following our battle. Because of that, I want you to distribute funds to help support each family for me."

Cyrus squirmed in his chair. "Sir, you have to support your own family and the coming new baby. You can't take money away from them and give it to strangers."

"It's alright. I told you that my family had wealth from the shipping business. My share of that will be sufficient for my wife and children. I didn't tell you everything about my time in Australia. While I was there, they discovered gold in New South Wales and other areas. I was among the first to prospect in a place called Hill End, west northwest of Sydney, and I processed a substantial amount of gold-bearing ore before that area was invaded in a gold rush by prospectors from all over the world. My gold is sitting in a bank in Sydney, waiting for me or my representative to claim it. You will be my agent and will claim that gold and use it to benefit our regiment's families. That enterprise will let me die in peace. Take this receipt documenting my ownership and this letter of agency to the Bank of New South Wales, in Sydney. They will issue you a bank draft for the current value of the gold I have stored with them. All the details required for payment are in the letter."

Danforth took the papers without examining them because he wanted to focus his attention on Stevens' soft words. "Your brother Charlie is here. Why not appoint him to be your agent?"

"That's out of the question. You mustn't mention a word about this conversation to him. Charlie would keep everything for the family. I need your loyalty to our regiment to assure that the funds are spent the way I desire."

"Very well, I'll take on your quest, sir."

"Two other things, no one is to know that the money came from me, and it must be distributed over a long period of time, so that the families won't realize that it came from a single benefactor."

"You're asking me to do the impossible, sir. How will I be able to remain invisible and still give the families their funds?"

"Be creative, Danforth. I believe that you will find ways to achieve my goal."

Cyrus shook his head. “I’ll try, but I don’t have your degree of confidence that I’ll be able to handle this quest.”

Stevens held out his hand for a confirming handshake. “All I can ask is that you try. Remember that your family and the several other Danforth families in the regiment are included in the distribution also. Now, I have to lie down. I took an opium pill halfway through our conversation, but it’s wearing off. Thank you for carrying out my last adventure for me. I doubt that we’ll talk again.”

CHAPTER 7 – DEPARTURE

Cyrus Danforth looked at his image in the mirror and wondered what he had gotten himself into. Here he stood, a hard goods store clerk from Fox Lake, Wisconsin, discharged from the Union Army after Gettysburg with a wooden replacement for his lower left leg, and he had been chosen to pursue a major quest that only started with a journey to Australia. He had never been out of Wisconsin before he joined the Army, and he had only a rough idea of what he would face on his trip to the other side of the world and back. At least Lt. Col. Stevens had given him a promissory note for the cost of his passage plus expenses, which Stevens' brother Charlie had funded. Cyrus knew that George Stevens had not wanted Charlie to know the purpose of his mission, but surprisingly, Charlie had asked no questions while supplying the funds. Danforth supposed his ready compliance to have been due to a combination of wanting to grant his late brother's dying wish and his military training to follow orders.

Cyrus knew that it would take time for the stump from his amputated lower leg to fully heal and for him to get completely acclimated to his wooden replacement, so he had deferred his journey until after the conclusion of the war. Now, in June of 1865, he knew that he had to take action on his adventure. He would follow the plan and trust that God would smile upon his endeavor.

The journey would begin in an hour with his friend and former comrade in arms, Edwin Cole taking him by wagon to the town of Prairie du Chien on the Mississippi River.

As the horse plodded along the road through the tall pine trees, Edwin displayed a big smile. "You single guys get to enjoy adventures while the rest of us have to stay home and raise our kids and crops. I envy you, but I'm satisfied with what I have. You'll probably get rich in that gold rush they have there. That's why you're going, isn't it?"

"You have me pegged right, Ed. I'm going to find out whether I'm lucky or not. I already feel fortunate to have gotten through Gettysburg with only half a leg lost. Poor George Stevens and a whole bunch of our other friends lost their lives there."

"In that sense, I'm fortunate too. I was wounded and discharged at the end of 1862, so that I was already a civilian when all hell broke loose at Gettysburg."

They emerged from the woods and slowed their pace as the road curved its way downhill toward Prairie du Chien and the river. Edwin wanted to be sure that his horse wouldn't stumble while descending the hill. After delivering Cyrus Danforth to the riverfront, he planned to stay overnight to enjoy whatever the town had to offer before returning to his wife and his tedious work routine.

When they approached the steamer dock, both men were surprised by the size of the crowd and the amount of activity they saw. The end of the war had brought the reopening of the southern portion of the Mississippi River, so that people and goods could once again travel by river to southern cities and the Mississippi Delta. It had been only a month since the surrender at Appomattox Court House, but already the number of Union military uniforms in the crowd had dwindled. This throng was primarily civilian and concerned with personal and business matters.

Cyrus climbed down from his seat, grabbed his carpet bag from the wagon bed, and gave Edwin Cole a hearty handclasp as he departed. He was alone and on his way.

His military training automatically took over as he approached the crowded dock. Instead of walking directly toward the ticket booth, he circled the crowd to get a general impression of its composition and then worked his way toward the booth by an indirect route. During his approach he picked out several likely swindlers and thieves as they scanned the crowd for easy marks. Without drawing attention to himself, he slipped into position at the ticket window immediately after an attractive woman passenger walked away. He figured that any hostile eyes would at least briefly be following her.

Once at the counter, Cyrus learned that the cost of a first class cabin fare to St. Louis was six dollars and forty cents, but that deck passage cost was half of that amount. He opted for the more expensive fare because he wanted privacy. The ticket clerk told Cyrus that he would depart aboard the steamboat *Annie Jacobs* in ninety minutes.

After leaving the ticket booth, Danforth made his way to a general store he had noticed while assessing the crowd. There, he purchased several hardware items plus a five barreled double-action Remington Elliot pepperbox revolver that he could conceal in his pocket. He had his Colt revolver from his Army days in his carpet bag, but that weapon was too large for concealment. He hoped he would never have to use the pepperbox pistol, but he had to be prepared.

Once within the privacy of his cabin on the *Annie Jacobs*, Cyrus Danforth went to work. He unstrapped his wooden leg and secured it in an upright position against his bunk. Then he reached into his carpet bag and withdrew the bit brace and auger bit he had purchased from the store. Working very carefully, so as not to crack his artificial limb, Cyrus drilled a deep half inch diameter hole down into the top of it. Then he removed George Stevens' bank agency letter and receipt from his pocket, folded them smaller, and tightly rolled them to fit into the drilled hole in his wooden leg. He plugged the end of the hole with a cork he had purchased. Danforth knew that his journey would be for naught should any adversary relieve him of those documents. He strapped his leg back on, and walked several times around the cabin to be sure that it was as comfortable and supportive as before. During his final preparation for the steamboat's departure, he hid the bit brace in a newspaper and walked to the entrance leading down to the engine room. There, he laid the newspaper on the deck while he bent down to adjust his boot. When he retrieved the newspaper and walked away, the tool remained behind. A crewman would pick it up, thinking it belonged below.

As the steamboat moved away from the dock, Cyrus Danforth strolled behind the people lining the railings, looking for anyone who appeared suspicious or likely to pose a threat. Not seeing anyone obviously out of character, he returned to his cabin. He would be reclusive during this first leg of his journey. On the *Annie Jacobs*, he had the luxury of privacy. That would not be the case on later segments of his trip.

CHAPTER 8 – ST. LOUIS AND WESTWARD

The St. Louis docks were much larger and busier than those in the Wisconsin riverfront at Prairie du Chien. Four steamboats were in pre-departure preparations, while another was discharging its passengers and freight as the *Annie Jacobs* approached the dock. Once ashore, Cyrus would inquire as to the location of the Wells Fargo stagecoach stop, and determine the schedule for coaches to California.

When he arrived at the Wells Fargo office, Cyrus Danforth learned that the first leg of his trip would not be by stagecoach but by train. The journey from St. Louis, Missouri to San Francisco, California began with a twelve hour train segment between St. Louis and Tipton, Missouri. The total trip to San Francisco was scheduled to take twenty-five days. Danforth purchased his tickets for the segmented trip and made his way to the railroad terminus.

As he approached the train, Cyrus laughed to himself at the optimism of the railroad firm. Painted on the engine, coal car, and each of the four passenger cars in large gold letters was *Pacific Railroad*. That signified enormous ambition for a train line that traveled only the one hundred and sixty miles between St. Louis and Tipton. The station platform was occupied by a large number of people of different backgrounds. He judged that most of them were making short trips, based on their assortments of items purchased in St. Louis stores and lack of baggage.

Cyrus gave the railroad credit for being businesslike when the train departed on schedule, but he realized that the more important test would be whether it arrived on time. He took a seat by a window at the rear of his car so that he could assess his fellow passengers. Once the train started on its way, he discovered that many of the people on board knew each other, and may have been traveling in groups. Several conversations were taking place among people standing in clusters around a few seated passengers. All of the speakers were talking very loudly so as to be heard over the bumping, grinding, and squealing of the engine and undercarriage mechanisms.

After multiple uncounted stops over a period of twelve hours, the train reached Tipton. Cyrus managed to nap for an hour or so along the way, but was awakened periodically by the shaking and swaying of the passenger car. The hard seat was uncomfortable, but he appreciated that he already had traveled hundreds of miles from his home in Fox Lake, Wisconsin, a small but significant start on his overall journey.

When Cyrus transferred to Wells Fargo's big Concord stagecoach at Tipton, he observed that the seats were more comfortable than those on the train, but that he would be in very close quarters with the other passengers. There would be a total of seven passengers on this trip, with only one of them, a cattle rancher, getting off in Tucson. The other five, two women and three men, would accompany him on the entire trip to San Francisco. He would do his best to be no more than surface friendly during the remaining twenty-four and a half days of the journey. He had a mission and didn't trust casual acquaintanceships.

The two women chose to sit across the narrow aisle between the facing seats from each other so that they wouldn't find themselves touching or locking knees with men. They were teachers, traveling separately, but striking up a friendship because of their common profession. One indicated she was from Boston, and the other claimed

Indianapolis as her home. Four of the five men exchanged only occasional terse comments, while the fifth, a slight bookish type started the trip proclaiming his views on a variety of topics. He was soon stared down by the other four men, including Danforth, so that the long trip proceeded in relative silence, punctuated only by soft comments between the women and occasional monosyllabic observations among the men. Cyrus wondered whether one or more of his seatmates had fought against him in the war, but he pushed that question out of his consciousness. *It will be difficult, but we have to learn to accept each other now that the war is over.*

The journey to San Francisco was divided by Wells Fargo into nine divisions, including the railroad trip to Tipton. However, there were many more stops, because each driver's responsibility was limited to taking the stage sixty miles from his home base before handing it off to a new driver. The first man would then trade off with a driver traveling in the opposite direction to guide that stage back to his home. By this procedure, none of them had to drive more than a total of one hundred and twenty miles, all of that being over a familiar stretch of road.

With the exceptions of discomfort due to intense heat while crossing the southwestern desert during early summer and the resulting body odors due to long hours wedged together in close quarters, the passengers survived their journey well. When the stagecoach finally pulled into the terminus in San Francisco, the six remaining passengers politely bid goodbye to each other, but most were more than happy to end their joint period of forced familiarity.

CHAPTER 9 – OCEAN VOYAGE

By the time Cyrus Danforth reached San Francisco, the calendar had shifted from July into August of 1865. When he reached the docks, Cyrus wandered back and forth among the booths hawking passenger bookings for the various lines, trying to get a feeling for the best way to go. He heard competing claims between lines that used sailing ships and those whose vessels were powered by steam. He also learned that some lines were well-regarded as being safe and efficient, while others had bad reputations. Conversations about the latest news concerned a recent disaster on July thirtieth. The side-wheeler steamship *Brother Jonathan*, overloaded with backlogged freight and more than two hundred passengers had run into stormy weather on its way to Portland and had struck St. George Reef near Crescent City, California. The ship sank within an hour after the collision, and even though it was close to shore, only one lifeboat had managed to get some of the crew and passengers safely to the Crescent City harbor. More than one hundred sixty passengers and crew went to the bottom that day. The conversations also concerned the large amount of gold that the ship had carried. Many wondered if it could ever be recovered.

Cyrus quickly got the message that ocean voyages, even coastal ones, were dangerous. How much worse could it be to travel the thousands of miles across the Pacific Ocean from California to Australia? Setting fear aside, Cyrus took the shipwreck as an omen that he would be better off in a sailing ship than a steamer. As he wandered on the docks, he asked several sailors and business people for their opinions and learned that the firm of Cole and Nagle used sailing ships for semi-monthly voyages to Australia. They had a good reputation and were continuously increasing their fleet to accommodate the many people interested in emigration and the Australian gold rush. He studied one of their advertisements posted on a public bulletin board:

FOR SYDNEY AND PORT PHILIP
Will sail on or about the 12th, the Medford-built live oak bark TARTAR, 650 tons, coppered and copper fastened. This spacious vessel is fitted up in the best manner. The steerage is spacious and airy ... cabin and houses on deck are very handsomely ornamented. She will be supplied, as all our vessels are, with an abundant supply of the best provisions. The owners will go with the vessel, which we presume will be a sufficient guarantee that the comforts of the passengers will be attended to.
She will carry an experienced Surgeon.
For further particulars apply to COLE & NAGLE, corner Front and Pacific Streets, San Francisco.

As Cyrus stood reading the announcement, he noticed that a woman standing slightly behind him and to his right was also reading it. He was surprised to see that she wore a long dark coat in early August. His reaction to the presence of the coat was followed by his recognition of its origin.

Cyrus turned toward the woman. “Excuse me, ma’am, but isn’t your garment a Union Army frock coat?”

“It is, sir. It belonged to my late husband who died at Gettysburg. I wear it as a symbol that he’s still in my heart.”

“Sorry for your loss. I too was at Gettysburg. A lot of brave men on both sides lost their lives there. The war is finally over now, and I hope people will be able to move on to peacetime pursuits."

She looked first at him and then at the advertisement on the wall. "You appear to be moving on. I saw you studying the poster. Will you be sailing to Australia?"

"I will. I figure I'll try my luck at gold mining. This ship, the *Tartar*, looks like a sturdy craft to get me there. Are you traveling there also?"

"I am, and perhaps on this same ship, but I don't expect to be mining."

He chose his words carefully. "I don't mean to intrude on your privacy or any of your plans, but if we are to be shipmates, perhaps we should introduce ourselves. I'm Cyrus Danforth."

"Fear not, Mr. Danforth; as a war widow, I've learned to assert myself with men in social as well as commercial situations. I'm Barbara Boynton."

"Pleased to meet you, Mrs. Boynton. Are you going to settle in Australia, or will you only visit there for a short while?"

"I'm open to both possibilities, but my initial activities will require a stay of at least two months. What are your plans, Mr. Danforth?"

"They're not yet firm. A lot will depend upon the opportunities I find after we arrive there. I'm afraid I'll have to excuse myself now in order to make the arrangements required prior to sailing. Perhaps I'll see you again on board the ship, Mrs. Boynton."

He started to walk away.

She called after him. "Mr. Danforth, I notice you have a slight limp. Would that be due to action at Gettysburg?"

"I parted with half of my left leg there, but I'm getting quite used to its replacement. Speaking of Gettysburg, what unit was your husband in?"

"Warren was in the 6th Vermont Cavalry. He was the best rider in his unit."

Cyrus waved and continued to walk away. *Vermont had only one cavalry unit at Gettysburg, and it was the 1st. That woman is lying. If her husband was killed there, I'll bet he was on the Confederate side.*

August twelfth found Cyrus climbing the gangway to the *Tartar* and being directed to his second class cabin below decks. He apparently was the first to arrive there, so he selected the lower bunk at the end of the narrow room and stowed his carpet bag and bedroll beneath it. He would have five cabin mates if the ship was fully booked. Because of that, he strapped on his Army holster and revolver underneath his coat. He also carried his smaller five-barreled pepperbox revolver in an inside pocket. He wanted to be prepared for anything, including dishonest fellow travelers.

As he walked through the sections of the ship that were open to passengers, Cyrus concluded from his infrequent encounters with civilians and the relaxed attitude of crew members that the ship would carry only about half of its maximum number of passengers. Some of the passengers he did meet appeared to be surly and potentially dangerous. He had not fought anyone since receiving his artificial leg. The pistols would be some insurance, but he would plan to exercise during rough weather to be sure he would be able to move abruptly on board the swaying ship if required to do so.

When the ship sailed, Cyrus discovered that he had only two other men in his cabin. One, giving his name as Rufus Klinger, was well-spoken and claimed to be an agent for a woolen mill, traveling to Australia to set up contracts for wool with sheep ranchers. He appeared to be no potential threat. The second man stood more than six feet tall, spoke infrequently, and said he was planning to get rich in the gold fields. He said his name was Schmidt but offered no given name. When Cyrus asked whether he had mined before, Schmidt laughed and said he would not be mining except on a social level. Despite his physical size, he was a gambler, not a laborer. Cyrus would keep his distance from both of his cabin-mates to avoid complications during their weeks of sailing.

The first few days of the voyage turned out to be easy for the passengers. The weather cooperated, allowing the ship to make good time. The total trip to Australia was scheduled to take thirty-five days, but the record for this crossing was thirty-three. The passengers at first lined the rails to observe their surroundings, but once they were out of sight of land, most lost interest, became bored, and opted for warmth and security below. Cyrus filled the endless sailing hours by exercising and observing his fellow passengers from a distance. Twice during the first three days, he thought he saw Barbara Boynton with two family groups and several single women. Cyrus didn't make contact with her because he wanted to avoid social involvements.

After five days, the weather became threatening and stormy. Passengers were restricted to the lower decks or their cabins. The crew no longer had time for interactions with the travelers. They were professionals and had faced the dangers of rough weather many times. Other vessels would reduce sail area and just try to stay secure from storms, but the reputation of the large clipper ships was that they clipped the tops of the waves rather than plowing through them. Somehow the crew managed to maintain full sail area during the stormy weather, although the effect on the passengers was dreadful. The cargo had been tied down to keep it from shifting in rough weather, but the passengers got seasick and bounced around when the ship tilted drastically. When the storms ceased, cleanups and repairs were the orders of the day.

Cyrus avoided meeting Barbara Boynton and getting dragged into her social group for three weeks. On the twenty-second day of the *Tartar's* voyage, he returned from eating to find Barbara waiting by his cabin door. She smiled at him, but had a hardened expression around her eyes. He had seen that hardness frequently in the faces of battle-weary soldiers.

"You've been avoiding me, Mr. Danforth."

"I've seen you at times, but you were always involved with a group of people, so I didn't intrude."

"In other words, you wanted to wait until you could be alone with me. If that's the case, you now have your opportunity."

"Mrs. Boynton, you're putting words in my mouth. I neither said nor implied that I wanted to see you alone."

"Call me Barbara, and I'll call you Cyrus. Formal addresses and surnames are not necessary within the close quarters of a ship. Are you saying that you don't want to see me alone?"

"I didn't say that either, Barbara."

"Good, we're past the name barrier. Now tell me why you didn't look for me, Cyrus."

"Are we being honest with each other, for a change?"

"What do you mean?"

"I said before that I wanted to avoid your social gathering, which was true, but I also had doubts about contacting you because you lied to me when we first met."

"How did I lie, Cyrus?"

"I'm sure you know the exact answer to that question, but let's start with the fact that your husband's 6th cavalry unit was not at Gettysburg. I'm not even sure that Vermont had more than the 1st cavalry regiment, which was there. If your husband did die at Gettysburg, for which, again, I'm sorry, he probably was on the Confederate side."

"You're pretty good at analyzing details. You're correct. I lived in Virginia rather than Vermont, and his unit was the 6th Virginia Volunteer Cavalry."

"Therefore, I avoided you because you might want to seek revenge against a former Union soldier for the death of your Confederate husband. By the way, I was wounded during the first volley of the first action at Gettysburg, so I didn't kill anyone."

Barbara Boynton removed her Union-issued frock coat and draped it over a railing. "Fair enough, Cyrus, my disguise is gone. To be honest, I did see you briefly as the enemy, but you mentioned that you hoped the end of the war would bring us all to civility, and I saw you differently."

"Now that we're being honest with each other, why are you really going to Australia?"

"I saw an advertisement looking for women who would be willing to go to Australia and possibly marry a settler there. The Australian government would pay all of the travel and initial residence expenses. I was running out of funds, so I accepted their offer. Is that so bad, Cyrus?"

"Not if it's the truth. I'm still not ready to completely trust you."

"I understand. Can we spend some time together during the rest of this voyage? I promise I won't involve you with a large group of people if you'd rather be alone."

Cyrus had already noticed that without the frock coat, Barbara looked much more feminine. Despite that hardness around her eyes, her dark curly hair and her small waist made her look fragile. "No guarantees that we'll end up trusting each other, and you'll have to seal your offer with a kiss."

"You drive a hard bargain, Cyrus." Barbara put her arm around his waist and pivoted her head upward to kiss him, at first gently, and then somewhat harder. She was pleased by his passionate response.

Cyrus gently separated himself from Barbara and told her that he had to attend to a task, but that he would meet her in the saloon in two hours. She looked disappointed, but he wasn't ready to completely revise his initial assessment of her without confirmation. He walked away without turning back.

After a brief stop in the saloon for a shot of fortifying whiskey, Cyrus climbed to the ship's deck. As he went outside, he felt a blast of moist air against his face. He scanned the horizon and the sky. The weather had moderated, but they were still running at less than full speed because of headwinds. The ship had its first class cabins at the deck level, and he needed to visit one of them. He turned toward the stern and made use of every available handhold as he eased himself toward his destination. A slip earlier in the voyage had taught him that an artificial limb may not completely cooperate on a wet deck. He knocked on the cabin door.

The door swung open at the hand of a silver-haired man wearing a smoking jacket. "Private ... I mean Cyrus Danforth, come on in. It takes a while to get away from military conversation style."

Cyrus entered and wiped his feet on the rug inside the door. "Thank you, Colonel Allen. If you don't mind, I find it more natural to include your former rank as recognition of your achievements."

"Well, I'll take that as a very fine compliment, coming from a Yankee."

"We may have won the war, sir, but it's time for us to do our best to put it behind us and indulge in normal relationships."

Colonel Allen gestured for Cyrus to take a seat on the ornate couch. "Let's sit together and take advantage of the plush furnishings in first class. It's a far cry from the conditions at Spangler's barn where they treated our wounds. I must say that I appreciated the doctors' attention to Confederate as well as Union soldiers. Would you care for some fine Kentucky bourbon? I made sure I had my daily ration of it during most of the war."

Cyrus assented and reached for the offered glass. "This is very good indeed. I may have to make my visits more frequent during the rest of our trip."

"Please do that, my friend. What brings you here on this occasion?"

Cyrus laughed. "I could say that I came for the friendship and the fine whiskey, but I did have a further motive. I'm checking some information I received from a fellow passenger that needs confirmation."

"By all means, I'll help if I can."

"You served in a command position in the Army of Northern Virginia. Would you know whether the 6th Virginia Volunteer Cavalry fought at Gettysburg?"

"Cyrus, you know how people like to brag about their exploits and paint their careers in exaggerated colors. There's no harm in that, but whoever said his 6th cavalry was at Gettysburg was telling you a tall tale. That unit fought well on many occasions, but not that time. Jeb Stuart had most of our cavalry units engaged elsewhere, which gave you Yankees a big advantage. You knew how the battle was going before we did, because we lacked sufficient cavalry for reconnaissance."

"Thanks, Colonel, that's what I thought had happened. By the way, are you traveling to Australia on vacation, or are you moving there?"

"No, Cyrus, I'm a re-assimilated American. We won't have two versions of our country in the future. I'm informally visiting Australia on behalf of the former Confederacy to thank the managers of their shipyards for assisting with repairs to the Confederate ship CSS Shenandoah and other naval vessels during the war. Thanks to the Union blockade, we had to go far away for safe harbors and maintenance. The war is over, but we like to thank our friends who supported us. It's the Southern code of conduct."

Cyrus raised his glass. "That is indeed a fine procedure to follow. If you'll touch up the contents of my glass, I'll drink to your having a successful trip and safe return."

As promised, Cyrus visited the ship's ornate saloon at the appointed time. As he entered, he saw Barbara Boynton talking with a mother and her daughter at the other end of the large room. Barbara responded to his arrival by excusing herself from her conversation partners in favor of walking to meet him. Cyrus noted that she had changed into a dress that was more colorful than the one she had worn earlier in the passageway. He wondered whether women felt that they needed a range of clothing to suit their various moods. He next wondered why he needed to analyze her every action. It had to be that honesty question coming up again.

As he approached Barbara, he said, "I hope I haven't kept you waiting."

She smiled. "I've only been here long enough to greet a few people I recognized. I discovered that there are some small tables near the corner of the room. We could sit at one of them."

"Fine, but would you like to have something to drink before we sit there?"

"Perhaps later; for now, I'll settle for getting you to sit with me for more than a few minutes."

Cyrus followed her to the table. "Forgive me if I lack some social graces. Three years of Army life during wartime will do that to you."

As they sat, she rested her hand on his. "If you'll let me, I'll help you overcome your shyness."

"Thanks for the offer. Tell me more about your late husband."

She withdrew her hand and sat back. "That's not the most romantic direction for our conversation to take, but I'll follow your lead. William was a farmer and a lover of horses. That's why he joined the cavalry during the war."

Cyrus avoided any change in his expression as his mind reacted. *She slipped there. Earlier she said her husband's name was Warren. I wonder whether she even had a husband.*

Aloud he said, "I enjoy riding horses, but I haven't tried it with my new left foot. When I get home, I'll have to add riding to my project list."

Barbara once again moved her hand to his. This time she grasped his gently. "I'd enjoy being on your project list."

"It appears as though you already are a project, although I'm not sure how far we'll be travelling together."

She squeezed his hand and then released it. "We've traveled a long way up to this point. Let's work on the *together* part of the project. I'd like some wine now to toast the project's success."

Cyrus went for the wine. When he returned, they touched their glasses together in a toast and then sat chatting about events that had occurred on the ship. Despite his suspicions about Barbara, Cyrus found that he enjoyed her company and her wit.

After their conversation became relaxed and effortless, Cyrus said, "I've enjoyed this interlude. If you have time later, I'd like to introduce you to a friend of mine."

Barbara smiled. "We have nothing but time on this voyage. I would definitely like to meet your friend."

"I'll see you here at four o'clock, and then we'll go visiting."

"I'll look forward to it, Cyrus."

CHAPTER 10 – INTRODUCTIONS

They walked along the deck with arms linked as a token of affection as well as a device for improved balance as the ship sped through the restless waves. Barbara made sure that their path never strayed beyond reach of a handhold for Cyrus in case he slipped.

Cyrus knocked on the cabin door. She squeezed his arm in anticipation.

The door opened, revealing Colonel Allen dressed in a tuxedo.

"Come in, Cyrus. Your visits are always welcome. I've looked forward to meeting your companion, but I believe that our paths have already crossed in the past. Please come in."

Cyrus said, "You know each other?"

"Yes, indeed. We used to call her Isabelle Number Two. Isabelle Browning worked with Maria Isabella Boyd, one of the Confederacy's best sources of intelligence on the operations of Union forces. They each had the nickname of Belle, so we would call them the BB girls. I hope you don't find that term offensive, my dear."

"In a way, your comments are a relief to me, Colonel. I hope they don't shock you too much, Cyrus. I've been traveling as Barbara Boynton because Pinkerton's Secret Service is looking to apprehend Belle Browning. After the surrender, the government in Washington said there would be no vengeance or recriminations against Confederate military personnel, but they didn't extend that amnesty to intelligence agents. I'm traveling to Australia to get beyond their reach."

Cyrus held her hand. “I brought you here because I hoped that Colonel Allen could help me unravel your tangled personal history. I certainly didn’t expect him to recognize you.”

Belle grasped his other hand. “So, you suspected something. How did I reveal myself?”

“For starters, even after you admitted that you weren’t from Vermont, you said your husband was at Gettysburg in a cavalry unit that wasn’t there. Then you changed your husband’s name from Warren to William.”

“I was a lot better at discovering and reporting information than I am at making it up. Cyrus, can I still mean something to you, despite my having been a spy for the other side?”

“The war is over. Everyone did what seemed to be the right thing at the time. A lot of good people on both sides died. The best thing we can do for them now is to learn how to live at peace with each other.”

Colonel Allen said, “Amen to that, brother.”

Turning to her Cyrus said, “It will take a while to have your real name, Belle Browning, automatically slip off my tongue. Are you sure you don’t have any other hidden mysteries or lies for me to work my way through?”

“Colonel Allen has confirmed my identity. That’s who I am. Thank you, Colonel for easing my way back to honesty, at least with Cyrus.”

“I’ll assist you two in one other way. I’ve been meaning to have a few beers with another old Army friend who’s on board. I’ll go get him and take him to the saloon for some reminiscing while we drink. I’ll be gone for at least an hour, maybe two. In the meantime, please feel free to take advantage of the comforts and privacy of a first class cabin. I’ll see you again soon, either singly or together.” He half-bowed to them and went out.

Cyrus and Belle stood for several minutes, holding hands and looking at each other. She spoke first.

"In answer to the question in the back of your mind, I did not focus my attentions on you as part of a plan to evade Secret Service. I can't put it into words, but you had something special that attracted me."

"Don't try to put your feelings into words. Your words have caused nothing but problems so far. Let's adjourn to the couch and get to know each other without words."

"That's very forward of you, Mr. Danforth. I can be forward too. If you have trouble adjusting my name to Belle Browning, you could always consider how Belle Danforth would sound."

"I already have. It sounds perfect."

CHAPTER 11 - ARRIVAL

Upon arrival in Sydney, Cyrus asked the shipping line for a list of reliable rooming houses. From that list he and Belle selected one run by Mrs. Olivia Ferguson. Belle surprised Cyrus by informing him that she would return to being Barbara Boynton and that he would have to be consistent in calling her that.

"Why do you want to use that name now that you're safely in Australia?"

She laughed and held his hand. "The first reason is that I wouldn't be safe using my own name. There are American agents and bounty hunters over here as well as at home. The second justification is that the Australian government paid for my passage under that name, and I'm still under contract to consider marrying a settler here."

"I find it hard to believe that with all the lies you told me, that part of your story is true."

"It's a great opportunity for a woman. I'll have my pick from a large number of men. By the way, do you consider yourself a settler? You gave me a story about coming here to prospect for gold. Were you completely honest with me?"

"You're enjoying this too much, Barbara. See, I'm cooperating with you. How long must this charade last?"

"My contract says that I have to entertain local suitors for at least two months unless I marry one before that time. I'll repeat my earlier question. Do you consider yourself a settler?"

Cyrus raised his hands palms upward in a gesture of submission. "I definitely am a miner and a settler. Let's head for the rooming house and see what Mrs. Ferguson has to offer by way of food, shelter, and entertainment. You'll have to be a casual acquaintance from the ship and spend most of your time on your own."

"Why, Mr. Danforth, I wouldn't have it any other way. Don't worry about my playing a part. That's how I contributed to the Confederacy's cause."

They found Mrs. Olivia Ferguson to be gracious and humorous, to the point of telling a few off-color stories when she felt relaxed with her guests. She had gray hair and a plumpish figure, but attributed both of those features to having spent two years as a cook in a mining camp. She claimed to be forty years old and proud of it. Most of the other boarders were somewhat younger rough-edged men, but Mrs. Ferguson assured Barbara that she wouldn't allow them to get abusive or romantically aggressive with her.

The house was a two-story type that might be described as rambling because it had undergone three additions on different sides of the original structure. Although Cyrus and Barbara indicated that they barely knew each other, Mrs. Ferguson winked as she assigned them to adjacent rooms halfway down the corridor from her own combined office and apartment. She would be this young woman's chaperone while Cyrus would act as her bodyguard. If Barbara and her bodyguard were to improve their relationship, that would be alright too. They appeared to be well-suited for each other.

That evening, Cyrus and Barbara enjoyed their first land-based dinner in weeks and mingled with the other boarders on an individual basis, being careful to sit separately and scatter their conversations widely.

On the following morning, Barbara left first, having determined the location of the government office that had covered her travel expenses. She would register her presence and start the clock ticking on her minimum required time for availability as a potential wife. She wondered how she would handle meeting a suitor who attracted her as much as Cyrus, but she quickly repressed that thought in favor of the Danforth fantasies she had generated during their voyage on the *Tartar*.

Cyrus enjoyed an extra hour of rest before he left the rooming house for his day's activities. His first goal was to locate the Bank of New South Wales, where he would later present George Stevens' receipt for his gold deposit and his letter of agency establishing Cyrus's right to claim the deposit's current value. For today, this bank visit would be limited to a reconnaissance mission.

The bank building turned out to be smaller and less imposing than he had expected. He had seen photographs of the banks serving California gold rush clients, and the sturdiness of those banks proclaimed their security and success. By contrast, the wood frame building housing the Bank of New South Wales projected the image of hasty frontier construction. Australia had only recently increased its population and importance as a British colony, and the quality of the roads and architecture showed it. He would defer entering the unimpressive building until a later time.

Cyrus next found a general store and purchased a small quantity of mining supplies. He had heard from some of the other men at the rooming house that tools and supplies were much less expensive in Sydney than in the minefields, where the few available stores overcharged the miners. He returned to Mrs. Ferguson's rooming house to deposit his purchases in his room and then went back out to find the offices of Cobb & Co. Stagecoach Lines. Once there, he purchased a ticket for the next day's coach to Bathurst. That was the closest stop to the gold fields at or near Hill End, one hundred seventy-three miles northwest of Sydney. Hill End was the location where George Stevens had mined his gold. Cyrus would have to rent or buy a horse for the rest of the trip using a narrow foot-worn way winding at least twenty-five miles up into the hills. It was called the Bridle Track, and its final six miles could only be scaled on horseback.

Cyrus could have selected a mining location that was more easily reached by stagecoach, but he chose Hill End because he wanted to travel the same path that Lt. Col. Stevens had taken. Besides, he didn't really expect to be successful at gold mining. Too many other people had been there before him, and he considered himself to be playing a part, establishing himself as a settler so that his marriage to Barbara/Belle would cancel out her obligation to the government. He continued to have mixed feelings about her, waiting for the next time he would catch her in a lie, but recognizing in her the mirror image of his own personality and the perfect partner for pursuing the quest George Stevens had given him. There was emotional attraction between them, but he wouldn't know whether it was love until they worked together to overcome obstacles over a longer period of time. At this point he could only tell himself that he wanted their relationship to become love more than he had ever wanted anything else.

He would not reveal to Barbara his mission to claim the gold in the bank until or unless they married.

On the morning of his departure for Hill End, Cyrus knocked on Barbara's door. She invited him in for a special goodbye, knowing that they would be apart for months. If there had been any doubt on either side of their desire for each other, it ended with the passion of that morning. He stayed as long as his schedule allowed and before leaving gave Barbara his pepperbox pocket pistol to use for protection in his absence.

That evening, while Barbara was out, Mrs. Ferguson advised all her male boarders to refrain from making any romantic advances toward Barbara. She was to be considered already committed to someone else.

CHAPTER 12 – TWO MONTHS

Two months without Barbara/Belle seemed like forever to Cyrus, as he worked his tiny standard claim of 13.5 surface square meters. It was located at the edge of a narrow creek, and he had to pay the government a monthly fee of thirty shillings to work it. When he first approached Hill End on horseback, Cyrus had visions of selecting a large unexplored tract to mine, but he soon learned that the government kept a tight rein on the gold rush miners and restricted them to designated standard plots. During his interlude as a miner, he did better than most, extracting enough gold dust and small nuggets to offset his expenses and have a minor amount of gold left over. He enjoyed the experience and adventure, but a job in Sydney would have yielded him more money in the same period of time and wouldn't have required an investment in equipment. As the end of the two months approached, he was more than happy to leave the mining business.

Barbara's two months could certainly be termed dynamic. The agency offset their relatively small number of potential brides by asking each of them to spend no more than thirty minutes with each settler client every evening at the social center. A few of the men who came to meet them were reasonable candidates while most were crude and unpleasant. Barbara quickly realized that the government was out to pacify the settlers rather than find them wives. If one of the women actually agreed to marry someone, it would mean that the agency lost six social contacts every evening. That would damage the program's legitimacy. Barbara felt like a prostitute who was protected from sexual advances at the social center, but who was on her own if settlers came after her elsewhere. She carried the five-barreled pepperbox pistol with her at all times. She hoped that she wouldn't have to use it, but she had already survived more than one life-or-death confrontation during the war and would not be afraid to act if required.

The first month and a half of what Barbara considered serial hostessing went fairly smoothly. Her late evening walks back to Mrs. Ferguson's establishment were rather agreeable, especially since another woman, Nellie Harris, walked with her for the first half mile of her way home. One evening, about two blocks from her rooming house, Barbara saw two men approaching from the other side of the street at an angle that would intercept her path. She didn't think she could outrun them in her social center dress, so she continued to walk as though unconcerned while loosening the drawstring on her purse, in order to grip the pepperbox revolver as she moved forward.

As the first man approached he said, "Good evening, Mrs. Boynton."

She recognized him as a sheep farmer she had met a few nights earlier. At that time he had used crude language and had acted as though he expected to own her. Barbara knew what to expect. She tightened her grip on the pistol. "Please don't block my way, Mr. Russell. I don't want to be late."

"You're going to be very late, Mrs. Boynton. I'm taking you home to be my wife. If necessary, Harold will carry you." He gestured toward his taller companion who had started to circle around behind Barbara.

Barbara withdrew her revolver from her purse, slid the purse handle up her arm to free her second hand, and pointed the pistol at the moving man. "Harold, move back next to Mr. Russell if you don't want to be shot."

That got Harold's attention. He stopped and looked to Russell for guidance.

Russell said, "She probably doesn't know how to use that thing. Grab her."

Harold took a stride toward Barbara, and she fired at his legs, striking him in his left knee.

"You won't be going anywhere on that leg for a while." The double-action revolver rotated the pepperbox to the next barrel position, and Barbara was prepared to fire again if necessary. "I suggest you take your friend home, Mr. Russell, unless you want more of the same or want to watch him bleed to death."

For a moment, Russell couldn't decide whether to charge Barbara or assist Harold. He hadn't considered the possibility of her being armed. Finally, he yielded to Harold's screams and curses at him. "You've won this time, but I'll be back for you with my gun. I'll take you home to be my wife, and I'll keep you chained down if necessary. What do you think of that?"

Barbara answered his question by shooting him in the right knee and walking away.

When she reached the rooming house, Barbara knocked on her landlady's door. Olivia Ferguson came out, wrapped in her robe.

"What is it, Barbara? You look shaken."

Barbara hugged Olivia and described the assault in a shaky voice.

Olivia said, "You go into your room, and I'll bring you tea. In the meantime, you let me take care of those men and their threats."

As Barbara walked away, Olivia struck the hanging steel triangle that served as her alarm bell. The eight male occupants filtered out of their rooms.

Andre Beauchamp, a sailor, was the first to reach Mrs. Ferguson. "What happened? Is the building on fire?"

Olivia told the assembling crowd of Barbara's assault. "We have to do something so that those two men don't come after Barbara again or send others to do their dirty work. They can't have gotten far away from the scene of the attack with leg wounds. Round them up and take them to the police station, or throw them in the harbor – your choice. Young women staying in this house have to be protected."

Andre and the others proclaimed their agreement. A few returned to their rooms for shoes and assorted weapons. Then they went out, returning in a much better mood ninety minutes later.

Andre found Mrs. Ferguson waiting for them with pots of coffee and tea. "They won't be bothering anyone again."

"What did you do with them? Are they dead?"

"I know some sailors from a ship that brings in Chinese miners. Those two attackers are now leaving port on their way to China. They'll have to behave well if they hope to actually get there."

The next morning, everyone around the breakfast table had big smiles for Barbara.

CHAPTER 13 - RETURN

Mrs. Ferguson barely recognized Cyrus when he limped into her front room carrying a large pack of miner's tools and equipment. During his two months away, he had modified his facial appearance by adding a shaggy beard and a heavy tan. She approached him as he lowered his pack to the floor.

"Mr. Danforth, you look so different."

"It's good to see you too, Mrs. Ferguson. Outdoor living and constant work do tend to change you. I'm very glad to get back to civilization in general and your establishment in particular. I trust things are going well here."

"They are now, but we had to handle some problems a short while ago." She summarized Barbara's assault and its aftermath.

"Is Barbara here now?"

"She's in her room. She hasn't left the house since that encounter. Barbara won't admit it, but she has lost some of her self-confidence." Mrs. Ferguson winked at him. "Perhaps you'll be able to improve her outlook. Go see her now. I'll have someone carry your pack to your room."

Cyrus approached the door and knocked softly. "Barbara, are you awake? It's Cyrus."

The door opened quickly, and she stared up at him. "You're not the Cyrus I knew, but even with that beard and broader shoulders, you're a welcome sight. Get in here stranger." She closed the door behind him and reached up to feel his beard. "That will be a bit scratchy, but I'll get used to it." Barbara pulled him toward her and kissed him.

They held each other tightly. Then Cyrus said, "Mrs. Ferguson told me about the men who ambushed you. She said you took care of them like the war-hardened soldier I know you to be."

She pressed her palm to his cheek. "I'm not too hardened for you, am I?"

"You're perfect for me, and that's why we should avoid any more artificial delays. Let's get married as soon as possible. I want to be with you to protect you from any future troubles."

She kissed him again. "That solitary mining interlude toughened you even more than your soldiering. Of course, I'll marry you, but we should discuss a couple of obstacles."

"We'll overcome them together. What are the problems?"

"First, I'm Catholic, and the Catholic Church in Sydney burned down in June, four months ago. Second, you want to go back to Wisconsin, and they'll try to arrest Belle Browning there, even if she changed her name to Danforth."

Cyrus smiled at her. "We've both overcome problems worse than those. First, I'm Episcopalian, and Australia being a British colony, we'll have no problem finding an Anglican Church. If the church difference bothers you, we can have our ceremony in Mrs. Ferguson's front room. I'm open to raising our children in either church. Second, I'll be marrying Barbara Boynton who will become Barbara Danforth. Everyone here knows you by that name anyway. As you may have noticed on the trip over here, Australia is a long way from Wisconsin. No one is likely to track you here and back again. If they do, I'll have the former soldiers of the 2nd Regiment Wisconsin Volunteer Infantry to stand in their way."

"And why, Mr. Shaggy Miner, would that Union Army unit stand up for me?"

"That's a secret you'll learn after we're married."

Per Cyrus's suggestion, the wedding took place in Mrs. Ferguson's front room. All the boarders were invited, with Andre Beauchamp acting as Cyrus's best man in recognition of his leadership in disposing of the men who assaulted Barbara. Olivia Ferguson was matron of honor, a duty she accepted with pride. Several of the wife candidates who had worked with Barbara also came and were enthusiastically welcomed by the male boarders. An Anglican priest, Father Paul Billingsley, performed the ceremony with Barbara's hearty agreement. Following the ceremony, Cyrus gave each of the male boarders a small gold nugget as a symbol of his thanks for their efforts on behalf of Barbara. Olivia Ferguson and Barbara served a variety of special hors d'oeuvres they had prepared, and Cyrus acted as bartender with beer, ale, and whisky generously provided. When Andre asked whether they would be taking a honeymoon trip, Cyrus announced that he and Barbara would be sailing back to the United States within the month, but that they did not yet have specific details for the trip. That announcement put a slight damper on the festivities, but it came after everyone had consumed a large quantity of food and drink, so its impact was minor. The normally straight-laced Olivia Ferguson looked the other way when couples drifted off to some of her rooms. She followed their example somewhat later with the merchant who had supplied the libations.

As a wedding present, Mrs. Ferguson gave Barbara the key to the connecting door to Cyrus's room so that the Danforths would have a honeymoon suite.

No one arose early the following morning.

CHAPTER 14 – BANK BUSINESS

When Cyrus awoke late in the morning following the wedding, he sat in bed staring at the dark curly hair of his bride. He touched her hair gently, and she stirred, stretching her arms above her shoulders.

"Good morning, husband. We'll have to go somewhere today to find privacy."

"Good idea, wife, but I've been sitting here thinking about a question I forgot to ask you."

Barbara raised herself to a sitting position, fully alert. "Don't tell me that you still don't trust me, even after I married you."

Cyrus gave her a light kiss. "I trust you. I simply need to clarify something."

She leaned back and arched her right eyebrow. "Go ahead, you have my full attention."

"Am I your first or your second husband? I reached my own conclusion that Warren or William, in your earlier background story, was a fiction, but you never confirmed my theory. Did he or any other prior husband exist in your life?"

"Nope, that was all window dressing. You're my first and only spouse. Would it have made a difference if I had said this was my second marriage?"

"No, but I like to get my facts straight."

"In that case, I'll admit that you didn't get me as a virgin, but I had no other marriage."

Cyrus pulled her toward him and hugged her. "I suspected that, but it makes no difference to me. We're together now and in the future. That's what's important.

One more question – will you mind being Barbara instead of Belle?"

"Not if you won't mind someone questioning the legitimacy of our marriage because I used a false name."

"I took care of that one. I had the reverend record your name in the official record as Barbara Isabelle Danforth. I also told him that Boynton was your name from a previous marriage but that I didn't know your maiden name."

"My name at birth was Isabelle Barbara Browning, so you did very well, Cyrus. I have a final personal question for you. Don't you ever take off your artificial leg?"

Cyrus laughed. "I have two answers to that one. The first is that I keep it on all the time because I want to learn to live with it as though it is my real leg. The second gets into the matter of trust between us, and you don't get that one until after we cuddle some more."

He pulled back the covers so that they could once again admire each other and then began to caress her. Barbara rolled over to match his actions and facilitate them. After a period of increasing activity, they relaxed and lay side-by-side, touching each other.

Barbara spoke first, "I love you and I trust you. Reveal your secrets if and when you want. I won't feel offended if you don't share everything. I certainly didn't in the past. I do, however, pledge to be as open as possible with you in the future."

"That's all I can ask. Now, let's get dressed. Then we'll take a walk to that park down the street, and I'll share some important information with you."

"Are you sure you haven't been a spy also? One of the first tricks I learned from Belle Boyd was to go to an open outdoor area before discussing secrets."

Cyrus responded by pulling her close for another kiss. "The war may be over, but we'll have an ongoing mission that will require all the skills that both of us have acquired along the way."

Olivia Ferguson rose early, prepared coffee, tea, and light breakfast foods, and then returned to her apartment and her new merchant friend. It had been seven years since her husband's death in a shipwreck, and she was ready for someone new. The merchant, Alex Bangston, was a promising candidate. She would not let him depart until he realized that she considered last night's coupling to have been serious rather than casual.

Cyrus and Barbara did their best to be quiet as they shared coffee and rolls at the dining room table. Then they left the house and walked toward the park, arm in arm, linked in a new shared adventure.

Once among the nostalgic samples of British gardens, they settled on a bench well-distanced from plantings that might conceal a witness to their conversation. Barbara gazed at Cyrus with love and anticipation.

"I'm ready to share your mission, whatever it may be."

He squeezed her hand and recounted his meetings with George Stevens and the commitment he had made to covertly support the families of the 2nd Wisconsin soldiers who had fought at Gettysburg and especially the families of those who had fallen there. He also told her about the gold at the Bank of New South Wales, and the documents hidden in his artificial leg.

As Cyrus finished his story, Barbara leaned toward him and kissed him. "You are such a unique person to take on that mission and to travel halfway around the world to take its first enabling steps. I thought I was an idealist when I worked as a civilian to support the Southern cause. You've taken on something that will require efforts from both of us plus future generations of our family. Of course, I'll support you in this, but when you agreed to do it, did you understand that the project has no end. It will go on forever."

"That depends on the amount of gold, Stevens has on deposit here. We may find that it's only enough for one-time minimum contributions to all the families."

"How many families would you have to support?"

"Slightly more than three hundred ..."

Barbara had retrieved a pencil and a sheet of paper from her purse. She wrote 300 on the paper. "How much is an ounce of gold worth?"

"About $19.00 ..."

Barbara did a few calculations. "For each family to receive $100.00 there would have to be about one hundred pounds of gold in George Stevens' account in that bank. Do you think he has that much?"

"The man was dying when we discussed this project. I didn't press him for details."

"Cyrus, you're a wonderful and compassionate man, and I love you, but you may have come all this way for an amount of money that will only provide a small gift to each family."

Cyrus's facial expression became stern. "I have faith that Stevens wouldn't have asked me to do this unless there was enough to make a difference for the families." Then he relaxed and laughed.

Barbara arched her eyebrow. "Why are you laughing?"

"We've just had our first argument. That means we're in this marriage for better or for worse. We're working through problems together."

"You're right; instead of worrying about what might be wrong with this mission, we should go to the bank and find out what we actually have to work with."

This time it was Cyrus who leaned toward Barbara and kissed her.

"Why, thank you Cyrus. What did I do to deserve that?"

"You said 'we' in discussing the project. We're a team now."

"And we always will be; now let's go to that bank to find out some facts."

They made their way to the Bank of New South Wales on Broadway, and asked to speak with the manager. That individual, a Mr. Edwin Williams, assessed Cyrus's now shaven but still-tanned face and broad shoulders, and asked whether they were looking to sell gold. Cyrus remarked that he did have a small quantity to sell, but that his primary purpose was to claim the deposit of gold that George H. Stevens had previously made with the bank. Mr. Williams suggested that they adjourn to his private office to discuss the matter further. Cyrus introduced his new wife, and they all went together. As they passed by a desk outside the office, Mr. Williams said something to his secretary.

Once inside the office, Mr. Williams offered them tea or coffee. Cyrus and Barbara each selected coffee, and Mr. Williams poured it for them from the silver coffee urn on his side table. He took tea from a matching pot. As they carried their cups to the conference table, the secretary entered with some papers. Cyrus and Barbara sat patiently while Mr. Williams spread the papers on the table in front of him and read them.

At last, the banker looked up at his two visitors and addressed Cyrus. "You say that George H. Stevens appointed you his agent to claim the current value of his deposited gold. What were the circumstances of that appointment?"

"He gave me this assignment as he was dying from wounds received during the American Civil War Battle of Gettysburg. Are those circumstances important?"

"They are because documented deathbed transactions carry increased weight in a court of common law. We have to consider the possibility that a relative might dispute your claim."

Barbara said, "I hardly think an American relative would argue with a transaction in Australia."

"Be that as it may, the directors of our bank have to concern themselves with all legal possibilities. May I see your documentation including your identification?"

Cyrus withdrew his Union Army discharge papers and George Stevens' documents from the inside pocket of his coat and handed them across the table. "Please forgive the lack of flatness on the account papers. I stored them rolled up for security reasons."

Edwin Williams took the papers cautiously, wondering where Danforth had stored them. He pulled their curved surfaces across the edge of the conference table to flatten them somewhat. "Your receipt appears to be the original. I recognize the signature of my predecessor." He next checked Cyrus Danforth's discharge papers and examined the letter of agency very carefully. Then he placed all the documents on the table, stood up, and extended his hand toward Cyrus for a handshake.

Cyrus stood and clasped the offered hand. "I assume this means you found everything to be in order."

"Very much so, Mr. Danforth. Even on his deathbed, George Stevens was shrewd enough to have two doctors witness his signature. I don't foresee any legal problems for the bank if we release his holdings to you."

Barbara looked up at the banker. "If it's not impolite to ask a direct question about the account, how much gold did Mr. Stevens deposit with you?"

"Keep in mind the fact that Mr. Stevens mined his gold before the rush started. He did much better than the many miners who followed him to the Hill End area. The file records eight deposits totaling 4,191 troy ounces, or in more common units at 14.58 troy ounces per pound, he has approximately 288 pounds of gold to his credit."

Cyrus and Barbara both sat down again.

She asked, “And in American dollars the price of gold is about $19.00 per troy ounce?”

Williams looked at the papers in front of him. “The current price is $18.93. The Stevens account is currently worth 79,335.63 American dollars.”

Cyrus asked, “What is the procedure for withdrawing that and closing the account?”

You said you are from the state of Wisconsin. We will issue you a bank draft backed by this gold, which may be reimbursed by our correspondent bank in Chicago.” He examined a different sheet of paper. “That would be the Merchants’ Savings, Loan and Trust Company.”

Barbara added the other bank’s name to her previous written notes. “Is there any chance that the Chicago bank might not settle on your draft?”

Williams said, “It’s a very reputable bank, even though it is only eight years old. The people there are well-regarded, and the draft is backed by gold, which gives them a guaranteed claim on our bank or on other banks that settle these claims. You will have no problems with this transaction.”

As they left the Bank of New South Wales with their draft for George Stevens’ funds and a much smaller one for the proceeds of Cyrus’s mining, Barbara squeezed Cyrus’s hand. “You were right as usual. George Stevens had enough on deposit to keep the project going beyond a minimal payment.”

He smiled at her. “Thanks for saying ‘as usual’.” That puts a long-term stamp of approval on our marriage. If we string out our donations to families over time and invest what we have not yet distributed, the magic of compound interest will keep the project going for a very long time.”

CHAPTER 15 - BACK IN THE FUTURE

Marie leaned forward on her rocking chair. "That's how it all started. Cyrus and Barbara Danforth returned to Fox Lake, Wisconsin and purchased a modest home. He went back to work at the hard goods store, this time as the manager, and she joined a local quilting group. They wanted to establish themselves as a sociable but humble family. Barbara revisited her earlier story about having grown up in Vermont, and did it effectively because interactions with others during her travels had erased any traces of a Virginia accent."

As Jeremy focused on Marie's words, he leaned forward, following her example. "How did they appear humble when they were giving money to soldiers' families?"

Debbie said, "That's Marie's point. They took their time before doing anything with the money, so as to blend into the local social fabric. They didn't want to attract attention, especially with Pinkerton agents searching for Barbara as a former Confederate spy."

Her words didn't change Jeremy's point of view. "Fine; they spent some time being unremarkable local folks. At some point, they started to give away money. People would have noticed that and treated them differently."

Marie eased the rocker backward. "You would be correct, Jeremy, if Cyrus and Barbara openly distributed money. You have to remember Cyrus's original conversations with George Stevens. George told Cyrus that he didn't want the soldiers' families to know the source of their unexpected income."

"How could Cyrus possibly give them money without their questioning him about its source?"

Marie winked at him. "They had to be very creative."

CHAPTER 16 - REUNION

The first postwar reunion of the 2nd Regiment Wisconsin Volunteer Infantry took place in a large barn in Fox Lake. Beer and other drinks flowed freely as the surviving soldiers and their families toasted friends who were no longer with them. Many of those in attendance were relatives of deceased soldiers, hoping to feed their melancholy for their lost men. Reporters from local newspapers and historians from the University of Wisconsin interviewed attendees selected at random plus surviving officers. In the barn's corner farthest away from the entrance and the band, poker tables drew enthusiastic participation by many of the veterans. Some were winners and some were losers, but one veteran had the worst luck of all.

Friends consoled Cyrus Danforth on his bad luck at table number one, and suggested that he might do better at table number two or one of the other card games. He muttered a few curses about his bad luck and then accepted their suggestion, excusing himself from the first game site to find a seat at another table. No one noticed Cyrus's wife Barbara standing in the shadows, recording the names of the men with whom Cyrus had played and the approximate amounts that he had lost to them.

Cyrus's luck appeared to remain bad as he entered the second game, and after another hour of losing, he repeated the process of switching to another table in search of a game and set of players who would reverse his losses. Those watching the games suggested that Cyrus should just quit and go home, because of his amazingly high losses. One former flag-bearer said that he hoped

Cyrus did better with his wife in bed than he did at playing cards. Barbara heard that remark as she stood in the background making notes and promised herself to be sure he'd be especially fortunate at home that night. The first stage of their plan was working well. Gambling was an easy and efficient way to distribute money to others without their realizing that it was a deliberate act. They would have to develop some additional distribution techniques to extend their assistance to men who didn't gamble and to families whose men had not returned from the war.

CHAPTER 17 - BACK TO SCHOOL

One evening, as they sat by the fireplace absorbing its warmth, Barbara set aside her needlework and suggested to Cyrus that he put down his book in favor of some conversation. Cyrus complied and wondered whether Barbara had some major announcement for him.

"Will our conversation focus on a particular topic, or are you looking to share the events of your day?"

"I'd like to touch a bit more on our personal histories as a starter. We've never discussed our educational backgrounds. How much schooling have you had?"

"So far, this sounds like a job interview, but I'll contribute that I finished high school and that I've learned a lot more from being in the Army and from books I've read. How about you?"

"I went beyond high school to a few classes at the University of Virginia, cut short when the war broke out. Young ladies in our social circles were expected to acquire education and cultural graces in order to attract a man of significant social standing. The war ended that outlook, at least for its duration."

Cyrus walked over to Barbara and held her hands. "Under normal circumstances would you have looked at me twice? I have no social standing."

Barbara turned on her southern flirtation voice. "Why, Mr. Danforth, your standing has been highly endorsed by an officer and a gentleman in the Union Army and another officer in the Confederate Army. I also have been studying your family tree where I have identified ancestral connections to people who came to America on the *Mayflower*. You would definitely be a good catch for me."

"I'm pleased to hear that, Miss Isabelle, but unless you've completely lost track of calendar time, we've already caught each other. Where are you going with the education questions?"

"Would you have liked to go to college?"

"Possibly, but I knew that our family couldn't afford it. The farm back in New York didn't produce much by way of cash crops. Dad and Mother and the rest of us worked long hours just to produce our own food plus a little extra to trade at the local store to pay our bills."

"When did you move to Wisconsin, and why didn't you take up farming here?"

"Lots of questions tonight ... I came to Wisconsin about three years before the war started. As to farming, that's why I moved. I didn't see great opportunity in being chained to a parcel of land. I wanted to be free to pick up and do something else when I felt the urge."

"Like going to Australia and mining gold ..."

"Like going to Australia and meeting the love of my life who's worth more than gold."

"Why thank you sir. Would you like to go to college now, after your time in the Union Army?"

Cyrus took his time before responding to her question. "I can feel you leading me down a path of logic. Where are you going with these questions? Let's skip ahead a few steps."

Barbara winked at him. "I like the way you see beyond my words. What I'm thinking is that an anonymous way of giving funds to families whose men served in the 2nd Wisconsin would be to fund scholarships at the University of Wisconsin. We could meet with the administrators there and set something up where applying students wouldn't know who supplied the money for their scholarships."

"That's an interesting idea, but how would we keep them from giving the money to people who had no connection with my regiment?"

"You work at a store, Cyrus. How do you get your suppliers to give you the number of rakes and shovels that you want, rather than some other quantity?"

"We send them an order."

"That order once accepted is a contract. We can do the same thing with the University of Wisconsin. We'll write the agreement to say that our scholarships are only available to students with a family member who served in the 2nd Regiment, Wisconsin Volunteer Infantry."

"I like your thinking, Barbara. We could set it up so that the university would take care of all the details. We would want them to give us a list of people we funded so that we would know what families would still need to get future support. We want to help as many families as we can."

She put her hand on his shoulder. "Some of the students would be discharged soldiers and some would be their children and grandchildren. If you don't want to go to college, some other member of our family might."

Cyrus put his arm around her waist. "I have no problem with your going to the University while I work."

Barbara shook her head. "I meant some future family member."

He stared into her eyes. "Are you referring to a family member who's in our near future?"

"Yes, my dear; I'm expecting we'll have a new Danforth joining us in about six months."

CHAPTER 18 - CAMPUS CONFERENCE

Paul Ansel Chadbourne, Chief Executive of the University of Wisconsin, tried to evaluate the couple that sat across the desk from him. "Let me get this straight, Mr. and Mrs. Danforth. You say that you want to give money to the university, but you don't want anyone to know that you've donated it. That's highly unusual."

Cyrus stiffened his posture. "That's an absolute requirement, sir. Should our names be publicized in any way, our support of your students would stop."

Chadbourne stared at Cyrus. "You don't want anyone to know the donor's identity, and you want to specify how we spend it. That doesn't sound like a donation. That's a contract. You'll give us money, but only if we do your bidding in spending it. We've never had such an arrangement before, and we haven't needed it. The Wisconsin legislature recently gave us funds to expand and reorganize our institution. Perhaps I'll decline to accept your funds. How would you react to that?"

Barbara Danforth gestured to Cyrus that she would like to respond, and he nodded his affirmation.

"Mr. Chadbourne, I've read about the actions of the legislature in the newspapers. As I understand it, the discussions among the lawmakers in giving you expanded funding centered on expectations that soldiers who served in the recent war and their children would want to attend the university to improve their condition in life. Is that not so?"

"That was one of their underlying concerns."

"Then you should look favorably upon our proposition, because our donations are intended to fund scholarships for veterans of one particular infantry regiment, their family members, and their descendants. That is exactly in tune with the thinking of the legislature."

Chadbourne stood and faced Barbara Danforth whose chair was to his right. "Madam, are you saying that you would be making more than a single donation?"

Cyrus answered. "That's exactly what she's saying. We will fund a number of scholarships each year for the foreseeable future, but we wish to remain anonymous, and the scholarships will only be available to veterans of the 2nd Regiment, Wisconsin Volunteer Infantry, their family members, and their descendants."

"If you want to open this up to their descendants, you would have to make continuing contributions for a long time indeed." He looked back and forth between his two visitors.

Cyrus said, "That is our intention. Will you work with us? A negative response would, of course, be followed by our informing the legislators of your disdain for veterans and their families."

"I understand, Mr. Danforth. The University of Wisconsin will welcome your donations and the accompanying rules for their distribution. My assistant will draw up a contract for us to review and sign next week. Your project is aligned with our charter to educate and improve the outlooks of the people of Wisconsin. Thank you both for your generosity."

Chadbourne shook hands with Cyrus and bowed to Barbara. "Feel free to visit us again whenever you feel our university staff might be of service to you."

As they left, Barbara said to Cyrus, "I couldn't believe that he was considering rejecting our money."

"He was showing us his position of power, but your revelation that there would be many donations and my suggestion that he might find the politicians turned against him changed his mind. It would be easy to grab for power with this money, but we'll stay in the background, put a limit on the number of scholarships each year, and let our account grow through investments. At twenty-four to thirty-two dollars per year for tuition, we should be able to fund a significant number of scholarships each year and still let our bank account grow."

CHAPTER 19 – BIRTH AND CHILDHOOD

1868 brought the arrival of Bruce Boynton Danforth. Cyrus had wanted the child's middle name to be Browning, but Barbara thought that would reveal her true identity, so they used her alias surname as his middle name and laughed about it when they were alone. Two years later, Bruce was joined by a younger brother, Daniel George Danforth. His middle name was a tribute to George Stevens, whose quest had led to Cyrus and Barbara meeting each other. Barbara had become so used to the reversal of her own given names that she no longer thought of herself as an Isabelle.

Young Bruce and Daniel turned out to be very close siblings. Daniel followed Bruce everywhere and patterned his personality and behavior after his older brother. As they continued to grow, it became obvious that Daniel was more athletic than Bruce, while the older boy did better at studies in the one-room schoolhouse they both attended. By the fifth grade, Daniel had grown two inches taller than his older brother, and because of his height, townspeople began to reverse their thinking as to which was the older brother. They both began to work at the hard goods store with Cyrus, stocking shelves and assisting customers with loading purchases onto their horse-drawn wagons. Each autumn, they would get a week off from school to help local farmers harvest their crops. Both boys grew muscular from this work and from fishing and hunting outings with their father.

After one such fishing trip, Bruce and Daniel entered the back door of their home, removed their muddy boots, and went to the kitchen to show their mother the long string of fish they had caught. When they didn't find her there, they yelled for her. Bruce went upstairs, while Daniel checked the cellar. Unsuccessful, they both returned to the kitchen as their father came in the back door.

Cyrus asked, "What's up boys?"

Bruce said, "We can't find Mother anywhere. We yelled for her, and looked upstairs and downstairs."

"Go see if she's outside somewhere. She may have visited Mrs. Steuben. If you don't find her nearby, go check the Steuben's house"

The boys ran outside. Cyrus put their string of fish in the sink and rinsed them with water from the sink-mounted pump. He knew that Barbara would object to the fish lying on the kitchen table. Then he started to check the other rooms for some indication of where she had gone.

When he found both her coat and her shawl in the closet, Cyrus began to consider the possibility that Barbara had left suddenly. The overturned chair and the sewing basket on the floor in the front room suggested that she might not have left of her own accord. He searched the front room for some kind of message or clue for him to follow in looking for her. When he saw the strip of cloth on the chair closest to the front door, Cyrus took it to be significant. It was pink ...

Pinkerton's Secret Service ... How can they still be after her? The war ended fifteen years ago.

Cyrus ran out the back door. The horse was still harnessed to the wagon they had taken on their fishing trip. He collected the reins from the tie-ring on the post, petted the horse's neck gently, and then climbed aboard. He caught up with Bruce and Daniel on their way back from the Steuben house. After they indicated that Mrs. Steuben hadn't seen Barbara or anyone else that day, he told the boys to wait at home until he returned in case their mother came back. Then he urged the horse toward town and the sheriff's office. Once there he tied the reins to a railing and rushed inside.

Sheriff Hanson looked up from his desk at the flushed face of the man facing him. "Hello, Cyrus; is something wrong?"

"Erik, I can't find Barbara anywhere, and there are signs of a scuffle at my house. Do you know of any strangers who might have been looking for her?"

"You're thinking someone kidnapped her? She could have gone for a long walk or a visit."

"It's too cool for her to have done that without taking her coat or her shawl. Please answer my question about strangers."

"I do try to keep track of people who don't belong here. This morning, there were a couple of fellows asking directions to the Steubens' house and a peddler of pots and pans. They're the only ones I've seen in the last few days. Why would someone from out-of-town be after her?"

"That's a long story that I'll tell you when we have more time. My guess is that the men asking about the Steubens could be the ones after her. The Steubens are our closest neighbors. What did those two look like?"

"They had black hats and coats, and one of them smoked a cigar."

"Did they carry weapons?"

Sheriff Hanson thought for a few seconds. "I can't say for sure because they had long coats, but those coats could have hidden gun belts."

"Did you see them come back through town after they left here?"

"I didn't see them, but they could have slipped by while I wasn't looking out the window."

Cyrus turned to go. "I'll assume they kept going past the Steubens' house after they took Barbara."

"Do you want me to go with you?"

“If you want to help, Erik, go the other way in case they did pass without you noticing them.”

He left, climbed on his wagon and headed west. As he climbed up, Cyrus’ coat folded back to reveal a holster with his Army revolver. Hanson took the hint and made sure he too was armed before going down the town’s main road eastbound.

Sheriff Hanson rode seven miles down the road without seeing the two strangers. He decided that they must have gone the other way. As he was about to turn around, he saw in the distance the peddler’s wagon taking a branch road heading southeast. He wondered whether he should pursue the peddler, but decided to turn back in case Cyrus needed assistance with the other two riders.

CHAPTER 20 – FRUSTRATION

Cyrus searched long and hard for the men who might have taken Barbara, but he found no trace of them. He had no idea where Secret Service agents would take their prisoners. When he returned home alone, the boys vented their emotions with screams and more than a few tears. It took Cyrus several hours to calm them down so that he would be free to plan his next move. In order to get them thinking instead of reacting, he told them how Barbara spied for the South during the war and why she still feared Pinkerton Secret Service agents.

Three hours after learning about his mother's secret history, Bruce approached Cyrus holding the latest newspaper. "Dad, didn't you say that you served in the same regiment as Governor Lucius Fairchild?"

"Lucius was our Colonel at Gettysburg. He was wounded and lost his left arm in the same action where I lost part of my left leg. He got elected governor of Wisconsin, but left that post eight years ago. I don't know what he's doing now."

"According to this newspaper article, he has been consul-general in Paris for the past two years. He's home now, but he'll soon leave again to become the ambassador to Spain. With all his government connections, wouldn't he be able to find where the Pinkerton people are holding Mother?"

Cyrus stood and hugged Bruce. "That's a great idea, son. He'll be at his home in Madison, I'm sure. You and Daniel will have to be on your own for a few days while I go to visit him. Can you handle that?"

“We'll be fine, Dad, and we'll go into town for our normal work schedule too. I'll tell the folks at the store that you were called out of town on a family emergency. They don't have to know about Mother's background, at least not yet.”

“That's good thinking, but are you sure you're not eighteen instead of twelve? Remind me to ask for more of your advice in the future.”

CHAPTER 21 - LUCIUS FAIRCHILD

When Lucius Fairchild greeted Cyrus, he did so with a warm and firm handshake. He semi-permanently held his artificial left hand inserted into his left coat pocket, but his right arm and hand were muscular due to their constant use.

"Hello, Cyrus, it's good to see you after all these years. I've heard a few confidential rumors about what you've been doing for the veterans of our regiment, and I thoroughly applaud your actions. If you were a politician like me, you'd tell the world about your good works, but you always were quiet and a deep thinker. How did you manage it?"

"There weren't supposed to be any rumors to hear, but too many people got involved, I guess. Credit my projects to some gold mining I did during the Australian gold rush."

"Is that so? We have more in common than I thought. We both lost a left limb in fighting on the first day of Gettysburg, my arm and your leg, and way back when I was eighteen years old, I went to California to strike it rich in the gold rush there. I stayed there for six adventurous years, but I didn't get rich in the process. Is this a social visit, or may I assist you in some way?"

"You're my last hope on a matter of personal urgency. Barbara, my wife has disappeared, and I'm certain that she has been kidnapped by Pinkerton's Secret Service agents. I'm hoping against hope that you or one of your associates would know where they take their prisoners."

"Cyrus, old friend, I'll do everything I can to get that information for you, but first you'll have to tell me why you think they took her."

Cyrus shrugged his shoulders. "I expected that response. The problem comes from the agreement to end hostilities at the end of the war. The powers that be in Washington promised that there would be no penalties or abuse to soldiers who served on the Confederate side, but they didn't extend that graciousness to civilian supporters of the Confederacy. Barbara's original name was Belle Browning, and she worked with Belle Boyd to provide intelligence on Union troop movements and actions to the Confederate Army. I trust that you will treat this information as highly confidential. I met her while she was running away to Australia to evade the reach of Pinkerton's people. Now, we're fifteen years into our marriage with two fine sons, and they've taken her from me. There have to be limitations on war-based arrests."

Fairchild gave a long low whistle. "I remember Belle Boyd and the damage her spying caused. She and her group were quite good at what they did. I believe she's in England, married to one of our former naval officers. Your wife's case is almost parallel to hers. Everyone did what they thought was patriotic during the war, so I'm on your side as far as saying that it's time to stop chasing ghosts. They call me a diplomat rather than a politician now, so I'll see whether I have the skills that should go with that title. Can you stay in Madison for a few days while I check my sources? You're welcome to stay here with me at my home. It gets little use while I'm abroad."

"Thank you, Lucius. I didn't know where else to turn for help in finding her."

The next day, Lucius Fairchild went to the Wisconsin State Capitol Building and talked with many of the people who had served in his administration as governor. He also sent several telegrams to friends and official contacts in Washington, DC. His in-person feedback from Wisconsin officials could be summarized by their collective experience that the Pinkerton people didn't want to share information with anyone. Because of this attitude, most officials didn't ask the Secret Service anything, for fear that they would be investigated by that mysterious agency. The ex-governor decided that he would have to rely on return telegrams from contacts in Washington for any useful information. He anticipated a delay of several days.

While they waited for return telegrams, Lucius and Cyrus spent time exchanging information about surviving veterans of the 2nd Wisconsin within the confines of Madison's finest saloons. Cyrus felt slightly guilty about enjoying beer and ale while Barbara was still missing, but he knew that camaraderie was the price of intelligence. Lucius was his only known source for the information he needed, so Cyrus had to keep Lucius happy. When the return stream of telegrams finally trickled in, they both grumbled about the results. *Even though Allan Pinkerton had left the Intelligence Service, their government agents were still commonly called Pinkerton men. The current Pinkerton organization was a private agency and could not be forced to divulge information ... officially, Pinkerton had no record of the incident in question ... Pinkerton's had thousands of operatives and was larger than the peacetime standing U.S. Army ... many of those agents operated on their own without sanction from the home office.*

After spending a week in Madison, Cyrus had no choice but to go home and wait for possible information from Barbara or her kidnappers. Perhaps this would play out as a ransom ploy. He would gladly meet the kidnappers' demands.

CHAPTER 22 – LOOKING BACKWARD

Jeremy and Debbie had listened intently to Marie's tale of Cyrus and his family. After hearing about Lucius Fairchild and the Secret Service inquiries, Jeremy rose from his chair and began to pace around the kitchen.

"Marie, I need to know whether they ever found Barbara. Can we jump ahead in the story? Cyrus and Barbara had a great family, and with her kidnapping everything fell apart. Was that the end of it, or did Cyrus find and rescue her?"

Marie turned to Debbie. "Your husband isn't the most patient man in the world." To Jeremy she said, "I'm telling you the story as it has been handed down in our family for generations. I'll skip some parts if you wish, but you might miss something that would be important to you later."

Jeremy looked puzzled. "Why would omitted sections bother me later?"

"I didn't ask you here just to tell you stories. We have a family problem, and I want you to act on it. Anyway, I'll yield to your anxiety and skip some parts."

Debbie approached her grandmother and patted her on the shoulder. "We'll try to be patient."

Marie smiled at Debbie and then continued. "Cyrus continued to search for contacts at the Pinkerton organization, but he had only limited results. He did find two veterans from his regiment who had moved to Milwaukee where they had become policemen. They knew several Pinkerton men who operated out of a Milwaukee office, but when contacted, those individuals couldn't supply information about Secret Service activities elsewhere. They sent Cyrus away with a promise to let him know if they learned anything about his wife, but that was the last Cyrus ever heard from them. He returned home, despondent, and vowed to be the best father he could to the boys in their mother's absence."

Jeremy said, "So that was it then. Barbara never returned, and Cyrus had to do his best without her."

Marie tilted her rocking chair forward. Her voice had a sharp edge. "A little patience, young man, if you please. I was about to tell you that Cyrus was alone with the boys for two and a half years. At that point he received a letter addressed simply to *Cyrus, Fox Lake, Wisconsin.* Fortunately, Fox Lake was small enough for the postmaster to know Cyrus. The letter was from a doctor in Memphis, Tennessee. He was writing to determine whether a story he had heard from a patient might be true. Doctor James Linton indicated that one of his regular patients, Mrs. Sally Priddle, a widow, had opened her home to a woman whom she had found collapsed on her doorstep. That woman had injuries from a recent beating. Mrs. Priddle nursed the woman back to reasonable health, but discovered that her houseguest couldn't remember anything about herself and could barely carry on a conversation. Dr. Linton wrote that he had suggested to Mrs. Priddle that the woman might have suffered some kind of shock and that she might regain her memories after a period of time. After some discussion, Sally had agreed to let the woman stay with her for a month or two if she helped out with chores and Sally's bakery business. After two months, during which the woman showed remarkable skills around the house, she remembered that her name was Barbara and that she recalled the name Cyrus and a place, Fox Lake, Wisconsin. However, that was all that she remembered.

Cyrus, of course, was overjoyed to receive Dr. Linton's letter and sent a reply that he would come down immediately to learn whether the woman at Mrs. Priddle's house was his missing wife. He told the boys of his destination and had Bruce drive him in their wagon to the Wisconsin Central Line station. That railroad would take him to Chicago, where he could connect to the Illinois Central Railroad for the rest of his trip to Memphis. Travel was getting much easier and faster than it was when he traveled by riverboat to St. Louis and stagecoach to the west coast on his way to Australia.

During his train ride, Cyrus kept asking himself whether the woman he would be meeting was likely to be his Barbara. It sounded too good to be true. He also shuddered at the thought that if she was Barbara, she had lost her memories of him and their family. He hoped she would at least recognize him.

He carried the two addresses that had been contained in Dr. Linton's letter. His plan was to go to the doctor's office first for further medical information and to possibly convince the doctor to accompany him. He also wanted to get the doctor's guidance in case of an unexpected reaction from Barbara. Then he, with or without the doctor's support, would go to Sally Priddle's house to see whether the woman really was his wife.

CHAPTER 23 - MEMPHIS

When Cyrus reached Dr. Linton's address, he found himself facing a modest white house with an added wing to the left of the front door. A sign by the front door read *Medical Entrance around Corner*, with an arrow pointing to the left. Cyrus followed the path around the corner of the house to an entrance bearing another sign *Open – Come in and remove shoes.* That sign bothered Cyrus because the removal of his shoes would show that he had an artificial left foot, but this visit was too important to let such a minor matter disrupt it.

When he went inside, Cyrus found one man waiting for the doctor. He removed his boots and took a seat across from that person. They nodded to each other, and Cyrus noticed a brown leather glove on the man's left hand, meant to conceal the fact that it was artificial. The man said to Cyrus, "Looks like we both got shot up in the war. Thank God it's over and we're one country again."

Cyrus smiled but didn't volunteer any information because he had heard that many southerners wanted to keep fighting when they were one-on-one with a Yankee.

At that point, the door to Dr. Linton's inner medical office opened, and the doctor escorted a middle-aged woman out. After she had left, Dr. Linton turned to the man who had been waiting longer. "Come on in Stephen." To Cyrus he said, "There's a newspaper on the shelf under the table if you want to read while you wait."

Cyrus responded that he would just sit and relax. His thoughts were churning in his mind so rapidly that he wouldn't have been able to concentrate on a newspaper anyway. At least he now knew what Dr. Linton looked like.

He appeared to be about forty years old, and he was clean shaven, probably because medical practices had started to pay attention to cleanliness and sanitation. So many people had died during the war because of unsanitary practices like using the same surgical instruments on many patients without cleaning them off in between operations.

After about twenty minutes, Dr. Linton escorted Stephen out and asked Cyrus to come into his office. Before Cyrus could identify himself, Dr. Linton said, "I don't know your medical complaint today, but we have improved versions of that artificial leg you're wearing. I could fit you with a more comfortable alternative."

Cyrus said, "Actually, Doctor, I don't have a medical complaint. I'm Cyrus Danforth from Fox Lake, Wisconsin, and we exchanged letters about the possibility that the woman at Mrs. Priddle's house is my kidnapped wife, Barbara."

Dr. Linton shook his hand. "I'm so pleased to meet you, Mr. Danforth. This has been my first experience with someone suffering amnesia because of a traumatic event or injuries. I hope that your presence will accelerate her improvement."

"Thank you, Doctor. I wanted to visit you before going to Mrs. Priddle's house to learn more about the circumstances of her arrival there, and to try to persuade you to accompany me in case Barbara has a bad reaction when she first sees me."

"My going with you sounds like a good idea, and I have no more appointments today to interfere with that. What else do you want to know?"

"Why do you think she went to Mrs. Priddle's house instead of somewhere else? How badly had she been injured and what do you think caused her bruises and cuts?"

I'm sure you have more questions than those, Mr. Danforth, but they'll do for a start. Mrs. Priddle lives in an isolated house that backs up against a forest. I suspect that your wife suffered her injuries inside that forest and stumbled out of the woods to head for the only house she saw. With regard to her injuries, she appeared to have been beaten by someone who used fists and a long weapon of some kind, perhaps a pipe."

Could it have been a branch from a tree?"

"Possibly, but I think its surface was smooth."

"Have Barbara's wounds healed?"

"She has scars that will be with her always, but she has physically healed. It's likely to be a long time before her mental wounds heal, if they ever do."

"One last question before we go over there, do you think she'll accept my story that I'm her husband?"

"I honestly have no idea."

CHAPTER 24 – MEETING AGAIN

Dr. Linton pulled his horse to a stop outside Sally Priddle's house and climbed down from the wagon, leaving Cyrus to secure the horse and follow him inside after a few minutes. Linton wanted to ease the potential shock to Barbara of having Cyrus arrive unannounced. Sally had seen them arrive through her window, and she realized the second man sitting alongside Dr. Linton in the wagon had to be someone significant. She sent Barbara into the kitchen to prepare a pitcher of lemonade and bring it out with some glasses.

When Dr. Linton knocked on the door, Sally opened it quickly and ushered him in. As she glanced over his shoulder at the wagon and the man next to it, the doctor whispered that he was Cyrus Danforth and quite likely was Barbara's husband.

Appreciating the implications of the encounter, Sally suggested that they arrange four chairs in a circle around a small table so that Barbara wouldn't be forced to concentrate on Cyrus, but would be sitting close to her two post-ordeal friends. They finished rearranging the furniture as Barbara returned with the lemonade. She adjusted to the new setup and placed her tray on the centered table. Then she greeted Dr. Linton, and as she turned to ask Sally Priddle for additional tasks she heard a knock on the door.

As Dr. Linton walked toward the door, he told Sally and Barbara that he had brought a visitor to meet them. He opened the door and greeted Cyrus by name, to indicate that they were already friends. With the open door blocking the women's sight lines, he gestured by a downward motion of his open palm that Cyrus should proceed slowly and softly. Cyrus responded with a slight nod. He entered and stood quietly while he waited for Dr. Linton to introduce him.

The doctor turned toward the women. "I brought a friend along with me. This gentleman is Cyrus Danforth from Wisconsin. He's visiting Memphis for the first time, and I thought he would like to chat with you and learn more about the area."

Seeing no sign of recognition from Barbara, Sally Priddle welcomed Cyrus and suggested he sit down for some conversation and lemonade. "I visited Wisconsin before the war. My late husband, John, and I both enjoyed our time in Milwaukee. I hope to get back there sometime."

Cyrus responded to Sally while facing in a direction that allowed him to study Barbara. He was relieved that this person was indeed his wife, but her stooped posture, massive array of arm and facial scars, plus closely cropped hair indicated she had been to hell and only partially returned. He made an effort to avoid staring at her. "Mrs. Priddle, I'm pleased that you enjoyed Milwaukee on your last visit. I'd welcome the opportunity to serve as a host and tour guide should you visit our state again. Have you been in Wisconsin, Barbara?"

"Maybe. Sounds known, but not sure. Things fuzzy lately."

Dr. Linton injected himself into the conversation. "Cyrus and I were talking, and he suggested that he may know you from the past. Take a good look at him, Barbara. Does he look familiar?"

She stood, moved toward Cyrus, and stared at him. Then she reached out her left hand and touched his cheek. "Did you have beard?"

That surprised him. "I did, but it was a long time ago in a place called Australia. Do you remember being there?"

Barbara shrieked. "Bad place. Men attacked me."

Cyrus slowly reached for the hand that had touched his cheek. "No. Good place. Bad men there. Do you remember anything else about Australia?"

"Friend had bad leg."

"What do you mean by that?"

"Don't know. It just came to me. Nothing more. This game is too hard."

Cyrus pulled up the left leg of his pants to reveal his artificial leg. His action surprised Mrs. Priddle, who looked away. "Did the bad leg look like this?"

Barbara pointed at Cyrus' leg and shouted, "Bad leg. Bad leg."

Dr. Linton leaned toward Barbara. "Look closely at Cyrus. Is he your friend from Australia?"

They saw Barbara's first smile since she had arrived at Sally Priddle's house.

"Friend and more. Safe." She stretched her left hand out toward Cyrus, and he grasped it with his right hand.

Sally Priddle said, "I think it's time for lemonade. Something good is happening here. Praises to God and love."

CHAPTER 25 - NEW BEGINNINGS

Cyrus remained in Memphis for more than three weeks, spending his days with Barbara at Sally Priddle's house and his evenings reviewing each day's progress with Dr. Linton who had insisted that Cyrus sleep in his spare bedroom to facilitate the process. James Linton genuinely liked Cyrus and hoped to build their friendship into the future, but he also saw Barbara's case as a significant medical study. Prior to the Civil War, his journals had contained no cases of mental anguish caused by physical hardships. A few military studies had recently appeared, but the application of those study results to civilian cases would be something quite new.

Initially, Cyrus was content to sit with Barbara and let her gain confidence from his presence. Then he started to ask questions, addressed first to Sally Priddle and later to Barbara directly.

From Sally he learned that Barbara had been virtually incoherent in her despair when she reached the Priddle doorstep and collapsed. Sally had gone to the door when she heard a scratching sound, thinking a lost dog from a neighboring farm was there. She had found the woman bruised, cut in several places, and completely filthy. Her clothes and shoes looked as though she had worn them without changing for a very long time. Her hair was so tangled and knotted that Sally had no choice but to cut it down almost to the scalp. Mrs. Priddle knew that Barbara would die of her wounds and exposure if someone didn't help her, so Sally accepted her new role as Good Samaritan and provided the necessary compassion. As

Barbara began to recover, Sally found her to be a welcome companion within the limits of their strained relationship.

Cyrus found that getting information out of Barbara was difficult and frustrating. She remembered very little from her time in captivity, and she didn't want to talk about the very few aspects she did recall. All Barbara wanted was to sit with Cyrus, hold his hand, and talk about feeling safe with him. He felt the way he had as a boy when his father brought home a stray dog. Cyrus and Lucky had loved each other, but they hadn't been able to communicate or share anything except new experiences. Barbara was his new Lucky, and he felt lucky to have found her again, whatever the future would hold for them.

During one of the evening sessions with Dr. James Linton, Cyrus learned that Barbara's behavior and communication patterns were much the same as those observed in veterans who had felt insecure and unable to cope with their intense warfare experiences.

Cyrus responded to James' observation. "Ordinarily, I'd say that your comparison of Barbara's mental withdrawal to similar military cases was very clever and insightful. But think of her experiences. She was kidnapped and presumably held in captivity for two and a half years. Most recently, she was beaten somewhere in the middle of a forest and left to survive by crawling out of unmapped woods in order to find a house and possible help. I'd say that hers essentially was a military experience. We don't know the real circumstances yet, but she essentially escaped from a military prison camp."

James Linton smiled. "You're right, Cyrus; they are close parallels. We won't know whether her case is more civilian or military until she regains more memories and shares them with us. You're becoming quite a student of physical and mental stress effects."

"That's because I've been officially out of the Army for more than twenty years, but I've continued to be on tactical missions of my own for almost all of that time. Barbara and I have had good times together, and we've raised a couple of promising lads, but behind the scenes, we've been on the watch for Pinkerton agents coming after her while we've also continued concealed efforts to assist members of my former regiment and their families." Cyrus gave James a brief sketch of his past life and shared adventures with Barbara.

After hearing Cyrus' story, James said, "You originally blamed the Secret Service. Do you still think that Pinkerton agents are responsible for her beatings and captivity?"

"No, James, it wouldn't make much sense. The Pinkertons are organized and relentless in their assignments. I doubt that they would beat a woman like this, but if they did and she escaped, they'd have groups of agents searching for her. I've pretty much convinced myself that her kidnapping and captivity was the work of a single man. I won't know anything about him until Barbara remembers more and shares with me, but that person will eventually pay with his life for what he has done."

"Are you saying that you follow the Old Testament teaching of an eye for an eye and a tooth for a tooth?"

"No, it's not that. I'm usually very merciful and forgiving. I consider her kidnapping and near destruction to have been an act of war against me and my family. I'm a soldier responding to that declaration of war, and I will win the final battle."

"Cyrus, I hear you saying that coldly and without emotion."

"It's not an emotional matter, James, and your reaction tells me you believe that I will succeed in my mission."

CHAPTER 26 – GOING HOME

Three weeks into their companionship sessions, Cyrus asked Barbara to go for a walk with him. Her response surprised and encouraged him.

"I'll go where you want, but not in trees. Danger there."

As Cyrus went for his jacket to put over Barbara's shoulders, Sally approached him and offered her shawl. She gave it to him and whispered, "This will be the first time Barbara has left the house and yard." He nodded his thanks and affirmation.

They walked along the road in a direction that increased their distance from the woods. Barbara held his arm and repeatedly touched the shawl until its texture became familiar to her. Her posture was much more erect than when he first saw her. After they had walked for half a mile, Cyrus suggested they sit on a stone wall by a farmer's field.

Once settled, Cyrus said, "Tell me who you think I am, Barbara."

She thought for a while and said, "You are a friend and more."

"How much more than a friend?"

"You are long time from before bad times friend."

"I'm even more than that to you. I'm your husband." He watched for her reaction.

She arched her right eyebrow as she had many times during happier days. "If you are my husband, I am your wife?"

"Yes, that's true."

"Did we live together?"

"Yes, in Wisconsin."

"Wisconsin. Wisconsin. Wisconsin. – Funny name."

"It will sound better after we go there. Wisconsin is home."

Barbara looked at Cyrus and felt his face with both hands. "We're going home. You and me. Am I Barbara Danforth, same name as you?"

Cyrus put his arms around her and gave her a gentle hug. "You are definitely Barbara Danforth, same name as me."

She reached out and returned his hug. "That feels good, home and husband, safe once more."

Cyrus held her hands in his. "Now, your husband wants you to relax and think back as far as you can. Do you remember anything about what happened to you since the time when someone took you from our home?"

"I walked and crawled from bad woods to Mrs. Priddle's house. She helped me. I needed her."

"Do you remember what happened in the bad woods or anything before that?"

"No, but doctor says maybe later."

Cyrus smiled and squeezed her hands. "Then 'maybe later' will have to be our motto. The important thing is that we're together again. We'll go home soon."

Two days later, Dr. Linton drove Cyrus in his wagon to pick up Barbara for the journey home. Cyrus had purchased a suitcase and a few changes of clothes for his wife. She cheerfully changed into one of them before they left Sally Priddle's house. Cyrus insisted that Sally accept an envelope with some cash to cover her costs while she aided Barbara, and he promised that they would correspond with her in the future.

As they drove to the railroad station, Cyrus made a similar pledge to keep in contact with Dr. James Linton. The doctor surprised Cyrus by saying that he hadn't taken a vacation for a long time, so he hoped to visit the Danforths in Wisconsin in about six months or a year. He hoped that at that point Barbara would remember more about her imprisonment ordeal. Cyrus had the impression that James wanted to write about Barbara's case as a medical study. He wasn't sure how he would react to having his wife's suffering documented and published, but he assumed James wouldn't proceed without his approval.

When they reached the station, James gave Cyrus a package from underneath a canvas cover in the back corner of the wagon. "I have a going home present for you. It's an updated version of your leg replacement. I think you'll find it more comfortable. I took measurements one evening when you fell asleep on my sofa. There are adjustment straps, so you'll be able to get the best fit."

Cyrus gave James an enthusiastic handclasp. "James, I don't know how I could have found Barbara and brought her to this point without you. We'll have to keep our friendship strong no matter what happens in the future. I'm sure the leg will be a welcome improvement. Thank you for everything."

Barbara held the doctor's hand and nodded her thanks too. Then Dr. Linton climbed onto the wagon and left.

After purchasing their tickets, Cyrus and Barbara had only twenty minutes to wait for their train, but sitting together on the waiting room bench, they felt it was much longer. Cyrus had prayed for this reunion for a very long time, and now it had happened.

CHAPTER 27 - WISCONSIN

After they changed trains in Chicago, Cyrus began to talk with Barbara about what she should expect when they arrived home. The most essential goal was to get her to understand or remember that she was a mother. Cyrus hadn't wanted to shock her with extra details of her life until it was necessary. He told her about Bruce and Daniel and watched to see how she reacted.

Barbara looked at the horizon through the train window. "I wondered if I was both wife and mother. Now I know. Bruce is the older boy?"

"Yes, he's almost fifteen years old. Daniel's almost thirteen. When you see them they'll look much taller than when you were taken from us, if you have memories of them."

"I'll try to remember. Doctor says seeing home and people may help me remember."

Cyrus put his arm around her shoulders. "Don't worry if you don't recall them right away. It will come with time as you get to know them again."

"I'll start with the names – Bruce and Daniel. Bruce is older and bigger."

Cyrus laughed. "It will be confusing, but even though Bruce is older, Daniel is taller. He grew faster than Bruce."

"So the taller boy is the younger, and the older boy is the shorter. Are they friends? Sally Priddle said she has never been a close friend to her sister. She said they argue when they see each other."

"Our boys haven't had that problem. They've always been good friends."

Barbara held his hand. “I like it when you call them our boys. We must have done many things together. How long have we been married?”

Cyrus thought for a few seconds and said, “It has been close to eighteen years.”

She squeezed his hand. “That’s a long time. I will try hard to remember.”

When they reached the closest station to Fox Lake, Cyrus asked Barbara to sit with their luggage while he hired a driver to take them the rest of the way home. When he returned to get her, he found Barbara fighting back a few tears.

Cyrus grasped her hand in an effort to calm her. “What’s the matter? Is this journey making you uncomfortable?”

“No, Cyrus, not the trip. I’m getting closer to having to be someone I don’t remember. I don’t know if boys will accept me as mother or how I will react to them. Will I remember home and neighbors? I can cope with you. You’re my island of safety, but I’ll have to be part of a world that means nothing to me. Anyway, forgive my tears. I think I was once brave, and I’ll have to become strong again.”

“Barbara, you were the strongest, most self-sufficient woman I ever met, and you will regain that inner strength again. You’ll have to start by knowing that I love you and think of you even when we have to be apart. We can’t always be together, so we’ll work on getting through these short separations.”

She squeezed his hand. “I’ll be better soon. I promise. Now, where’s our ride?”

The wagon was a springseat buckboard type with only a single bench seat for them plus Bill Whitehorn, their driver. Cyrus sat next to Bill with Barbara on the right end of the seat, so that she wouldn’t have to sit next to a strange man. During the trip, Barbara spent her time looking at the fields, woods, and houses they passed while Cyrus talked about unimportant things with Bill. Barbara felt relieved when the wagon slowed and stopped in front of an isolated house with a porch that wrapped the front and right side of the building. She would no longer have to listen to the men talk.

They climbed down, and Cyrus paid the driver. As the wagon pulled away, Cyrus turned to speak to Barbara, but she wasn't there. He experienced a slight shudder at the thought of her going missing again, but then he saw her walking the length of the porch from the front to the side of the house. Cyrus picked up the luggage and climbed the porch steps.

"Cyrus, I know this place. No seats here now, but I sat here in past on soft chair."

Cyrus set down their bags and hugged her. "Your chair is in the barn. I'll bring it back after we get settled inside. I took your chair away when I had the boys paint the porch. We're going to be fine. You're home now, and your memories will return."

"Are the boys here? It sounds empty."

"No, they're at work in the hard goods store. We'll have a few hours for you to spend here alone before they return. Let's go inside and visit all the rooms to see what seems familiar to you."

Cyrus watched Barbara as he held the door open for her to enter. He saw her look into the sitting room to their right and then up the stairs on the left wall and down the hallway straight ahead.

She said, "This house much different from Sally's. More chairs in front room because more people live here. Does hallway go to kitchen? I want to see kitchen."

Cyrus led her down the hall to the kitchen and opened the door wide for her to enter. He expected her to look first at the stove, but she went to the sink.

"You, I mean we, have a water pump next to the sink. I can pump water for washing there. Much better than having to pump water outside and then carry it in like at Sally's house."

Cyrus walked over to the sink and worked the pump handle up and down until a forceful stream of water splashed into the sink. "When we first moved here, I installed this so that you wouldn't have to carry water buckets from outside. We're the only people on this side of town to have this setup."

She looked at the stove and then shook her head. "Can't remember this. Does it burn wood or coal?"

"We burn wood from the pile on the back porch. The boys and I cut trees and branches from the back end of our field and pile it out back for the stove and the fireplace."

"I remember now. Colder here than where I was."

"Do you remember anything about where you were?" Cyrus hoped Barbara was on the verge of remembering more.

"Just Sally Priddle's house. Everything before that is gone."

Cyrus was about to ask a few more probing questions when the back door opened and the boys rushed in. Together, they shouted, "Mother, you're home!"

Barbara backed up slightly at their outburst and looked a question at Cyrus.

He said, "Boys, your mother has been through some terrible ordeals, most of which she can't remember yet. Just stand next to each other quietly, so that she can get used to seeing you again."

The boys followed instructions, a little awkwardly, not knowing how upright their posture had to be.

Barbara looked at their faces and sizes and then said, "Daniel, the taller one is on left and Bruce is on right. Am

I correct? Be patient with me. I hope to remember the past soon."

Bruce gently hugged her. "Welcome home, Mother. You were correct. I'm Bruce, and that stringbean is Daniel. You won't remember that we used to try to get out of doing our chores, but we know you'll need our help more now, and we'll do our best to be around when you want an assist with anything, right Dan?"

Daniel put his hand on his mother's shoulder. "He always was the speechmaker, but he's right this time. Anything you need, just call on us. We've missed you so much."

The boys and Barbara enjoyed a tentative communal hug and then backed away.

Cyrus said, "You boys can start by refreshing the woodpile out back while I reacquaint your mother with the rest of the house. Later, you can tell me how things went at the store while I was gone."

After the boys ran out the back door, Barbara said, "They're wonderful. With them and you I feel much safer now. Just keep me from being alone too much. I was alone for a very long time, and it was painful."

Cyrus wasn't sure how to react to that nugget of information, so he filed it away in his mind as he led Barbara upstairs to the second floor rooms.

CHAPTER 28 – TRANSITIONS

Cyrus felt relieved to have Barbara back in the Danforth household, but he and the boys felt tension at the same time. Barbara was back, but she was incomplete and fragile. At times she screamed in her dreams and woke herself and everyone else. She was relearning how to live in their family. Because of that, Cyrus and the boys tried to avoid any minor conflicts when they were with her. Conflict caused Barbara to withdraw from socializing for several days at a time. Their new family relationship improved with time, but the old easy-going banter and spontaneity were gone.

Occasionally, Cyrus would slip questions into his conversations with Barbara to see whether she was regaining memories of her kidnapping and captivity. Usually, she resisted sharing whatever had come back to her. The one breakthrough came when they were together in the hard goods store looking for a new rug beater and a cast iron fry pan that was bigger than the one they had used when the boys were small.

They had already picked out the rug beater. Barbara carried that device, swinging it as they walked over to the kitchen section of the store. As they approached the shelves, Cyrus said, “We have a new supply of pots and pans that just arrived so you'll have a lot to choose from.” As he turned away from the pans to look at Barbara, he saw that she had stopped and stiffened with a strange expression on her face.

Cyrus grasped her hand. “What's the matter, Barbara? Did I say or do something wrong?”

She reverted to her earlier limited speech pattern. "You said pots and pans. Peddler of those came to house and took me away."

Cyrus stared at her with mixed feelings. "Barbara, you're starting to remember. That's very good." As he reached for her arm, he mentally kicked himself. He had made a big mistake when she disappeared. Sheriff Erik Hanson said at the time that the only strangers he had seen were two men with long coats and a peddler of pots and pans. He had chased the men with the long coats because their description fit that of Pinkerton Secret Service agents. He should have gone after the peddler instead of the other two. The sheriff said he saw the peddler's wagon when he searched in the eastbound direction. Cyrus knew now that he might have spared Barbara from her long ordeal if he had chosen to go after the other stranger, but he had not suspected the peddler of being dangerous.

"Where did he take you, Barbara?"

She limply leaned against him. "I don't know. Very long ride. Tied up. Pots and pans hitting me as we rode. We go home now. Don't want new pan."

Cyrus agreed, seeing the misery in her expression. He had learned something basic and important, but he didn't know whether the information about the initial kidnapping would lead to the return of more of Barbara's memories. Even without them, he understood an additional key fact. The kidnapper had gone directly to their house in disguise to catch Barbara off guard. She had been targeted because of something in her past.

CHAPTER 29 – NORMALIZATION

Cyrus hoped that Barbara's reaction to the pots and pans comment would lead to additional bits and pieces of lost memories. He revealed the new information to Bruce and Daniel in the hope that they would notice and share additional comments from their mother about what had happened to her. The problem was that while Barbara regained her day-by-day calm outlook and comfort with their family activities, she had no more obvious flashes of memories. At least, her screaming episodes disrupting their sleep subsided. The Danforths were learning to live together based on the present and future, while disregarding the uncomfortable hole in their past.

All of the turmoil over Barbara's kidnapping and the rehabilitation period after her return had diverted Cyrus' attention from his program of support for veterans of the 2nd Wisconsin regiment. Once he believed Barbara could cope with his being away, Cyrus returned to the University of Wisconsin in Madison to see whether any improvements could be made to distribute benefits to more families. The scholarship program assisted those families that sent their children to college, but it had little benefit for farmers and trades people.

In Madison, Cyrus met Professor William A. Henry who was Wisconsin's first professor of agriculture. They spent time together, both in Henry's office and at several local drinking establishments, discussing the way the raising of wheat had generated abundant cash for the state's early farmers but had depleted the nutrients in the soil. Because of this, the quality and quantity of wheat raised on each acre of farmland was decreasing. Professor

Henry advocated that wheat farmers in the southern part of the state consider a change to dairy farming. He had used the university's model farm to experiment with new dairy methods and had pioneered the use of cylindrical silos for storing cattle feed during the winter. Professor Henry also worked on bacterial testing of dairy products and practical techniques for milk pasteurization.

As they exchanged ideas over their drinks, Cyrus found himself agreeing with William Henry's ideas and his plan to have those considering a shift to dairying take short courses at the university, including winter courses that he would schedule when farmers had the most down time from their field work. Cyrus offered to extend his scholarship program to the farmers' courses including support benefits for their families who had to maintain the farms during the university sessions. This offer excited Professor Henry, while relieving some of Cyrus' guilt over losing interest in his regimental support mission while he concentrated on Barbara's problems.

When Cyrus returned home, he asked Bruce how Barbara had been during his absence.

Bruce shrugged. "She keeps surprising me. Mother has never been particularly athletic, but she has taken over our wood-chopping chore. She still lets us gather the logs, but insists on splitting them for fireplace and stove use herself. She told me she has to build up her strength for emergencies."

Cyrus said, "That either means that she's still not feeling secure in our home, or that she expects another future attack from someone. I'll talk with her to see if I can get her to share her thinking."

He went upstairs to their bedroom, expecting to find Barbara sitting in her chair by the window, either knitting or reading. When she wasn't there, he looked for her in the kitchen and the cellar. Cyrus began to wonder whether she had left home without telling the boys, when he saw the barn door open. He went into the barn and saw Barbara grooming one of their three horses, Sunshine. She had already worked his coat with the hard brush, and she was finishing her effort with the soft body brush.

Cyrus asked, "Was Sunshine looking bad that you're giving him the full treatment?"

"Not too bad; Moonglow was much worse. Daniel had him in the mud by the creek when he went fishing. It's good to have you home again. I can brush your horse, Starburst, later."

"I wasn't gone that long, Barbara. Does it still bother you when I'm away?"

"Not as much as it used to. I'm concentrating on getting strong again so that I'll be able to travel with you. I don't feel I'm carrying my share of the load when you go and leave me behind."

Cyrus nodded his understanding. "I wasn't worried about your lack of strength. It was more a matter of whether you would be comfortable away from home. Do strange places disturb you?"

"It gets easier each time I see new places and people. It will never be like before, but it gets easier."

Cyrus took advantage of this opening to ask questions. "Are you beginning to remember more about when you were away from us?"

"Don't tiptoe around the subject, Cyrus. You make it sound as though I was off on a vacation. I don't remember anything after that man took me away, but I get a sense of dread every time I think about it."

"Dr. Linton thinks that your mind shut down the memories because they were so bad."

"That may be true, Cyrus, but I'm working on getting my new life with you to be more normal. It's not what we had before, but it gets closer as time passes. That's the most I can offer you right now. At least my hair looks like it did in that old picture you have."

He reached over and fingered her dark curls. "This is our first open discussion about what happened to you. Earlier, you had trouble communicating what you felt, and I was afraid that too many questions would build a barrier between us."

"That might have happened. It took a long time for me to feel part of the family again. I'm sorry if I hurt you or the boys by still being alone even when I was with you."

"But you are back now. We all can relax with each other?"

"I'm back, Cyrus, but be very gentle with me in the bedroom. I know things happened to me that make me reject aggressive advances. I don't have many memories, but that instinct kicks in when I feel sexually cornered."

He held her in his arms and caressed her back until Sunshine stomped his feet and whinnied his request for more grooming attention.

CHAPTER 30 – LETTER

Several weeks later, Cyrus returned from the post office with a letter from Dr. James Linton. He hurried into the kitchen and kissed Barbara while she was cutting carrots for their soup.

"Watch out, Cyrus. It's not a good idea to surprise someone while she has a knife in her hand. I do appreciate the kiss, though. You must be in a good mood."

"I received a letter from James Linton today, and it contained some surprising news. James married Sally Priddle. While you were living at Sally's house they got to appreciate each other, and they kept seeing each other after we returned to Wisconsin. What do you think about that?"

"I think that's great news. They're both good people, and we owe them a lot for taking care of me. We'll have to send them a congratulations letter."

"I don't think we'll need to do that. The second part of James' news is that they're coming from Memphis to visit us in two weeks. We can temporarily move the boys in together so that we'll have a spare bedroom for the Lintons."

"It's not quite that easy, Cyrus. You'll have to get a new bed that's big enough for the two of them, and I'll have to store some of the boys' clutter in a different location while they're here. I think it would work out best to have Bruce move in with Daniel. We can put both beds in Daniel's room. It's big enough. You can get a double bed and put it in Bruce's room."

"Then, you're willing to have them stay here?"

"Of course I am. They did everything possible for me. Besides, the nearest family that takes in boarders is miles away. It will be different spending time with them now that I'm myself again. I still remember Sally's recipe for oatmeal cookies. I'll surprise her by serving them."

"I know James will be pleased to see how far you've come. He was very interested in your case from a medical viewpoint."

"Well, he'd better be coming here as a friend. I don't want anyone studying me as a curiosity. I've had quite enough of that."

James and Sally arrived from the train station in Bill Whitehorn's springseat buckboard, reminding Cyrus of his own return home with Barbara. The two couples enthusiastically greeted each other. Barbara led Sally into the house while the men carried the luggage up to the new spare bedroom. When Cyrus and James came back downstairs, Barbara and Sally had already settled in front of the fireplace with a pot of tea and cookies.

James laughed when he entered the room. "This is a much more relaxed scene than we had at Sally's house. Barbara, you've come a long way since your captivity ordeal. It's so pleasant to visit you now."

Cyrus said, "You won't get our complete domestic picture until Bruce and Daniel return. They're on a fishing trip with some friends and won't return for a few days. They will be back before the end of your stay. In any case, we want to congratulate you and wish you many happy years of marriage."

James looked to Sally for guidance, and she nodded her consent. "Cyrus, this is more than a social visit. We have information about what happened to Barbara that will affect both of you. What we have to say required our coming for an in-person visit."

Barbara stood. "Go ahead, James. I'm strong enough to take whatever you have to share with us. I'll apologize in advance for any bad reactions I may have to it."

Cyrus moved over and held Barbara's hand to show his support.

James took his cue from Cyrus and moved closer to Sally on the sofa. "A little more than a month ago, I organized a search to try to find what happened to Barbara in those woods outside Memphis. Earlier, the sheriff's people had explored those woods about a mile deep without finding anything. My group extended that search to five miles, where we found a small stone cabin."

Cyrus looked at Barbara for any reaction, but saw none.

James continued. "Cyrus, you once told me that you would go after the man who declared war on your family by kidnapping and mistreating your wife for so long. You won't have to. We found his remains inside that cabin. He's dead."

Barbara sighed but said nothing.

Cyrus asked, "How do you know he was the kidnapper?"

"The cabin had a back room without windows where we found chains with shackles fastened to the wall. The chains were long enough for a shackled person to reach a half whiskey barrel that was used as a toilet. The shackled person could also reach a pump to obtain water and a bucket that held some old ears of corn."

Barbara interrupted. "...one ear of raw corn on a good day, often none. Then I had old empty cobs and bad water."

Cyrus said, "You remember!"

"It's beginning to come back. Keep talking, James."

"The man, or rather his skeleton, was dressed in a Confederate officer's uniform."

Barbara jumped in again. "...not an officer or even a soldier. He deserted and hid 'til the war was over."

Cyrus asked, "How did he die?"

James asked, "Can you remember? Do you want to answer that question?"

Barbara shook her head negatively.

"The prisoner was smart and strong. Over a long period of time she used her chain as a tool, scraping at the mortar between the stones in the cabin wall. She finally dislodged a graspable stone and smashed him in the head when he came close to her."

Cyrus said, "I'm surprised he came that close."

Barbara gasped. "You have to come close to rape someone. He didn't know I still had strength. I took a terrible chance. If he didn't have the shackle key in his pocket I would have died of starvation. At that point it had to end, either way."

Cyrus hugged Barbara. Then he said, "Bad memories are returning. Let's have some drinks. I know I need some strong whiskey right now. We can continue discussing this later tonight or tomorrow. This is too much for her."

She kissed his cheek. "Not too much, Cyrus. Drink first; then we'll talk more. It's coming back to me. I have to talk about it right away, or I might forget it all over again."

CHAPTER 31 – MEMORIES

After several rounds of drinks, including a small whiskey for Barbara, they gathered once more in the front room, this time arranging the seats to face Barbara, who indicated that she was ready to share memories that were emerging from hidden recesses of her mind.

She told them that she would stand and might move around while she talked because she was not yet comfortable with sitting for long intervals. "Now that I'm aware of many of the things that happened to me, I realize I may have caused it all."

Cyrus said, "You can't blame yourself for any of this."

"Let me explain, Cyrus. You and I came to Wisconsin with my name changed and using my story of having been a war widow before we met and married. Our goal was to keep me hidden from anyone who might be after me because of my wartime spying for the South. As we lived happily together and the boys grew older, I felt I needed to share my contentment, so I wrote a letter to one of my best girlfriends from school days. Apparently she told others about my new life, even though I asked her to keep my story secret."

Sally said, "I've often found that the quickest way to spread gossip is to tell someone it's a secret."

Barbara nodded her agreement. "From my spying days, I should have known to trust no one. Anyway, news about my new life reached John Hackamore, a snobby guy I had dated once or twice in school. Yes, he did claim that one of his ancestors invented the hackamore headpiece for horses. Anyway, this guy bragged a lot, but when the war broke out, he deserted and took off for Mexico so that no one could make him fight. He later claimed that he had served the Confederacy fighting in New Mexico, but others who were there proved him a liar. Much later, when he learned about my marriage, he ranted and raved about a southern girl marrying a Yankee and turning her back on the Confederacy, even though the war had ended fifteen years earlier."

Dr. Linton said, "He was insecure because people laughed at his wartime cowardice, so he decided to show them all by going after you."

"I didn't recognize him when he came to the door in his peddler's get-up, and he knocked me out as soon as he realized I was home alone."

Cyrus hit his left hand with his right fist. "...that cowardly bastard."

Sally asked, "Did he take you to your old home town so that he could brag about capturing you?"

"Far from it, Sally, he took me to a mountain shack in the northwest corner of Georgia. He was nervous about someone catching him, but he turned his nervousness into aggression toward me. He kept screaming that it was my fault that he was in a dangerous situation."

Cyrus walked over to Barbara and held her hand. "You don't have to answer this if you don't want to. I'll understand. I do have to ask how he treated you during all that time you were gone. Was it always as bad as at the end?"

"In many ways it was worse earlier. He beat me and raped me almost every day. This made him feel superior, and he bragged about going out and raping other women on the days when he left me alone. He talked about two widows of Confederate soldiers that he visited regularly, and said that they were better than me because they remained loyal to the southern cause."

Cyrus said, "You suffered like that every day for two and a half years?"

"Not every day. I finally kept him away from me by getting pregnant. I couldn't believe it, but Hackamore turned romantic at the thought of having a baby with me, and he left me alone after he realized I was pregnant. He actually started to treat me like a human being."

James said, "He was living in a fantasy world anyway, and your pregnancy changed the nature of that fantasy. That's why you survived your ordeal for so long."

Cyrus got serious at the mention of her pregnancy. "What happened to the baby? Why did he treat you so badly at that place near Memphis if you had a baby together?"

"After all he had done to me I was in terrible shape to handle a pregnancy. I eventually gave birth to a baby girl, but she was born premature, and her hands were deformed. She had only the second and third fingers on her left hand and the thumb and forefinger on her right hand. I named her Lynnette, but he refused to call her anything at all. He referred to her as 'it.' He was furious because the child was imperfect."

Sally leaned forward. "Did your daughter die?"

"Somehow, I persuaded Hackamore to let me raise her for a year so that she would have a chance to survive. Then he could put her into an orphanage. There were many such places after the war. Many children had lost both parents or been displaced so that they had no one to care for them. Hackamore was mad at both himself and me for not being able to have a normal child, but I think he agreed because he realized she was part of him, whether deformed or not."

Cyrus said, "I'm amazed that he went along with that. Could he have had a shred of decency after all?"

"He agreed to give her to an orphanage, but when he did deliver her there, he refused to supply a family name for the child."

James said, “They probably took that as meaning the child was the offspring of a teen, possibly due to incest.”

Cyrus approached Barbara. “What orphanage was involved? We may be able to get her back.”

Barbara shook her head. “He only said that he took her to an orphanage rather than drowning her in the river like an unwanted cat.”

“It had to be someplace located in or near that northwest corner of Georgia you mentioned. We'll search through all the orphanages in that area.”

“That won't work. After Lynnette was born, Hackamore took me to another place in the mountains. I don't know whether it was north or south of that Georgia cabin. That's where we were when he took her to the orphanage.”

James said, “I may be able to get a list of the licensed orphanages, but there are many informal ones operated in small towns by good-hearted individuals without credentials.”

“Anyway, Barbara, we'll do our best to get her back. I promise.”

“Cyrus, you're willing to go after her even though she is the daughter of that evil beast?”

“She's the daughter of that evil beast and the love of my life. I'll settle for that. How soon after you lost Lynnette did he move you to that stone cottage near Memphis?”

“He dragged me off to that place right away – I think he was afraid the orphanage people would track him down and call the sheriff. He was always aggressive with me, but he was afraid of almost all outsiders. He'd parade around in that Confederate officer's uniform he bought when he was with me, but he wore old farm clothes when he went anyplace where there were normal people.”

Dr. Linton nodded. “He held you in captivity to prove to himself that he had power, but he knew he deserved scorn from everyone else for his desertion and his antisocial behavior."

Sally patted her husband on his arm. "James, this isn't a medical seminar. Barbara doesn't need evaluations; she needs compassion."

"Sorry, Barbara; I fell into my professional mode. Of course, I sympathize with everything you were subjected to. How long was it between the child's departure and the resumption of the beatings?"

"Right away ... he hated me and he needed to beat and rape me to prove that he still had some power. I knew it wouldn't end until one of us was dead."

CHAPTER 32 – GRANDMA MARIE

Marie paused her storytelling, both to take some refreshment before continuing and to see what impact her tale was having on her audience. The answer to her second goal came quickly from Jeremy.

"What terrible ordeals Barbara endured! She was an amazing person. You're not going to end the story there, are you?"

Marie turned to Debbie. "That's an interesting reaction, coming from your impatient husband who thought my story was so long that we should skip parts of it."

Debbie stood and stretched. "I'll apologize for both of us. We tend to like our information in short bites, and then we want to take action on it. Your story requires us to absorb a lot of family history so that we'll be prepared for your assignment. I'll take a break now, but I'm sure it will be a while before we even know what you want us to do. I do admire Barbara and know that I couldn't have held out for two and a half years of torture and captivity like she did."

Marie said, "I'm with Cyrus. I need a cool drink if I'm to keep talking, but I'll use that drink as a chaser following a shot of whiskey because of the stressful things I'm telling you."

After about ten minutes, Debbie and Jeremy once more sat across from Marie in her rocking chair. Jeremy had hoarded two extra drinks for consumption during the course of Marie's continuing story.

Marie looked back and forth between her two listeners. "Before I continue, do you want to ask any questions about what you've already heard or about things you anticipate?"

Debbie responded. "Am I getting too far ahead if I ask how I'm related to Cyrus, Barbara, and their boys?"

"Just a tad, I'm afraid. I'll use my 'patience' answer to that one, but feel free to ask other questions."

Jeremy said, "I have a comment instead of a question. Having heard Barbara's story up to this point, I have to admit that I never understood how much pain and suffering some people, especially women, are able to bear. The Danforths and their wives are sturdy stock."

Debbie said, "The men are pretty special too. Cyrus lost half his leg at Gettysburg and then treated it as a minor inconvenience for the rest of his life. Then look at how willing he was to accept Barbara's daughter with her kidnapper, if they could find her."

Marie leaned her rocker backward. "That's my cue. Let's continue the family story."

CHAPTER 33 - FAMILY MEETING

After the Lintons left to return to Memphis, Cyrus and Barbara called the boys to the front room for a family meeting. Bruce and Daniel hurried in because they knew that the topic would be something important.

Cyrus said, "Bruce and Daniel, as you may have gathered from overheard comments while the Lintons were here, your mother has regained her memories of almost everything that happened to her while she was held captive away from us. You two have been great at carrying on all of your chores and keeping up the house when I've had to be away in the past. We both want to thank you for that, and we want you to know that we think of you as almost adult in many ways."

Bruce asked, "Are you going to tell us everything that happened to you, Mother?"

Barbara walked over to the boys and hugged them both. "We'll tell you about some things, but that's where the 'almost adult' description comes in. Some of the things that happened to me are too serious for your ears at this time. Your father and I will tell you sometime, but not for a few years yet."

Cyrus saw their disappointment. "You'll get the gist of what happened today, but not all the gruesome details. You'll have to understand that your mother had to overcome many obstacles to be with us again. I'll let her tell you as much as she feels you should know right now."

Daniel interrupted. "Mother, if talking about it bothers you, we'll wait for some future time. We don't want you to do anything that makes you uncomfortable."

Bruce said, "Wow, even the younger guy has feelings. He's right though, Mother. Don't tell us any more than is required for the purpose of this meeting. We do know you're going to give us some important news."

Barbara laughed, and everyone relaxed. "You two are so sweet to me, but I don't want any more tiptoeing around points of conflict. We've been doing that ever since your father brought me home. It's time for us to be open and honest whenever we can. Do you agree, Cyrus?"

"Yes, but leave out some details."

She nodded her agreement. "On that fateful day, you three were out fishing together, and I was home alone. I answered a knock at the door and found a peddler of pots and pans on my doorstep. Once he learned that I was alone, he knocked me unconscious, tied me up, and threw me inside the back of his wagon. He wasn't a real peddler, of course. He was an evil man from the town where I grew up in the South."

Bruce asked, "How did he know you were here?"

"I made the mistake of writing a letter to an old girlfriend, and she shared my secrets with others. Anyway, this man took me all the way to a mountain cabin in northwest Georgia and held me captive there for a long time. He was cruel to me and beat me ... and eventually he got me pregnant, and I had a baby girl."

Bruce said, "So much for avoiding details. Please go on."

"This little girl, Lynnette, had deformed hands, and my captor wanted to get rid of her. I convinced him to let me keep her until she was strong enough to survive, and then he gave her to an orphanage. I have no idea where that orphanage is."

Cyrus said, "We asked for this family meeting because you two boys are going to have to be on your own again while we try to locate that orphanage and bring Lynnette home."

Daniel patted Bruce on his shoulder. "She's our half sister. I'm not the youngest one in the family anymore."

Bruce remained serious. "Are you going to tell us how you finally got away from your kidnapper, Mother? We know that Dad found you in Memphis after Dr. Linton wrote to him. That's a long way from Georgia."

Cyrus said, "We'll leave that story for another time. I'll just say that we're not going to have to worry about him in the future."

Bruce finally smiled. "Like I said earlier, so much for avoiding details. That saves our having to go after him."

Cyrus said, "When I called you almost adult, I didn't mean to imply that you were ready to go to war or on a manhunt."

Bruce said, "Dad, when it comes to defending the family, we all pitch in. I'll bet you had a few boys my age in your Wisconsin infantry regiment."

"Thankfully, the war's over, but I get your point. Your words echo some that I've spoken in the past."

Barbara stood to get their attention. "Let's get back to why we called this family meeting. Your dad and I are going to try to locate Lynnette and bring her home. We may or may not be successful. We may have to make additional attempts to find her in the future. You boys have two questions to answer. Will it bother you if we are away for a month or more?"

Daniel answered, "We were by ourselves about that long when Dad went to Memphis to find you and get you ready to come home. We're able to handle things around here on our own. You can even leave us a list of painting and repair jobs you want done while you're away. Are you with me on that, Bruce?"

"Sure."

Barbara said, "Now for the second and more important question –please be completely honest in your answers –

will you boys accept Lynnette as part of our family if we find her?"

Bruce said, "Of course, mother; she's your daughter and our half-sister."

Daniel added, "On top of that, I know that you should have someone female around you. We're a rough and tumble lot."

Cyrus applauded their answers. "Well said, boys, but remember that Mother told you Lynnette's hands are unusual. She doesn't have all of her fingers. Will that bother you?"

Bruce said, "It won't bother us, and we'll make sure no one else dares to pick on her for that. If you find her and bring her home, we'll welcome her. As you said, we're almost adult. It will be good to have a young kid in the house again."

CHAPTER 34 - MISSION

True to his word, Dr. James Linton mailed Cyrus a list of legally registered orphanages. Cyrus examined the list and circled the ones that were in the areas they would be visiting on their journey. On the day they were to depart, Barbara made the boys a special breakfast of buckwheat hotcakes and bacon because they would have to eat their own cooking for so long. Then she and Cyrus bid the boys goodbye with hugs and handclasps. After the exchange of goodbyes, Bruce and Daniel loaded their parents' luggage and camping gear into the wagon.

The first leg of their trip would be the longest. They would travel from Wisconsin to the northwest corner of Georgia without contacting any orphanages, on the assumption that Hackamore would have rid himself of Lynnette at an institution near to the place where he held Barbara. She said that they moved to a different location before he abandoned the child, but northwest Georgia gave them a starting place.

In Dalton, Georgia, they located two orphanages. The larger one, Cathedral Central, was on James Linton's list of registered facilities, and the other consisted of an extra wing built onto Rhonda Milquist's house.

Cathedral Central turned out to be in an old warehouse formerly used to store bales of cotton prior to shipping them out of town by railroad. The organization was not housed in a church, let alone a cathedral. Barbara and Cyrus entered the building and asked the woman in a front office for assistance. Cyrus let Barbara control the conversation.

"Excuse me, ma'am, we're from out of town, and we're looking for a young girl who may have been brought here. Would you have information on children who are or were here?"

"Good morning. I'm Thelma Jonas, and I'm the latest in a string of supervisors here, so I have some records that I inherited, and I know the current children. May I have your names?"

"Certainly. I'm Barbara Danforth, and this is my husband Cyrus."

"Are you seeking a child to adopt?"

"We're looking for a particular little girl who would be about four years old now. She would have been brought here about three years ago. Her name is Lynnette, but the man who brought her may have given you a different name for her."

Mrs. Jonas stared at them. "I take it that you're not familiar with the way our organization works. We call ourselves Cathedral Central because we work with churches of many different denominations to place children with their members. We rarely have children living here for as long as the three years you mentioned. We promote interest and then put our children on orphan trains, usually headed to the Midwest, where potential parents can view the children at each stop and adopt them."

Barbara and Cyrus exchanged shocked glances. Then Cyrus said, "The little girl we're seeking has deformed hands. Would you have shipped her out on such a train?"

"I'm sorry to learn of her handicap, but it may help you to find her. No, we don't ship children with physical problems on our trains, because they don't have a high chance of being adopted. Usually, we transfer such children to a local orphanage that might be willing to keep them for a longer time. You would have to ask them how long they house children before they give up on placing them."

Barbara asked, "If an orphanage gives up on placing a child, what happens to him or her?"

"We try not to discuss such cases, but unadoptable children have been released from orphanages to live by their own wits on the streets."

Cyrus asked, "How many of those street children actually survive to adulthood?"

"I have no way of answering that question. It's an unpleasant topic, but we do the best we can with limited resources."

Barbara thanked Mrs. Jonas for her assistance and candor. Then she and Cyrus left to visit the local home orphanage run by Rhonda Milquist.

The Milquist home had a fairytale feeling to it. The small white house with the neat picket-fenced and landscaped front yard was overshadowed by a much larger and taller blue two-story addition behind it. It reminded Cyrus of a church that had started small and then built a huge expansion as it attracted more members. A sign in front indicated that the little house served as the office of the combined structure.

As they entered the front door, they heard the attached spring-arm-mounted bell jingle. Footsteps, descending the enclosed staircase rhythmically, announced that their presence had been detected. A fortyish woman who carried herself like an athlete appeared in the opening at the foot of the stairs. She had curly prematurely gray hair and wore a smile above the flowered apron that covered her skirt. Rhonda Milquist was a dynamo of average height who greeted them with enthusiasm.

"Welcome to Casa Milquist. That's not its official name, but it started out as my home, and I like to think of it as home for our young residents." A series of thumps, scrapes, and shrieks coming from the direction of the large structure behind the house announced the active presence of those children.

This time, Cyrus took the lead, mimicking Barbara's inquiries at their first stop. "Good morning. We're Cyrus and Barbara Danforth, and we're trying to locate a little girl who would be four years old and would have been placed in an orphanage about three years ago. Her original name was Lynnette, but we're not sure whether the person who placed her in an orphanage might have assigned a different name to her."

Rhonda Milquist introduced herself and said, "You two are focused on a particular child. Was she taken away from someone in your family because of a hardship situation?"

Barbara said, "She is a distant relative. We only recently learned that she had been placed in an orphanage, and our visit to Cathedral Central has cast a shadow on our hopes of finding her. They said they ship most of their children out on orphan trains to the Midwest for adoption. Do you do the same thing, or do you have children living here for a number of years?"

"We take a different approach, Mrs. Danforth. Most of our children are local, and we try to give them the chance to grow up where their families have lived, so we do keep them for a number of years and try to find local homes for them. Is your Lynnette from this area?"

"She was born in this area, but her family is from somewhere else. One other thing I should mention by way of identifying her, she was born with incomplete hands. She has missing fingers."

Rhonda said, "That may help us to guide you in your search. We don't have a child that matches her description here, but I do remember receiving a flyer about a home that offers sanctuary to children with physical problems.

Let me check my files for that paper." Rhonda went into the next room.

Cyrus patted Barbara's shoulder. "This may be a break for us. If there's an orphanage that specializes in handling children with physical defects, she may have been transferred there from a different home somewhere else. I'm feeling more optimistic than I was earlier."

Rhonda Milquist returned with several sheets of paper. "I have the flyer I mentioned, and I also have a letter from a friend who runs an orphanage in Chattanooga. She wrote that she had transferred three children to the specialized home. The name of that place is Stalwart Haven, and it's located in Murfreesboro, Tennessee, on the road to Nashville. I've written the details for you on this sheet of paper. The woman to see there is Paula Goffert.

CHAPTER 35 - STALWART HAVEN

When Cyrus and Barbara approached Stalwart Haven, they noticed how different it was from Rhonda Milquist's orphanage. If Rhonda's place reflected a fairy tale, Stalwart Haven cast the shadow of a haunted house. The front yard was bare ground highlighted only by a dead oak tree from which hung the ropes that formerly supported a child's swing, but no seat connected the two dangling support ropes. Broken porch stairs supporting a long white ramp led to the dark brown porch of a black house. Although the house was black, Cyrus noticed a charred area, even blacker, next to one of the upstairs windows. Once on the porch, visitors approaching the front door clanged a ship's bell for attention in the absence of a knocker or doorbell.

Barbara did the honors of bell-clanging, following which they stood looking at each other while they awaited a response. After a couple of minutes, they heard a woman's voice yell that she was coming. As they waited for the door to open, Cyrus noticed that the doorknob had been set very low. The door opened, revealing the reason for the low doorknob. The woman who answered the door was in a wheelchair.

"Good morning. I'm Paula Goffert. Welcome to Stalwart Haven."

Barbara shook Paula's hand. "Hello, Paula; we're Barbara and Cyrus Danforth. We've learned from the owner of another orphanage that Stalwart Haven is a sanctuary for children with physical problems of various sorts."

"Not physical problems, Mrs. Danforth, physical differences. Someone who looks or functions differently should not be considered as having a problem."

Cyrus walked over to her and lifted his left pants leg to show his artificial limb. "I agree with you, Paula."

"Well, if you'll pardon the expression, that puts us on an equal footing. What can I do for you folks?"

"We're here looking for a girl who would be four years old. She was placed in a different orphanage three years ago, and we wondered whether she might have been transferred here. Her hands from birth have had missing fingers. Her original name was Lynnette, but she might be called something else now."

"Come on in, and we'll discuss your case further. Sometimes people shun children who are different, but I see that you are serious in your search. Tell me why you are looking for this girl."

Cyrus spoke before Barbara could. "We want to adopt her. She's a distant relative, and it's time to give her a proper home and family. Do you think she might be here?"

"After three years, she would be here if she's still in an orphanage. I call this place a haven because most institutions discard unadoptable kids to survive on their own, while I give them a home without time limits."

Cyrus asked, "Do you have a child who matches our description of Lynnette?"

"I do, but before you get your hopes up, tell me how many fingers your girl has on each hand."

Barbara said, "Two on each hand. Is your girl a match and what do you call her?"

Paula smiled and said, "Wait here." Then she rolled her wheelchair over to a doorway where she called out to someone. A woman about twenty years old approached Paula and listened to her instructions. Then Paula returned to the Danforths. "Louise will bring a child for you to meet."

They waited ten minutes, and then Louise came through the doorway walking hand in hand with a young girl. As they approached, Cyrus and Barbara saw that Louise had a limp due to one leg being slightly longer than the other.

Paula noted their exchange of glances. "Yes, Louise works for us now, but she also grew up here after her parents turned their backs on her. She is a beautiful young woman."

Barbara nodded to Louise and knelt down to be at the same level as the little girl. "Hello, I'm Barbara. What do they call you?"

"My name is Martha, but they call me Martha Number Two because there's an older girl here who is another Martha."

"How old are you, Martha?"

Martha held up both of her hands.

Barbara said, "I count four fingers. Are you four years old?"

Martha said, "Yes I am. I don't need to count on fingers. I can count up to ten, and I know the alphabet too."

"You're smart. I'll bet you learn from all your friends here."

Martha nodded. "Do you have children, Barbara?"

"I have two older boys named Bruce and Daniel, and I'd like to have a daughter just like you."

Martha looked a question at Mrs. Goffert, who smiled and nodded back to her. Then Paula Goffert asked Barbara, "Do you think our Martha is your Lynnette?"

Barbara said, "I do. We want to officially adopt her." She looked at Cyrus, and he nodded back to her. Then she and Paula went into the office to discuss details and legalities while Cyrus introduced himself to Martha. While they talked, Cyrus realized that he was chatting with the little girl but staring out the window at storm clouds in the distant sky.

CHAPTER 36 – EXPANDED FAMILY

Before they tackled the long ride back to Wisconsin, Cyrus stopped in Nashville to let Barbara buy some additional clothes for their newly adopted daughter. Paula Goffert was good to her young charges, but she had neither the wherewithal nor the need to provide them with extensive wardrobes. Cyrus gave Barbara money to cover her purchases, but he remained outside the store while Barbara and Martha shopped. He didn't feel comfortable picking out clothing for a girl, and he thought that this would give his wife and daughter a chance to get to know each other better. He was surprised when they emerged from the store carrying four large packages.

He asked, "Barbara, did you buy clothes for the boys too? How many outfits does a little girl need?"

Martha said, "Mother was very good to me."

Cyrus exchanged smiles with Barbara and realized that his daughter would have a major impact on their family life.

When they headed their wagon northward again, Martha asked about Wisconsin and the stories she had heard of long snowy winters. Cyrus assured her that she would be able to cope with the snow and might enjoy making snowmen and being outside in cold weather. During the long ride Martha sang songs she had learned at Stalwart Haven, and Barbara taught her a few songs that she remembered from her childhood. Martha did her best to feel part of her new family by sprinkling every conversation with a large number of Mothers and Dads.

On the second day of their journey, Barbara felt close enough to Martha to talk with her about what she would like to be called.

"Martha, you're old enough to have a second name."

"I already have a second name, Mother. Mrs. Goffert said that I'm now Martha Danforth."

"She was absolutely correct. You are Martha Danforth, but you can have both a first name and a middle name. My name is Barbara Isabelle Danforth when I include my middle name."

"I never had a middle name. What will it be?"

Cyrus understood what Barbara was doing, and he waited to see whether she would be successful.

Barbara said, "You are a very special little girl because you have had two first names. Did you know that?"

"How can I have two first names, Mother?"

"When you were brought to the first orphanage, you were called Lynnette. At some time they forgot that name and started calling you Martha. You are both Lynnette and Martha."

"I don't think I want to be two different people. It's confusing."

"Your father and I agree. We want you to choose whether you want to be Lynnette Martha Danforth or Martha Lynnette Danforth. You can be either one."

She thought for a while and spoke both names softly to herself. "Mother and Dad, if I was Lynnette first, that should be me first name. I'll be Lynnette Martha Danforth. Everything is new and different now, so I'll have my name different too."

Cyrus looked at Barbara and smiled at her obvious satisfaction.

When the wagon finally approached the Danforth home in Fox Lake, Wisconsin, Lynnette was asleep, leaning against Barbara. Cyrus reined in the horses, climbed down, and removed the canvas that covered their belongings in the back. As he started to unload, Bruce and Daniel ran out from the rear of the house shouting their greetings. This woke Lynnette, who started to cry over the sudden commotion. The boys, seeing that their parents had brought home their half-sister, ran to see Lynnette, which made her cry harder. After Barbara quieted her sons and calmed her daughter, she introduced Lynnette Martha Danforth to Bruce and Daniel.

Bruce spoke first. "Welcome, Lynnette. I'm your oldest brother, Bruce. This tall guy is your brother Daniel. We'll show you around the house and barn when you're ready. We cooked fish we caught for our supper, and there's enough for everyone."

Barbara helped Lynnette down from the wagon. "Do you want to eat or see your bedroom first? You'll be in a bedroom with a big bed that we use when we have guests staying with us."

"Can we eat first, Mother? I'm hungry. Besides, I never ate a fish before. They didn't have fish at Stalwart Haven."

"Fish it will be. I want to see how well the boys cook when they're on their own."

Daniel said, "We've actually become creative. In a few days we'll make our chicken and fish stew for the whole family."

CHAPTER 37 - SETTLING IN

On the evening of their homecoming the Danforths sat around the fireplace exchanging stories and songs. Cyrus told the boys about their trip, and Daniel related Bruce's encounter with a swarm of bees. Lynnette contributed a story about her friends at the orphanage playing Hide and Seek with her.

When it was bedtime, Barbara took Lynnette up to her bedroom and showed her the closet and all her new clothes neatly arranged on hangers.

Lynnette put on her pajamas and said, "Mother, I know I shouldn't do it every day, but for just tonight, would it be alright if I jumped up and down on my new bed? I want to feel it's my own."

Barbara subdued her smile and said, "You may jump four times while I'm with you, but we won't want you to do it in the future because the bed might break, and you might get hurt."

Lynnette ran to the bed and jumped up and down on it exactly four times. Then she ran to hold her mother's hand. "I did what you said, Mother. Mrs. Goffert and Louise taught us to obey instructions."

Barbara squeezed Lynnette's hand. "Thank you for being so good. I'll depend on you when it comes time for you to have chores to do around the house."

"I like doing chores. At Stalwart Haven I made my bed, dusted, and swept the floor. Sometimes I didn't like sweeping, because dust makes me sneeze, but I still did it."

"We'll talk more about chores during the next few days, but now it's time for you to go to sleep."

"I'm ready, Mother, but just this once, would you sleep with me? Everything is new and different, and I'm afraid I might forget where I am when I get up in the morning. If you sleep with me, I won't be scared when I wake up."

Barbara said, "Let's walk down the hall and say goodnight to your father. I'll tell him that I'll sleep in with you tonight. It won't take you long to get used to your room. I'll help you fix it up the way you like it tomorrow, and after that, you can sleep with a doll I made for you."

CHAPTER 38 - BODYGUARDS

Lynnette followed Daniel and Bruce whenever they were at home. She especially enjoyed riding high up on Daniel's shoulders when they were outside or in the barn. At Stalwart Haven, she had to stay inside the building except for special times when Louise and some of the older children led them outside for a picnic or group games. In her new home, she could go outside anytime she had a parent or a brother with her.

One day, Bruce and Daniel took her with them to the general store to get some flour and vegetables. They walked along State Street with Lynnette between the two boys. From time to time Bruce and Daniel picked her up by her arms and swung her with her feet off the ground. She felt like a circus performer. Once in the store, Bruce went to the counter to order the supplies while Lynnette roamed the store, looking at all the pretty and unusual things with Daniel trailing behind her.

Lynnette picked up a harmonica and was looking at all the holes along its edge, when a farmhand saw her and called out, "Hey, look at the freaky little girl. She has only two fingers on each hand."

Daniel reached him first, and Bruce was only a few steps behind. Each grabbed one of the man's arms, startling him. Then Bruce said, "I suggest you apologize to our sister."

Several women murmured comments about the man's behavior and the audacity of boys confronting the man.

The farmhand didn't know whether to fight, to flee the store, or to apologize as requested. Ed Mitchell, the store owner, who was also the postmaster and a deputy sheriff, joined the group and broke the tension.

"Marty, I'm sure your mother told you to think before you speak. This sweet little girl is Lynnette Danforth. She's Cyrus' daughter, and I'm sure you don't want Cyrus and his boys to stay mad at you. Why don't you just tell her you didn't mean what you said?"

Outnumbered, Marty said, "I'm sorry, little girl. I wasn't being mean, only surprised."

Lynnette smiled and said, "I know. Some people don't understand how some of us are different and have to work harder to do things."

Ed laughed. "Are you sure she's only four years old? Everybody, let's get back to normal now. Marty, here's a big red apple on the house. Bite into it the next time you're about to cause trouble. Lynnette, here's a bag you may fill with candy to take home."

Bruce and Daniel released Marty's arms and at the insistence of the store owner, shook hands with him. When they paid for their purchases, Ed told them to throw in the harmonica that Lynnette had been examining when Marty made his remarks.

When they returned home and the boys told Cyrus what had happened, he said, "I knew that something like that would happen sooner or later. Ed did a good job of calming everyone down. I'll buy him a beer next time we get together."

Bruce asked, "You're a businessman, Dad. Do you think Ed took control of the situation because it was bad for business, or did he do it out of concern for Lynnette?"

"I'm sure it was some of both. People don't like to shop in a place where fights break out, and Ed's a grandfather who knows how important it is for children to feel confident and comfortable with others. Let's say that he saw trouble developing, and he headed it off. Speaking of heading off, weren't you boys going to teach Lynnette how to fish today?"

"We were, but Lynnette said that having been in an orphanage, she'd rather have her father take her fishing the first time. How's your schedule for today, Dad?"

"I was going to replace broken slats in the fence, but if you'll handle that one, I'll take Lynnette fishing."

"Consider it done. Afterwards, Dan and I will rig a swing on the maple tree for her."

"Use the new rope in the barn. The old stuff may not be strong enough."

CHAPTER 39 – GROWING UP

Jeremy tilted his kitchen chair back as he listened to Debbie's grandmother.

Marie said, "I'm in a rocking chair, so it's fine for me to lean back, but if you break my kitchen chair, I'll be a bit unhappy."

Debbie reached over and pushed her husband's chair upright. "Jeremy, it looks as though you're having trouble staying in Grandma's good graces today."

"Sorry, Marie; your story of Lynnette fitting so well into the Danforth family led me to relax, and when I rest in a straight back chair, I tend to lean backward. It's an old habit."

"It's a bad habit. You're going to hurt yourself when a weak chair leg breaks."

"Anyway, I relaxed when I realized that Lynnette was so well accepted into the Danforth family and lived happily ever after with them."

Marie leaned forward in her rocker and glared at Jeremy. "You're not a good listener; you're taking my words and running with them to your own conclusions. Jeremy, this is not a fairy tale, and real lives don't often turn out perfectly."

Debbie asked, "Are you saying that something bad happened to Lynnette?"

"Both good and bad things happen to all of us as we grow and mature. Cyrus was very proud of his daughter, and Lynnette did very well, both in family relations and in school. During Lynnette's growing-up years, Cyrus' brother and sister, Ralph Danforth and Emma Stanton, moved to Wisconsin from upstate New York. Their parents had died shortly after selling the farm, leaving Ralph and Emma free to move their families to Wisconsin. Ralph's son Alexander and Emma's daughter Rosemary were close in age to Lynnette, so the three of them became very close friends. As they grew into their teen years and beyond, the three cousins were influenced by people with different backgrounds and started to get into trouble.

Rosemary wanted to fit in with the socially elite girls at school, but the price of popularity in their circle was a fancy wardrobe. Rosemary's father and mother practiced a frugal lifestyle based on having been raised on farms, so she stole money from the fabric store where she worked to buy clothes. At first, she took only a few dollars a month, hoping the shop owner would blame the shortage on bookkeeping errors, but as she became accepted by her richer friends, she increased the amounts she took from the cash box. When Rosemary's mother asked her about her stylish clothes, Rosemary said she had borrowed them from a friend at school. For a while she got away with this story, but then her mother told her she was not allowed to borrow clothing anymore. Thinking she would simply change clothes when she was away from home, Rosemary agreed, but soon discovered that she wasn't as good at deception as she had thought.

One morning, when Rosemary entered the fabric shop to start work, she found her boss, Sarah talking with Ed Mitchell, the owner of the general store. As she entered they both turned and stared at her.

Rosemary said, "Good morning; is anything the matter? I'm on time."

Sarah said, "You're on schedule, but keep your coat on. You don't work here anymore. I've been aware of your cash shortages for months. Each time you work, I count the cash right after you leave. You know Ed Mitchell as the owner of the general store, but he's also a deputy sheriff, and I've given him a summary of your thefts."

"I'm sorry. I didn't mean to hurt your business. It started as just a dollar or two, but then it became a habit. Are you going to arrest me, Mr. Mitchell?"

Ed referred to the sheet of paper in his hand. "According to Sarah's accounting, that dollar or two has grown to one hundred and fifty-seven dollars. I'm sure the actual amount is higher, because she didn't catch your shortages right away. In answer to your question, I'm not going to arrest you now, but I am going to take you home to your parents and let them decide whether they would rather repay Sarah or have me arrest you. To allow for errors, we'll round off the repayment amount to two hundred dollars."

Marie continued her narrative. "Rosemary's mother, Emma, told Ed they would repay her daughter's thefts and would increase the amount to two hundred and twenty-five dollars as a further apology to Sarah. She also told Rosemary she would have to dress like a working farmhand when attending school for the balance of that school year and do additional chores every day until she had repaid her parents with her labor for the reimbursement amount."

Debbie said, "I'll bet that wardrobe change bothered Rosemary more than anything else. She was one Danforth who wasn't completely honest."

Marie said, "She wasn't the only one who got into trouble. I told you that Rosemary was very close to her cousins Alexander and Lynnette. They also had their problems."

Jeremy said, "Not Lynnette – I had her down as a happily ever after story."

"I'll leave Lynnette's story for last. Alexander got into trouble partly because of her. From high school on, he was Lynnette's defender. Whenever someone picked on her because of her deformed hands, Alexander would give that person a beating. When the trouble-maker was female, Alexander would spread unsavory rumors about her. These actions were effective, but they led to retaliation against Alexander by others who wanted to fight him. Eventually, he became so good at fighting that he moved to Milwaukee and became a boxer."

Debbie said, "That's not a bad thing, Marie. Alexander knew how to defend himself, and he turned it into a boxing career."

"He was fine for a while, but he didn't have many fights that paid more than a few dollars. Only a few boxers got to be featured and paid well. The fight game wasn't entirely honest either. After Alexander had been in it for a year, a promoter approached him with the opportunity to fight some of the higher level opponents if he agreed to throw the fights. They called it taking a dive. He would always lose, but he would make a lot more money by making the featured fighters look good. They told him that if he agreed, they would later promote him as a winner after the betters expected him to lose. Alexander needed money, so he became a patsy for the featured fighters. At least he outsmarted the promoters by investing his payoffs instead of spending everything. After two years of canvas diving, he had enough investment income to quit boxing and learn how to build and maintain automobile engines."

Jeremy asked, "What about Lynnette? How much trouble did she have?"

Marie said, "You're very concerned about her. Without going into too many details, Lynnette's trouble was that she trusted people too much, and they took advantage of her. She had a string of serious love affairs with unsavory characters, eventually leading to her giving birth to a son, Theodore Cyrus Danforth, in 1901."

Debbie said, "Ted is my great-grandfather's name."

"Yes, he was my father-in-law, my wonderful Greg's father."

Jeremy said, "Then Lynnette must have stayed unmarried, because Ted kept the Danforth name. Is that true, Marie?"

"Not exactly. In those days the stigma for an unwed mother was tremendous. Lynnette gave Ted the Danforth name at birth because he was the product of a casual liaison, and she wasn't sure who the father was. If she had singly raised Ted to adulthood under the Danforth name, Lynnette would have lost any social standing she had, as an unmarried mother. Fortunately, her knight in shining armor rode in to save her."

Debbie said, "Great-grandpa Ted remained a Danforth because Alexander married Lynnette. She married her first cousin."

Marie said, "I assumed you'd figure that one out. Alexander had always taken risks to protect Lynnette, and he did it once more. The obvious reason is that he had always loved his first cousin, but marrying within that relationship was considered almost as bad as a woman having a baby without a husband. Lynnette and Alexander simply neglected to tell anyone that they were cousins. They made a pact with each other to avoid potential genetic problems by not having additional children. It was a terrible condition for Alexander to accept, because he wanted children with Lynnette, but he loved her enough to avoid taking genetic chances. Ted was the Danforth who lived happily ever after."

Jeremy said, "He must have known the facts of his birth and his parents' marriage, or you wouldn't be able to tell us this story."

"Lynnette and Alexander didn't inform him until he turned twenty-one. Ted later told me that he had suspected something because he didn't look like Alexander. He took the revelation in stride."

"Grandma, I mean Marie, are you going to take your story through Ted's life and up to the present?"

“No, Debbie, we’ve reached the end of my family history. Now it’s time for me to tell you what I want you to do for me and the family.”

CHAPTER 40 - ASSIGNMENT

Marie eased herself up from her rocking chair and rubbed the small of her back. "That chair is comfortable while you're in it, but the transition to standing can hurt your back. Anyway, we're not going to spend time talking about my creaky joints."

Jeremy said, "You move very well, Marie."

"Debbie, did you hear that? Your husband complimented me, but omitted the 'for your age' that he was thinking. Remind him of that when you two add a few years and start to slow down."

Debbie said, "I'm sure Jeremy didn't mean to imply that. Sometimes he's like that Marty in your story who commented on Lynnette's hands without thinking about the impact of his words."

Jeremy cleared his throat. "Excuse me for interrupting, but I'm right here. You can talk to me instead of about me. Marie, I didn't mean to imply that you've slowed down. I couldn't relate a family saga as well as you did."

Marie patted Jeremy on the shoulder. "Don't feel bad about my comments. I haven't had a man around to badger for a long time. They say that old habits die hard, and they're right. Let's gather around the table, and I'll explain why I need your assistance, assuming you're still willing to put up with my teasing."

As they sat, Marie opened a nearby cabinet door and removed a file folder.

"I told you all that family history information so that you would have the cast of characters and the background information you'll need for your assignment."

Debbie said, "Even without the assignment, I learned more about my family today than ever before. Cyrus and Barbara were special people, and their children had strong personalities too. I did a family tree study that went back as far as Ted, but now I know my older ancestors, and I feel that I know them as people and not just names in boxes on a diagram."

Marie opened the file folder. "Your project starts with the information in this folder, which came from your father, my son, Max. As a retired doctor with extra time on his hands and the desire to do something independently from Trish, he got interested in DNA testing and analysis. He grew up with the family tale I related today, so he decided to find out how much DNA difference there would be between descendants of Bruce and Daniel and our branch, which stems from Lynnette. Since Lynnette had a different father, he expected to find some resemblance to Bruce's group in the charts, but not as many similarities as between offspring of Bruce and Daniel."

Jeremy nodded. "I studied DNA testing in college, and that premise sounds correct."

"It's what one would expect, but it didn't match Max's results. There was no resemblance between the charts for Daniel or Bruce's families and those for our family, stemming from Lynnette."

Jeremy asked, "Even though Lynnette married Alexander Danforth?"

Debbie said, "Remember, they agreed not to have children together because of the first cousins stigma. Ted's father wasn't related to us, and we don't know his name."

Jeremy crossed out a link on the family tree diagram he had drawn on his notepad. "That means that Lynnette wasn't family, and Barbara made a mistake in selecting her at the orphanage."

Marie applauded. "Thank you, Jeremy. You've reached the correct conclusion and determined your assignment. I want you two to find out whether Barbara selected an unrelated orphan to raise as her daughter because she made a mistake or if she did so intentionally."

Debbie leafed through her many notes. "That adoption happened in 1885 at a home-based orphanage. Even if we had been there when Lynnette was adopted, we wouldn't know what was going on in Barbara's mind."

Marie smiled. "I didn't say the assignment would be easy."

CHAPTER 41 - STARTING POINTS

After they returned to their Parkville, Illinois apartment, Debbie brought out two bottles of beer and some pretzels for a relax-and-review session. She and Jeremy faced each other from opposite ends of the couch.

"So, Jeremy, what did you think of Grandma Marie, her family history, and her assignment for us?"

"After receiving her less-than-enthusiastic comments about my behavior and responses, I think we had better do a bang-up job on this project. I don't want to stay in Marie's doghouse forever."

Debbie extended her leg and rubbed his knee with her shoeless foot as though petting a dog. "She was just giving you a hard time to tell you that you have to earn your way into her inner circle of favorite relatives. I'm there already, of course, thanks to my stellar behavior as a child."

"Fair enough, star-baby; you get the job of compiling a record of Lynnette's interests and activities after she married Alexander at the end of Marie's story period. Some items may come from your memories and some will require that you check with your dad or Marie."

"That's an interesting project, but aren't we supposed to study what happened when Lynnette was adopted? Does that have anything to do with her adult life?"

"I'm trying to be thorough. We can't time travel back to 1885, so I'm suggesting that Lynnette may have learned about the circumstances of her adoption, and your study of her adult life might reveal what she knew."

"I accept your task, Jeremy. What are you going to do while I'm checking family memories and records?"

"I'll head in the other direction on her timeline. I wonder whether there are any records of Martha's arrival at that orphanage. Don't forget, she was called Martha before Cyrus and Barbara adopted her."

Debbie said, "I'll make copies of the notes that we both took during the story-telling session with Grandma. She had lots of details in there that might prove useful later on."

"You're not quite comfortable with calling her Marie, are you?"

"Expect me to go back and forth with what I call her for a while. As a kid, I didn't even know her given name. I've called her Grandma all my life. She claims that our calling her Marie makes her feel younger, so I'll have to get used to doing that, but it will take some time."

"Adjusting family traditions from years past to current perspectives is what our assignment is all about."

CHAPTER 42 – YOUNG MARTHA

Jeremy Hadley initiated his computer search for early records of the Stalwart Haven orphanage or the state of Tennessee and quickly realized he had a problem. He found an official posting that read: *Tennessee did not begin keeping birth records statewide until 1908. The larger cities in Tennessee did keep earlier birth records: Nashville (beginning in 1881); Knoxville (beginning in 1881); Chattanooga (beginning in 1879); and Memphis (beginning in 1874).*

Stalwart Haven was in Murfreesboro, which was Rutherford County, but that county was near Nashville in Davidson County, so it was possible that Martha's birth would be on file in the early Nashville records, although Marie's story only suggested that Barbara and her captor had moved an unknown distance from the northwest corner of Georgia before the baby arrived. Jeremy would assume that they had moved toward Nashville, because Martha ended up in that area.

Jeremy found the early birth records for Nashville, within Davidson County, which listed each child's name, father, mother, date of birth, file number, and race. The list was compiled alphabetically by surname, and he noticed immediately that very few of the entries had first names for the children. This data lapse reminded him that he didn't even know whether Martha had been the girl's given name from birth, or if it had been assigned to her at Stalwart Haven. The only actual fact Jeremy had was that the girl would have been born during the last half of 1881. When he saw that there were very few records for 1881, which was the first year of record keeping, Jeremy knew that he would have to look elsewhere.

He next tried searching on the name Stalwart Haven, but found results pointing to the demise of a racehorse rather than an orphanage.

Jeremy did get one positive result from his searching. He discovered a site that posted requests for information about adopted ancestors for genealogy tracers. He posted the information he had available: approximate birth date and possible states and counties of birth; names given to the child by the orphanage and adoptive parents; names and residence locations of adoptive parents; and where the adoption took place. He included his email address in case someone with information about Lynnette Martha Danforth wanted to contact him.

It wasn't much progress, but at least it left open the possibility that someone would contact him in the future.

CHAPTER 43 - ADULT LYNNETTE

Debbie began her study of Lynnette's adult life from family documents and public records. She soon discovered that Lynnette had been both unconventional and a major influence on those around her. She was graduated from the University of Wisconsin, where she had overloaded on coursework to complete her studies by 1900. Following graduation at the age of nineteen, she moved to Chicago, where she entered teacher training studies at the Cook County Normal School in Englewood, on the city's south side. The newly appointed principal there, Arnold Tomkins, didn't care for their practice school that trained student-teachers. He felt that teaching candidates should have real world experience in the Chicago Public Schools, preferably in poor and immigrant neighborhoods. At that time the five thousand teachers in Chicago's schools served two hundred and fifty thousand students, so student-teachers were well received at all schools.

Lynnette was assigned to teach English to German immigrants at a school on Chicago's north side. Her only foreign language studies had been in French, but this turned out to be somewhat useful for communicating with immigrants who came from the border areas between France and Germany. She taught children during the day and adults during night school classes. Fewer than half of her adult students were female due to then-current feelings that women should be housewives not needing education and because in many families men were the first to move to a new country with the plan of sending for other family members later.

Lynnette enjoyed her job, both for the satisfaction that comes with teaching others, and for the realization that she was learning at least as much as she was teaching to others. Her students were eager to talk about their personal histories and lifestyles in Germany. They were happy to be in America, but still praised the Old World that had denied them opportunities and, in many cases, acceptance. Most of those who had become United States citizens considered themselves to be German rather than American. Many of Lynnette's students were highly educated and enjoyed discussing history and philosophy with her.

Lynnette shared the student tales and discussions with her cousin Alexander Danforth during his frequent visits from Detroit, where he worked for the Henry Ford Company. During his most recent stopover, Alex brought news that his boss was talking with outside investors about turning his business into a corporation to be called the Ford Motor Company.

Alex had always been Lynnette's primary source of support during troubling times. On many occasions she had wished that he wasn't a close relative so that she would be free to consider him for a romantic relationship. They had always been close, and each seemed to understand the other's thoughts before they emerged as spoken words. The unspoken words she had sensed during his latest stay had been that she really didn't know very much about her adult male students and that she should protect herself by avoiding out-of-class contacts with them.

Debbie thought about Grandma Marie's earlier discussion of Lynnette having had a series of liaisons with unsavory characters before she became pregnant from one of them. It would make sense that some of those affairs involved her adult immigrant students. That would suggest that Debbie's branch of the family might have some German ancestry. She wondered whether Lynnette would have considered affairs with her German students to be flings or romances. They would have happened in 1900 and 1901, when women were supposed to be paragons of virtue and restrained in public. Lynnette must have been way ahead of her time. She seemed more a child of the 1960's than someone from the Victorian era. According to family records, Great-grandfather Ted was born in 1901, and Lynnette married Alexander in 1905 when Ted was four years old. Perhaps they had decided to marry so that Ted would have both a mother and a father at home when he was old enough to go to school. The records show that Lynnette Danforth of Chicago, Illinois married Alexander Danforth of Detroit, Michigan on June 17, 1905. At least their marriage month was traditional, if nothing else was.

In September of 1906, Ted Danforth enrolled in kindergarten in the Detroit Public Schools. Debbie reasoned that the family had moved to Detroit shortly after Lynnette and Alexander's wedding, because Alex had been working for Ford Motor Company since its incorporation. From Ford records, she learned that his title was Manager of Quality Assurance. That meant that he had a position with good income and Lynnette would have been free to pursue various interests. Debbie doubted that Lynnette would have been content to stay at home, but would have found new interests and projects in Detroit.

Debbie knew from her earlier research librarian work that it is sometimes useful to search something arbitrary and then sequentially add or subtract key words until something useful is found. She went to Google and entered *Lynnette Danforth.* Not finding anything useful, she typed *Lynnette Danforth, politics.* Her search results included several entries about the Women's Suffrage movement, but nothing specifically about Lynnette. Then she entered *Lynnette Danforth, protest*. This search result included a series of photographs of protest marches and people with picket signs. She eliminated all of the modern photographs and saved interesting protest photos from the first two decades of the twentieth century. Then she enlarged the pictures on her screen to study them more closely.

After thirty minutes of studying photographic images, she telephoned Marie.

CHAPTER 44 - ANALYSIS

When Jeremy returned to their apartment after visiting a local adoption agency, he found Debbie sitting on the couch drinking coffee while reading a magazine.

"Hi, Deb. I'm back from my face-to-face sessions with local adoption experts. Nothing useful. They didn't think that many records still existed from nineteenth century adoptions. You look comfortable. Are you taking a break, or did you give up for today?"

She put her magazine on the coffee table and stretched her arms. Then she walked over and gave him a kiss. "I'm goofing off because I've already learned quite a bit about Lynnette. I deserve congratulations. She was way ahead of her time and made a big impact on others. I'm proud to call her my great-great-grandmother."

"It sounds as though your results are better than mine. I pretty much struck out on adoption records. The 1880's are just too far back to expect results for a specific case. Adoptions were also informal events back then, and many were never legally recorded."

Debbie said, "You get credit for suggesting that I might find useful information for our assignment by studying Lynnette's adult life."

"Then you have found something."

"I learned that Lynnette and Alexander moved to Detroit from Chicago after their marriage. Alex worked for Henry Ford. In Detroit, Lynnette got involved in the women's suffrage movement and took part in protests."

"That's interesting, but how will it help us learn whether Barbara Danforth deliberately adopted the wrong child?"

"I found interesting photos of suffragists protesting in Detroit around 1910."

"Do you think you have a photograph of Lynnette?"

"You can help me decide that." Debbie took Jeremy's hand and led him over to their large screen television. "I connected my computer to the TV so that we can see enlarged photos. Stay here while I put up a couple of pictures."

Jeremy waited and soon saw a group of about twenty women in old fashioned clothing carrying picket signs about women deserving the right to vote. "It's up on the big screen."

"Look at the woman carrying the third sign from the right."

"I see her. Her face is pretty clear."

"Now look at her hands holding the sign."

"I see two fingers on each hand. She's holding the sign's post at the top and bottom between two fingers at each position. It may be Lynnette. How do we prove that?"

Debbie smiled. "I called Marie and had her email her only photo of Lynnette. I'll put them up side by side."

The protest photo moved toward the left on the screen, and a portrait photo of Lynnette moved onto the screen from the right.

Jeremy said, "The two pictures weren't taken at the same age, but I'd say they show the same woman."

Jeremy examined the image on the TV screen with a magnifying glass. While he did that, Debbie started to set the table for lunch.

Jeremy shouted, "Yes!"

Debbie dropped a soup bowl and watched the shattered pieces spread across the floor. "Damn! Now we have only three. I don't think they sell that pattern anymore. Thanks for startling me, Jeremy."

"I'll buy you a whole new set of dishes. You found the answer to our assignment. I'll be in Marie's good graces finally."

Debbie walked over to Jeremy after picking up the large pieces of the soup bowl. She would have to vacuum up the small shards and chips. "I didn't see a breakthrough when I looked at those photos."

"The answer to Marie's question is that Barbara Danforth deliberately selected the wrong child to adopt. I remember the details from our notes at Marie's. Lynnette had only the second and third fingers on her left hand and the thumb and forefinger on her right hand. The person in this picture has two thumbs. She has the thumb and middle finger on her left hand plus the thumb and forefinger on her right hand. Barbara had to notice that the girl's left hand was different."

Debbie said, "She must have felt so guilty about losing her birth daughter that she jumped at the chance to have a daughter who was almost like Lynnette."

CHAPTER 45 – RETROSPECTION

Cyrus sat in the rough-hewn rocking chair he had made many years earlier. He looked across the hearth at Barbara, sitting in the upholstered chair, knitting a scarf, her face red and flashing as the flames rose and fell. Neither spoke for what seemed like a very long time.

Finally, Cyrus said, "I must be the most patient man you have ever known."

She set aside her knitting and looked up. "You are indeed patient, but why do you choose this moment to mention it?"

"It has been several years since the children grew up and left home, and you have yet to answer my unspoken question."

"How do you expect me to answer a question that has not been spoken?"

"This question dates back to the day we adopted Lynnette."

"Oh, that question ... I thought we had moved well past it."

"We have, in many ways, and its answer will have no effect on my love for you, but I think it's time for us to completely understand each other."

"I completely understand you, Cyrus, and I appreciate your devotion over all the years since then. I truly do."

"I'd like to know the entire story before my time is up."

"Now, don't talk as though you're about to pass away. You're in good health, and I expect we'll have many more eventful years together. Besides, we should look toward the future, not the past."

Cyrus leaned forward in his rocker. “If you don’t stop teasing me by pretending there’s no story to tell, I might have to put you across my knees and spank you.”

“Very well, seeing that you still have a spark of liveliness in you, I’ll share my secrets.”

“Good, the first unspoken question is why did you choose to adopt Lynnette when you knew she wasn’t your daughter?”

Barbara laughed. “Hasn’t she been a fine member of our family and a devoted daughter to both of us?”

“She has grown to be a beautiful woman with spunk and willpower. I love her dearly, but you selected her rather than continuing our search for your own birth daughter.”

“Yes, I did, and there’s a very good reason for my decision.”

“I’d appreciate your sharing it with me.”

“I selected Martha to be our daughter and become Lynnette Martha Danforth because I had no daughter of my own.”

CHAPTER 46 – DISAPPEARANCE

Cyrus stared at Barbara. "You did it to me again, and this time it worked for the better part of a lifetime."

"I'm afraid so."

"When we first met, I caught you weaving stories about a nonexistent husband serving first on one side and then the other during the Civil War. Haven't we been important enough to each other to put aside any recurrence of such fictions?"

"I avoided it for as long as possible, but then I was forced into fictional cover stories by my past."

"That's a mysterious statement. You'd better tell me the whole story so that I'll be able to decide what to believe."

"The day I disappeared from here was more complicated than it seemed. You at first believed that I was kidnapped by Pinkerton agents, and then after you found me three years later, I said the peddler took me. Neither of those stories is true, although with my limited memories at the time, I confused reality with my cover story."

Tension showed in Cyrus' face. "Then what actually happened?"

"The peddler of pots and pans did come to our house, but he was neither sinister nor remarkable. I told him I wasn't interested in his wares, and he went away. The two strangers with the long coats were Pinkerton agents, but they didn't kidnap me. I went with them willingly."

Cyrus stood and walked toward her. "If you weren't taken by them, why didn't you leave us a note, and why did you upset the furniture to make it look as though there had been a struggle?"

"Relax, and sit back down, Cyrus. I meant you no harm. You knew that I was a spy for the South during the Civil War. You and I were together for many years during which I appeared to be worried about Pinkerton agents coming after me. That fear of the Pinkertons was actually my intelligence cover story. The fact is that as the war wound down, several of the top people at Pinkerton convinced me that the future required a united America if we, individually and collectively, were to grow strong and flourish. In short, I became a covert Pinkerton operative, assigned to lead a normal life until events occurred that would require my unique talents and history. I knew the day might come when I would have to leave you for a special covert assignment, but I never told you in advance."

"Was that because you didn't trust me to keep your secrets?"

"Hardly. I thought that the Pinkerton people were alarmists, and that their fears would never be realized. I didn't tell you about the possibility of my being called away because I thought it would never happen."

Cyrus felt angry. "But when it did happen, you set the scene to make us conclude that you had been kidnapped, rather than giving us some hint of the true reason for your disappearance."

"A spy needs a cover story. For me to do my job on this mission, I had to make it look as though I was kidnapped and then escaped after I arrived at my destination. My adversaries were smart and in touch with friends everywhere, including Wisconsin. I was sure they would send someone to check whether I had been kidnapped or not. In order to deceive them, everyone here had to believe that I had been forced to leave."

"Damn it, Barbara, what was so important that they had to have you on this so-called mission in the first place?"

"Did you ever hear of Quantrill's Raiders?"

"Sure. They caused a lot of death and destruction in the western Border States towards the end of the Civil War with their bushwacking guerrilla attacks. They were disgruntled Confederates, some of whom weren't really military men. Quantrill had no officer training, but eventually the South made him a captain. They massacred a lot of people in Lawrence, Kansas in 1863."

"His Raiders included men who went to Texas after the war and tried to continue secession there, claiming that Texas had the right to become a separate country again. Other Raiders became outlaws after the war, especially the gang headed by Cole and Jim Younger working with Frank and Jesse James."

"I know some of that, Barbara, but I think I read that Cole and Jim Younger along with some others including another Younger brother from California were arrested after a botched bank robbery in Minnesota. They're still in prison."

"Right you are. That bank was in Northfield, Minnesota, and they messed up the robbery four years before my apparent kidnapping. What most people didn't know was that Frank and Jesse James were part of that venture too, but they got away, and the Youngers never said anything about them."

Cyrus shrugged. "I still don't see where this has anything to do with your so-called kidnapping."

Barbara walked to the fireplace and added another log. Then she turned back to Cyrus. "The James boys were Pinkerton's nemesis. In 1875 a group of Pinkerton men went to the James family farm, hoping to catch Frank and Jesse there. Those two brothers were away, so the raiders decided to burn down the house. They used a fire-starting device that exploded rather than flaming up after it smashed through the window. The James boys' younger brother, Archie, was killed and their mother, Zerelda, was badly wounded. The bad publicity about killing and wounding innocent people made the Pinkertons stop chasing Frank and Jesse and keep their operations low key for a long while."

Cyrus said, "I can't say I feel sorry for Pinkerton and company. They got away with making their own rules for a long time. That botched raid just made them a bit more careful about how they operated. Continue your story, Barbara."

"We're getting to the crux of it. After the James brothers escaped capture following the Northfield bank robbery in Minnesota, they headed for Nashville, Tennessee, where they took up farming and lived quiet lives for three years. Then Jesse got restless and started up a new gang. Frank would have been happy to continue farming, but he went along with Jesse and his new recruits. They robbed a stagecoach and a store in Kentucky. The Pinkertons got interested as soon as they learned the gang was headed by Jesse. That's when they came after me to help them infiltrate the gang because of my Confederate spy background. They figured rightly that I would be welcomed as a past foe of the government in Washington. The gang members had all been Confederate soldiers or sympathizers."

"So, the Pinkerton agents took you to Tennessee, where you acted out your escape from their custody? That business about the northwest corner of Georgia was made up later?"

"The Nashville area where the farm was located wasn't too far from that Georgia spot or the home where we eventually adopted Lynnette."

"At this point, should we say Lynnette or Martha?"

"She's always been Lynnette in my mind. Even a cover story becomes real if you tell it enough times."

Cyrus nodded agreement. "What happened after you arrived at Frank and Jesse's farm? How did you connect with them? Did you take part in any robberies?"

"Slow down. I'll answer questions one at a time. After I made my so-called escape, I connected with a gang member I knew from wartime encounters. I was hiding out in an inn with guest rooms above the tavern area, and I met him when I came downstairs for food. We talked as I ate, and he told me what he was currently doing. I told him I was on the run from Pinkerton agents and asked to join him.

"Once at the farm I was welcomed, but they didn't expect me to do robberies. I was just supposed to be sympathetic to their cause. They did draw on my wartime anti-government knowledge when Jesse, Bill Ryan, and Wood Hite, Jesse's cousin, robbed a federal paymaster in Alabama. Then after Bill Ryan got drunk and boasted about the amount of money taken from the paymaster, he was arrested near the James farm. At that point, the rest of the gang, with me trailing along, headed to Missouri, where the James brothers had grown up."

"Does that story make you a criminal too?"

"I was merely an undercover agent for a private law enforcement group. It was as legal as you could expect in those days."

Cyrus held her hands and fixed his gaze on her eyes. "So everything you told me earlier about your kidnapping was a lie or a cover story. How did you end up near Memphis?"

CHAPTER 47 - ACTUALITIES

Barbara almost lashed out at her husband for calling her earlier story a complete lie, but then she decided her better path was to continue her summary. "As I said earlier, the gang decided they would be safer in their home state of Missouri than in Kentucky or Tennessee. They had friends and relatives there, as well as supporters from their old Confederate raider days. We all moved to Missouri in late March of 1881 and lived quiet lives until July of that same year, when some of them robbed a Rock Island Railroad train, killing a passenger and the conductor during the action. Two months later, they held up a train on the Chicago and Alton Railroad. That robbery was a bust, resulting in very slim proceeds and the arrest of two members of the gang, Creed Chapman and John Bugler.

"By this time, I was considered trustworthy by everyone, especially since I was older than they were. I wasn't quite a mother figure to them, but they gave me respect from a slight distance because I was beyond the age of romantic interest for most of them. After the Chicago and Alton robbery, I disappeared from St. Joseph, Missouri, where Jesse had his home and made covert contact with the governor, Thomas Crittenden. I told him that I thought a large reward would affect the loyalty of some of the gang members. He said that state law wouldn't let him post such a reward, and I suggested that Pinkerton might use its influence to help him raise contributions from private companies."

Cyrus interrupted. “Are you saying that in addition to being a hidden agent for Pinkerton, you had the backing of their top managers?”

“Of course not, but they told me I could talk as though I did. Jesse James had been an aggravation to Pinkerton due to the earlier botched raid on his mother’s home and the lost business that resulted from it. I was pretty sure they would back me up. Besides, the governor would mention Pinkerton in any negotiations, not me. I’d be back doing undercover work when he tried to get reward money.”

“How much did he raise?”

“The railroads kicked in five thousand dollars, and the express companies matched that amount. Ten thousand dollars was a big temptation for gang members, and it was more than enough to get Charley and Bob Ford interested. It amused me that Bob Ford was the youngest member of the gang, and he talked about growing up idolizing Jesse. Yet, he was the one who took him down.”

“I vaguely recall something about Jesse James being shot in the back. How did it happen?”

“Bob and Charley Ford were living at Jesse’s house using the names of Bob and Charles Johnson. At that time Jesse was using the alias of Thomas Howard. The gang had few members left, between arrests and infighting. Dick Liddil had recently killed Jesse’s cousin, Wood Hite, during an argument about the Fords’ widowed sister Martha Bolton, and Bob Ford had been on Liddil’s side during the gunfight.

“One day in April of 1882 everyone had breakfast in the kitchen, and then the Ford brothers and Jesse went into the living room. Jesse might have suspected something wasn’t quite right, because the Fords hadn’t said anything about the fight and murder of Wood Hite. He’d learned about it from a newspaper. Jesse liked things to be neat at home, so he climbed up on a chair with a cloth when he saw that the picture above the fireplace mantle was dusty. That gave Bob Ford his opportunity, and he killed Jesse with a shot to the back of his head behind his ear."

Cyrus said, "So that's the real story. By the time I heard it, the shot was to the middle of his back. Were you there, Barbara?"

"No, I lived in a different part of town. I got the story from Zerelda, Jesse's wife, who ran in after she heard the shot. She was terribly upset. She knew he was an outlaw who could be killed during any robbery, but it was a shock to lose him like that."

"I didn't hear anything about a wife."

"She's a good-hearted person. I wondered how they had met but never found out. One odd thing is that Zerelda is an unusual name, but both Jesse's wife and his mother had it."

"Maybe that's what attracted him to his wife when they first met."

"That's possible.... I have to say that Bob Ford's shot brought Jesse's life to an end and mine to major trouble."

CHAPTER 48 – JOHN BLANDON

Barbara Danforth continued her story after adding another log to the shrinking stack in the fireplace. "Cyrus, a while ago you accused me of having made up everything about the period when I was gone and of having faked my injuries and health condition."

"I didn't accuse you ..."

"You did; but I'll try to help you understand what happened." She sat in silence while she composed her thoughts. "My problems resulted from my friendship with Charley Ford. Bob Ford and Dick Liddil had killed Jesse's cousin, Wood Hite. Then Bob shot Jesse with Charley in the same room. Because I talked and joked with Charley at times, some of the gang members took me to be supportive of the Fords. This was especially true of Clarence Hite, Wood Hite's surviving brother."

"I can see that, Barbara. If someone kills your brother, you hate him and anyone friendly with him."

"The situation was complicated by the fact that Clarence Hite and Charley Ford had been close friends in the past. Clarence didn't attack anyone following Jesse's murder, but he voiced his anger to one of his friends, John Blandon, and John decided to take action for Clarence. Unfortunately, I was his target."

"What did he do?"

"You know most of that story, Cyrus. Contrary to your earlier accusation that I made everything up, the story of my captivity near Memphis was completely true. The only difference was that the man I called John Hackamore was actually John Blandon, Clarence Hite's friend."

"I wondered about the name Hackamore."

"When I told you about him, my mind hadn't completely cleared, so I chose a name that easily came to mind. It must have been due to all the horseback riding I did when I was young. I picked a false name because John Blandon's name might have been tracked back to the Jesse James gang. My thinking wasn't exactly right, but my past training kicked in. I knew I had to hide my undercover work."

"Why?"

"Because other gang members might have come after me. I guess I didn't mention that I used my real maiden name, Belle Browning, when I was doing undercover work. My reputation as a Confederate spy by that name got me accepted."

Cyrus stood and went over to Barbara. Taking her hand, he raised her up from her seat so that he could hug her. "Then all my anguish over your condition when I saw you in Memphis was well-founded. You did go through all of those terrible tortures."

"Yes, Cyrus; it was even true that I was kidnapped, but not from home. I was kidnapped from St. Joseph, Missouri and taken to Tennessee, ending up in that stone torture cabin deep in the woods."

"And the rapes?"

"Unfortunately, they happened. I started to count them with marks on the floor, but I lost count before long."

"What about the Confederate officer's uniform on your captor's skeleton?"

"I don't know why he started to dress up like that. Perhaps he started to feel guilty about what he was doing to me and justified it as my being a prisoner of war. Left-over war uniforms and supplies could be bought in any town."

"You do know how much we missed you, Barbara?"

"Of course, Cyrus; and it was your love that pulled me through that whole period. I had to survive to get back to you. I felt that way even after memories of your face and the location of our home had been beaten out of me."

"I'm sorry I had doubts. You really are a hero, Barbara."

"I'm not the only one in this family. That's why I married you."

CHAPTER 49 – FAMILY SECRET REVISITED

As they gathered in Grandma Marie's kitchen once more, Debbie took as significant Marie's sitting with them around the table rather than holding court from her customized Danforth family rocking chair.

At the table, Debbie and Jeremy deferred to Marie to start the discussion.

"Welcome back, you two detectives. I'll have to admit that your call requesting a new discussion took me by surprise. I figured that it could only mean one of two things. Either you gave up on my assignment, or you completed it. From the grins you were trying to hide as you came in the back door, I'll assume that you have answered the question of whether Barbara Danforth knew that Lynnette wasn't her daughter at the moment when she and Cyrus adopted the four-year-old. If you have succeeded, you did so in a surprisingly short time, so I congratulate you.

Debbie nodded to Jeremy to present their results, knowing that he wanted to impress Marie and feel more accepted.

"You're correct in judging that we found an answer to your assignment question, Marie. It was a challenging problem, but in the end, we got lucky."

Debbie interrupted. "He's not giving himself enough credit. We found the answer because Jeremy has a fantastic memory."

Marie said, "Before we worry about giving credit, deserved or otherwise, how about taking me step-by-step through your research approach and then lead me to your conclusion. Go ahead, Jeremy."

"I'll do that, Marie, but before I get started, I want to emphasize that our conclusion relies on the details of the family history you gave us. Are you sure that all your details were correct?"

"Jeremy, every time I think I should accept you without any more teasing or needling, you throw me a curve ball. Of course the details in my story were correct."

"Fine, then so is the conclusion I'll present shortly. To get started, we divided our efforts, with Debbie examining the details of Lynnette's life as an adult while I tried to dredge up facts about what went on during the orphanage visit and adoption. I would be looking into ancient history, while Debbie would look at Lynnette's adult period, which was recent enough to have documentation."

Marie said, "That's an interesting division of labor, but what did you hope to get from Debbie's study of the adult Lynnette?"

"We were hoping to get an answer to your question about the adoption that would have a high probability of being correct. The one person who might have the absolutely true answer was Lynnette herself. I guessed that Barbara might have told her daughter about the adoption details, and that Lynnette might have revealed them in something she said or did."

"A unique perspective; please continue."

"I'll continue by confessing that my search for specific facts about the adoption went nowhere. I searched for the name of the orphanage, Stalwart Haven and found only the story of a racehorse named Ms. Stalwart that retired, died, and was buried in Our Mims Retirement Haven in Kentucky. It turned out that statewide, Tennessee didn't even start documenting adoptions until 1908, and earlier local records were fragmentary."

Marie frowned. “You are going to get to some success in this story, aren’t you?”

“As you told me more than once, you’ll have to be patient. Debbie trained as a research librarian, and she was looking for useful information on grown-up Lynnette in a period that had newspaper files and records. Debbie gathered major amounts of information, and we went over it together. To make our long story short, ...”

Marie said, “I’d appreciate that.”

“... we found a magazine photograph of Women’s Suffrage protestors. You remember that Debbie asked you to email her a scan of your photograph of Lynnette?”

“Sure.”

“We compared your picture of Lynnette to that of a woman protestor who had only two fingers on each hand, and they matched.”

Marie smiled. “Great. Now we have two photos of Lynnette. How does that help us?”

“You said that the family history story you told us was completely accurate.”

“It has been confirmed by other Danforth family members who heard it independently from their parents.”

Jeremy slapped the table top. “That’s what I wanted to hear. You told us that Lynnette had two fingers on each hand, the thumb and forefinger on her right hand plus the second and third fingers on her left hand.”

“That’s correct.”

“Well, Marie, the woman we identified as Lynnette in the protest photograph has two thumbs. She has the thumb and forefinger on her right hand and the thumb and middle finger on her left hand. Barbara had to know that the four-year-old she adopted was not her daughter. She had different pairs of fingers on her incomplete hands.”

Marie stood. “Congratulations, you two. You’ve met my challenge. We have proof of what was going on in

Barbara's mind in 1881. That's pretty spectacular detective work. I might have to give your agency a recommendation."

Debbie said, "Hold it, Grandma. We answered your assigned question. Now you'll have to answer ours. Why is the deliberate adoption of a different child as Lynnette important?"

CHAPTER 50 - ENVY

Marie suggested that they all take a break and something to drink before she responded to their question. Debbie sensed that she was hesitant to verbalize her feelings.

"Take your time, Grandma. If you don't feel up to continuing our conversations today, we'll come back another time."

Marie said, "Thanks, Debbie. You were always my favorite granddaughter."

"Don't let her con you, Jeremy. I'm her only granddaughter. Seriously, Marie, would you prefer to keep going or have a postponement?"

Marie poured coffee into all three of their cups. "We'll continue. My hesitancy isn't due to something physical. It's just going to be an unpleasant discussion. Drink your coffee while I frame my thoughts."

She wrote a few notes on a pad of paper while Debbie and Jeremy silently ate her homemade chocolate chip cookies and sipped their coffees. After a few minutes, Marie put down her pen and read what she had written.

"I have enough to start our discussions, so here we go. When Cyrus and Barbara decided that it was time for them to retire from operating their fund for the benefit of families of the Second Wisconsin Regiment, they had to decide which child should take it over for them. They selected Lynnette because she was good at mathematics, had been a teacher, and had connections with the University of Wisconsin. Daniel had not gone to college because he was more interested in farming and did not enjoy bookwork. Bruce was probably the most intellectual of the three, but he wanted to travel the world and study with European philosophers. There was no doubt that Lynnette was the best choice at the time."

Debbie said, "From what I learned about her, she would have been dependable and would have stood up to bankers or others who wanted her to invest the foundation's money in risky ways."

"Lynnette was a good manager, and under her guidance, the fund grew quite large. That's the problem. We have so much money that people want to take it away from us."

Jeremy responded to Marie's comment by doing some calculations on his smart phone. "I have a future value calculator here, and it emphasizes what you said about the size of the fund that originated with George Stevens' gold. The original withdrawal from the bank in Australia was about eighty thousand dollars. If we say that Cyrus Danforth was very generous with contributions to 2nd Wisconsin veterans and their families, he might have dispersed as much as half of the money during his first two years back in Wisconsin. I doubt that he distributed so much money that rapidly, but I want to be conservative in my calculations. If his investments and interest at banks earned him four percent per year over the hundred and fifty years since then, he would have increased the fund back to its original eighty thousand dollars within seventeen years, and from that point on, he would have had more than his original balance to use for distributions, while the value of his holdings kept growing until they would be about fifteen million dollars today. If the funds earned a six percent return, they would amount to two hundred and eighty-one million dollars today. I don't know the actual foundation figures, but they must be holding huge amounts of money and valuable investments."

Marie smiled. "You're pretty good with numbers, Jeremy, but while Lynnette was managing the foundation, she made early investments in stocks of new companies that are huge today. Your estimates are very low. The foundation value exceeds two billion dollars."

Debbie whistled a long low tone. "No wonder you said that people want to gain access to some of that money. Are you talking about outsiders or family members?"

"The foundation is well secured against outsider raids on its treasury because we operate through major banks and investment houses. Our problems lie within the family tree. For many years we were so good at hiding the foundation's activities that most members of Bruce and Daniel's branches of the family thought that we had run out of money and ended our support of 2nd Wisconsin families back when Lynnette was still alive. If your father, Max, hadn't started playing with DNA analysis the other Danforth branches would still be in the dark. Once your father compared the DNA of Lynnette's descendants with those Bruce and Daniel's offspring, and found no similarities, he told other relatives that the 2nd Wisconsin project still existed and that they had a valid argument for taking over its control. Several Danforth relatives from both Bruce and Daniel's branches were more than happy to argue that Lynnette's branch should not have control of the funds. My position as the trusted manager of the secret fund was undermined by my own son."

Debbie looked up from her note-taking. "Now I understand why you wanted to know whether Barbara had deliberately adopted the wrong girl as Lynnette. The other family branches would have a stronger argument for foundation control if Cyrus and Barbara mistakenly thought Lynnette was Barbara's birth child."

Jeremy said, "That one flew right over my head. Why is it stronger one way than the other, Debbie?"

"If Cyrus and Barbara incorrectly thought Lynnette was the daughter born to Barbara, Bruce and Daniel's descendants could argue that as blood relatives Bruce or Daniel should have been chosen to run the fund. If Barbara knew that Lynnette wasn't her child, then the selection was made with the parents' eyes wide open to the circumstances, and they selected Lynnette even though they knew she wasn't a blood relative. They deliberately chose her because they thought she would do a better job. How's that for thinking like a lawyer, Jeremy?"

"I get it now. If Lynnette and her offspring had screwed up and run the foundation out of money, no one would care. The problem is that they turned a little pile of gold into a huge one; and now everyone in the family knows about it and wants part of it. Those folks knew they'd need a good argument to change fund management, and the DNA results convinced them they had one."

Marie had listened patiently, but now spoke up. "Jeremy, you painted your picture with too broad a brush. I know of only two people who are trying to gain control of the foundation, one person from each of the other two family branches. There might be a couple more who have kept their interests hidden. Most family members in all three of the branches are satisfied with the present arrangement."

Jeremy said, "And you are you the current fund manager, Marie?"

"It has been formalized as a foundation now, but yes, I am. You folks have a stake in this too, because it will soon be time for me to retire from that job, and the leading candidate to replace me would be Debbie."

CHAPTER 51 - ASPIRING MANAGERS

Debbie Danforth Hadley had a shocked look on her face as she stared at her grandmother. "How can you consider me as a possible manager of your project? I didn't even know about the foundation or the family secret mission until you asked us here to do investigative work."

"I had no more warning before I was given the job. Be that as it may, there's a large fund and mission that will need your attention soon. We also want to avoid big legal battles within the family."

Jeremy stopped writing and took a fresh sheet of paper. He kept his pen poised for new notes. "Who are the two people from other parts of the family who want control of the fund?"

Marie said, "The first is Patricia Danforth Flynn, Pat Flynn to most folks. She's a rising star in real estate development, and I'm betting that she'd find a way to invest our money in her housing and office building developments if she got control of the foundation."

Jeremy drew two columns on his sheet of paper. He used *Bruce* and *Daniel* as the headings for the columns. "Does Pat belong to Bruce's part of the family or to Daniel's?"

"Put her on Daniel's side. Prior to her generation, most of Daniel's descendants were farmers. Pat and her brother Lester were the first in their line to go to college and graduate school. Lester is a customs broker in Milwaukee. He and Pat sold the family farm. Lester used his portion to start his business, while Pat bought a land parcel in Milwaukee's far northwest suburbs and built a housing development, smaller homes suitable for retirement living."

Debbie said, "Pat sounds like a savvy businessperson. There's a big demand for low maintenance homes for retired people."

Marie agreed. "She's full of energy and works on several projects at the same time. If she were to manage the foundation, it would be a very part-time activity for her. She also likes to cut corners on ethics if it makes her more money."

Debbie wrote that statement on her pad and underlined *part-time*. "If I were running the foundation, it would be a part-time effort for me also."

"That would be fine, but I wouldn't feel it necessary to constantly check your actions as I would if Pat were in charge. Less than a month after her father's death, Pat sold a farm that had been in her family for generations. She might make spur-of-the-moment changes to long-term foundation investments also. Someone would have to monitor all the stocks and bank balances if she were running the fund."

Jeremy looked away from the notes he had made about Pat. "I'll summarize your comments as indicating that you don't think she's trustworthy. Who's the contender from Bruce's family?"

Marie realized that Jeremy felt free to assert himself and no longer worried about impressing her. She smiled to herself over his relaxing. "The candidate from Bruce's family is Jonathan Danforth. He really is a candidate, because he's in politics, having unsuccessfully run for Congress last year. Like most politicians, he tries to give himself every possible advantage with the voters. Jonathan grew up with the family name of Debka, his mother, Carolyn Danforth, having married an Eastern European gentleman. As soon as Jonathan decided to pursue politics as a career, he legally changed his name to Danforth."

Debbie said, "He's not the first politician to change his name to one that's more mainstream and easier to pronounce. He is a Danforth, even though it's conventional to take the father's name. Society isn't as rigorous about that as in the old days. It's no longer unusual for a woman to keep her father's name after marriage."

Jeremy had been entering Jonathan's notes into his column for Bruce's family. He looked up and asked, "What don't you like about Jonathan, Marie?"

"Don't assume that I view him negatively, Jeremy. As far as I know, Jonathan is a good man with many positive attributes. I don't particularly care for politicians, but I've known a few good ones. I simply don't feel there is any reason to remove control of the foundation from Lynnette's branch of the family. Barbara and Cyrus selected her to manage the fund, and that job was passed down to others in her immediate family; first Ted, then Gregory, and then me. Thanks to your research, I have a strong argument for keeping control in our branch of the family tree."

CHAPTER 52 – PATRICIA DANFORTH FLYNN

Patsy Flynn, you'd better pinch yourself to make sure this isn't a dream. Now that we know that Lynnette Danforth's DNA didn't match the family's patterns, we've got us a strong case for taking over that big foundation. Think of how many homes and museums and company buildings we could construct with that treasury behind us – all for the benefit of those Civil War soldiers' families of course. I can make a case for almost any project being beneficial to their descendants. We'll hire a bunch of them in every new company and in the construction crews too. That foundation is a huge truckload of gold, and I want to be its driver.

The question now is whether I'll have any competition. Most of the people from Daniel's branch are hard workers and aren't interested in straying outside of their career fields ... or farm fields for that matter. Uncle Harry might be competition, but he's past the age of lifestyle flexibility – I think that's forty-two per the article I read. On the other hand, Marie Danforth is running the foundation now, and she's a grandmother of adults. It's weird that at Danforth family gatherings when you hear whispers about the foundation and its work, it's described as the family secret, but people in the banking and investment industries must know about it, as does the administration at the University of Wisconsin.

Maybe I should approach Uncle Harry to see whether I can pay him to stay out of the competition. He's a greedy old bastard; I'm not sure that would work. Maybe I could dig up some dirt on him that he wouldn't want publicized. I might have him if I combined those two approaches. I've hidden the skeletons in my own closet pretty well. I don't think he'll be able to turn my own tricks against me. If nothing else is successful, I could claim that he sexually molested me as a child. That always taints the alleged pedophile for life, even when there's no evidence. – Of course, it might taint me too, as being someone out of control. I'd better forget that approach.

There's always the possibility that I might have competition from Bruce's branch of the family, but they're dreamers and philosophers for the most part. I doubt that they'd want to be labeled as money-grubbers. They think too much of their reputation as a family of intellectuals. There's more to intelligence than way-out thinking. I'll show them a thing or two about getting your way and controlling a source of power.

CHAPTER 53 – JONATHAN DANFORTH

Jonathan knew that some people were calling him a loser because he unsuccessfully ran for the local congressional seat. He didn't agree with them. In his mind, that loss was the price he had paid for name recognition. He would tackle another campaign, either for Congress or for some other office, and next time people would know his name and his personality. Initially, he had to force himself to voice his views in public, but now he knew both the words and the rhythms that energized voters.

When he wasn't running for office, Jonathan supported himself by selling cars in a Milwaukee Ford dealership. His success at this business had increased since the election because many car shoppers felt that they were befriending a celebrity when they shook hands with him on a vehicle purchase. Losing had actually paid off for him.

Selling cars could be lucrative, but not nearly as much as owning a dealership or two. Without overtly expressing interest, he had listened with interest as several family members debated the possible takeover of the family foundation by someone from Bruce or Daniel's branch of the family. He knew that his cousin Pat was drooling over the possibility of getting her hands on the foundation's charity funds, and he had heard rumors of other candidates equally eager to control the family project. He had kept his own interest hidden, but he suspected that the current foundation manager, Marie Danforth, had identified him as a potential competitor.

He didn't know how much the family's charity funds had grown, but they had been invested for a very long time, so the balance must be substantial. Automobile dealerships were a good investment. If he became the foundation's manager, he might make a case for establishing a dealership that trained descendants of 2nd Wisconsin soldiers in all aspects of the car business. That would give them good careers and make money for him too. He could even become the advertising spokesman in television commercials to enhance his personal celebrity status.

At this point he was only daydreaming, but he would keep the idea simmering on the back burner for a while. His dreams and concepts had been oversized from youth onward. He had a strong feeling that it wouldn't be long before he saw his business and government ideas get implemented.

CHAPTER 54 – PRESSURES

One afternoon, Jonathan sat at his desk in the Ford showroom sending follow-up emails to people in his area who had clicked online Ford advertisements. Cold contacts of that type rarely led to car sales, but they gave him something useful to do while he waited for live customers to show up. As he was completing his fourteenth message, three men wearing baseball caps and black leather jackets entered the showroom. It was Jonathan's turn to make the sales pitch, so he stood and greeted them.

"Welcome, gentlemen. I'm Jonathan Danforth, and I'll be pleased to answer any questions you may have."

The man who had walked in slightly ahead of the other two shook Jonathan's extended hand briefly. "We want to see a black Ford Expedition, and we'll need a test drive."

Jonathan brought up the inventory screen on his computer. "We don't have a black one on the lot right now. I can get one from another dealership within hours, but we can do the test drive in that Ruby Red Metallic model parked in the second aisle. Will that work for you?"

"Sure."

"May I have your names? I'll also need to see and copy the driver's license for the person who will be driving."

The lead man said, "I'm Manny, and these two are Sam and Tony. We mainly want to get a feeling for the size and comfort of the car, so you can do the driving. Is that red car set up with three rows of seats?"

"It has three rows, and the third row is our special seat that folds flat into the floor when the driver pushes a button on his console."

"That sounds real good. Let's take that ride."

Jonathan went into the office and pulled the keys for the red Expedition. While he was in there, he panned and zoomed the security camera to take close-up pictures of each of his potential customers. He didn't quite like the bearing of these men, but his job was to sell cars, not to judge the buyers. One more adjustment on the security camera aim, and he captured the license plate of the car they had parked outside. Most customers appreciated the convenience of their reserved parking spaces in front of the showroom window. They didn't realize that cars in those spaces offered unobstructed views of the numbers on their cars' plates to the security cameras.

As requested, Jonathan drove the car while Manny sat in the front passenger seat. Tony sat in the second row, while Sam occupied the third row seat. As they drove, Jonathan kept up his salesman's chatter about the various features of the car, but when they approached the domes of Mitchell Park Conservatory, Manny interrupted and told Jonathan to pull over and stop in the park.

After Jonathan complied, they all got out of the car, and Manny said, "Danforth, you come over here and talk with me by this tree, while Sam and Tony examine the car."

Sam and Tony took their cues and opened the tailgate and other doors. After they had investigated the car's interior, they examined the engine.

While the other two were checking the car, Manny said, "Danforth, you did a good job with your political campaign for an amateur, but you made a few mistakes."

Jonathan said, "I have the feeling that you guys aren't interested in a car at all. This road test was intended to get me away from the dealership. What mistakes did I make, and why do they matter to you?"

"I see that you don't beat around the bush with fancy talk. That's good. You gave us your dealer's pitch, Danforth, and now I'll give you mine.

"I represent a group of business people who would like to see you succeed in politics and in financial affairs. We can help you achieve success if you'll cooperate with us, or we can draw the public's attention to your political failings and ruin your political career. The choice will be up to you."

Jonathan doubted that his three passengers would physically attack him. The park and conservatory were filled with tourists and local visitors. He'd stand up to them and see what happened next. "Manny, you do remember that I campaigned for Congress on a law and order platform, with emphasis on ethics in politics. I'm not about to be shaken down by underworld characters."

Manny applied sweetness to his voice. "That's exactly why I said you made a few mistakes. You didn't check out the people who gave your campaign major contributions. If we were to publicize the fact that you received $35,000 from a convicted drug dealer and $10,000 from a pimp who forces innocent girls into prostitution, your ethical law and order routine would be rejected by the public. You wouldn't be able to run for any office again. That's the bad news for you. The good news is that none of this has to be known if you'll listen to the people I represent and cooperate with us on a few simple projects."

Manny was right. He hadn't checked the sources of his contributions. He had just been thankful when his meager bankroll increased enough for him to complete the campaign. He'd bluff his way through this. "You're right, Manny; I should have checked earlier. Now that you've brought the source of those contributions to my attention, I'll return their money. Better late than never."

“Good luck with that, Danforth. We know that your treasure chest was empty by the date of the election and you have a bunch of loans to repay. You gambled that you’d win and get a Congressman’s salary plus off-the-record add-ons. You lost, and now you need help from someone like me. I’ll make it easy for you. All you have to do is listen to our propositions and give them careful consideration, and I’ll buy the Ford Expedition that the boys are examining. That transaction should give you a start toward those refunds you want to make. We’re not bad guys. You may like what we’re proposing.”

“Thanks, but no thanks, Manny. I’ll be my own man or I’ll stick with selling cars. I have other places I can turn for a loan to get me out of this bind.”

Manny surprised him. “That’s the proposition we want to discuss with you. We’re sure we can engineer your takeover of that foundation in return for a small fee.”

“How small a fee?”

“Good. You’ve agreed to work with us. Now we’re just negotiating the fee.”

“I never said that.”

“I have it recorded.”

CHAPTER 55 – LOAN QUEST

Marie had reacted to Jonathan's telephone call by inviting him to visit her for lunch. They had previously talked only at large family affairs, and she looked forward to evaluating her politician relative across the kitchen table. He had said that he wanted to discuss a business matter, so she assumed this would be his presentation on why he should take over the responsibility of managing the family foundation. She wondered how many other relatives would come to her to pitch their cases for replacing her. She would be ready to counter his arguments.

Jonathan's appearance and bearing when he arrived surprised Marie. She had seen him on television when he was running for Congress, and he had always been stylishly dressed and upbeat when he spoke. Today, he arrived in blue jeans and a red checkerboard flannel shirt, and the tone of his voice was almost apologetic as he greeted her.

"Hello, Marie, I hope I'm not intruding on your schedule, but I felt it was time for us to get to know each other better and to discuss something serious that I'm facing."

She would try to cheer him up. "Come on in Jonathan. The family has grown so large that those of us in different branches of the family tree hardly ever see each other. I'd like to get to know you better."

"Thanks; I'd like that too. I'm sure you heard at least newscast samples from my campaign speeches when I unsuccessfully ran for Congress. I was an idealist hoping to be the kind of politician the public can trust. I'm afraid

I was a little naïve about how politics and the election process work."

Marie pulled a kitchen chair away from table. "Have a seat, Jonathan. This table has been the scene of many serious Danforth family discussions over the years. You might call it Family Central. It sounds as though we have some current problems to work through. Are you still bothered because you lost the election?"

As Marie studied his facial expression, Jonathan said, "Oddly enough, that never seemed much of a problem. I knew that I had only an outside chance of winning, and I felt that I had won name and viewpoint recognition that would help me when I ran again. I'm just now realizing that during my first venture into the political arena, I was being set up to fail if I ever ran for an office again."

Marie opened a bottle of root beer and passed it to him. "That sounds serious. Who was doing what to damage your political career?"

Jonathan told her about the visit of the underworld types to the car dealership where he worked and about their revelations about large sums of tainted money included in his election contributions. He continued, "If I run again as an independent crusader, they'll say that I've been telling lies about my ethics and honesty because I've been supported by drug and prostitution money. They want to blackmail me into doing their bidding."

"What do they want you to do?"

"I'm sure they'll have an unending list of goals for me, but their first target is for me to try to take management of the family's foundation away from you and others in Lynnette's branch of the family."

Marie sipped from her bottle of root beer as she studied Jonathan's eyes and demeanor. "How do you feel about trying to take over our charity work?"

"I'll admit that I fantasized about running the foundation at one point just because it contains a huge amount of money, but I know that I'm not the right person for that job. I do want to help people, but I wouldn't feel comfortable dealing with financial heavyweights. I want to help people overcome obstacles by improving government laws and systems, not by throwing money at them. I'm sorry if my last comment suggested that I don't appreciate your charity work. I do value it, but it's not the right path for me."

Marie said, "I'm afraid that I did a bad job of evaluating your outlook. I assumed that you would be one of the relatives who would argue that foundation management should be taken away from Lynnette's branch of the family because she was adopted rather than a Danforth by blood ancestry."

Jonathan reached across the table and patted Marie's hand. "Those discussions and arguments are indeed going on in the other family branches, but my opinion is that you folks have done a fantastic job of running the charity distribution work for many years, and it would be silly to suddenly change the management, rather than train new people over time to run it properly. Those people could come from any part of the family, but the important requirements are training and purposeful continuity."

"I'm glad to hear you take that stand, Jonathan, but how will you fend off the criminals if you don't tie in with them and try to take over foundation management?"

"I figure I have two ways out. I could give up politics, but they might still brand me as unethical because of those tainted campaign contributions. My other option led to my visit here today. I'd like to simply and quite publicly refund the tainted contributions to those unacceptable contributors, but I don't have the funds to do it. I wanted to ask the foundation to loan me the money at a normal rate of interest, and I would pay it back over time."

Marie smiled. "I expected you to say that you wanted to take over management of the foundation, but you're merely asking for a loan. Ordinarily, I would have no problem with your request, but as a politician you should be able to see that it's important to avoid any suspicion or appearance of impropriety. I don't want people inside or outside the family to think I bribed you to give up your interest in managing the foundation."

Jonathan said, "I didn't think of that scenario or realize that you were such a skilled diplomat, but I suppose that's necessary for you to run the family gatherings. I could declare publicly that I am not interested in the position of foundation manager, should it become available. However, this might encourage other family members to try for the post by implying that it is or will be an open position. As an alternative, the foundation could name me a consultant for development of new projects, and I could work on proposals for faster distribution of the funds. The only reason for family members to try to change the management is because we have accumulated money much more rapidly than we can distribute it. Isn't it time to identify new projects which are still in line with the original marching orders from Lt. Col. Stevens?"

"You know more about the family secret and the foundation than I thought. Let's go with your second suggestion. Jonathan, you are hereby appointed to be a consultant, and I'll announce it to the family. This might cause some of the ambitious ones to back off of their quest for managing everything. Let me know how much money you need to refund those tainted donations, and I'll give it to you as an advance on your consultant billings."

CHAPTER 56 – REACTIONS

Pat Flynn stared at the email in disbelief. Marie Danforth had announced to the family that Jonathan Danforth from Bruce's family was going to be working as a project development consultant to the family foundation. Her scream filled the empty room. "Jonathan, you S.O.B., you aren't going to get away with stealing my chance to run that foundation. I see what you're doing. You're worming your way into management slowly and gradually. I won't let you do that! I'll find a way to stop you."

A prolonged ring of her doorbell interrupted her shouting. *Had someone heard her from outside her house? Did they think she needed help?* She straightened her hair and approached the front door. Through the glass insert in the door she could see that a large man was standing there. He gave a second long push on the bell button.

"I'm coming. I'm coming."

When she opened the door she saw a man wearing a gray suit over a black knit turtleneck shirt. In the background she saw two other casually-attired men standing next to a large red car at the curb.

She tried to assess her visitor. "May I help you?"

He said, "My name is Manny Ortega, and I'd like to talk with you about a possible construction project and a suggestion for a joint venture. May I come in?"

Pat's outlook as an individual made her regard this stranger with caution, but her real estate development persona smelled an opportunity. She invited Manny to enter her house.

"What may I do for you, sir?"

"Call me Manny, and I'm here to discuss what I can do for you."

"That sounds as though you got me to invite you in under false pretenses. Whatever you're selling, I'm not interested."

"Would you be inclined to talk with me if the subject was a certain family charitable foundation containing major amounts of cash and other assets?"

Pat responded cautiously. "I heard you say that you had a construction project to discuss. I don't know you, so I'm not interested in conversing about that foundation."

"Let's say that I'll need a small office building for processing investment proposals once you become the manager of that family foundation."

"And why do you think I'll be moving into that position? I've already learned that my cousin is being trained as a consultant to that group."

"You must mean Jonathan Danforth. We've already had some meetings with him, and his uncooperative attitude portends an unpromising future for him."

"*Portends* – You have a more elaborate vocabulary than I might have imagined, Mr. Ortega. How and why would you expect me to be, as you say, cooperative?"

"Call me Manny, and I'm counting on your assigning a much higher priority to taking over that foundation than Jonathan did. If you do become the fund's manager, you'll need an organization to legitimize any possible projects that reduce the asset balances. We're good at disguising cash flows behind legitimate project buffers."

"In plainer words, you're proposing a money laundering service."

"For a small fee – a negotiated percentage of the cash that is flowing."

"You weren't listening to me earlier, Manny. I have a smaller chance of running that foundation today than I did yesterday. Cousin Jonathan is now a consultant to the foundation and will have the inside track if there is to be a management change."

"And you weren't listening to me, Pat. I suggested that Jonathan might have an unpromising future."

"How would you remove the promise from his future?"

"I wouldn't remove anything, but a partnership between you and the group I represent might make it more likely that Jonathan Danforth might have some kind of accident."

"Are you suggesting that there would be a cause and effect relationship between that partnership and an accident?"

"Certainly not. I represent an investment group, not anything unseemly."

"As they taught me when I grew up on my family's farm, you have to scatter many seeds to be sure that at least one will grow. I'll let you be one of those seeds, Manny, if you convince me that you represent a legitimate organization. Then you'll have to fertilize that seed until it produces better results than the more conventional seeds I've planted. If a different seed flourishes better than yours, I'll probably walk away from dealing with you if I get to be the foundation manager."

"That's fair enough, Pat, but no other seed will produce better results than ours. And once we plant our seed, there won't be any walking away."

CHAPTER 57 - PRECAUTIONS

The more Marie talked with Jonathan about his outlook and the veiled threats aimed at him by Manny and his associates, the more she felt that he needed assistance and protection. Jonathan was the strangest of creatures, an idealistic politician, and although it was refreshing for her to spend time with him, she felt he would never succeed in the cannibalistic world of politics. Marie knew that any protection for Jonathan would have to be skillfully organized before it was proposed to him, or he would refuse it. She waited until the week following his visit before she took action.

She keyed in the phone number and waited for the now-familiar Sandley Agency greeting. This time it was delivered by Debbie.

Marie responded, "You both sound professional when you answer the telephone. You have that part of the business under control. My inquiry for the day concerns whether you two are real detectives, capable of handling some strong-arm types in a threatening encounter."

"Hello to you too, Grandma. I'm pleased to announce that both Jeremy and I have had martial arts and small arms training from off-duty military trainers. We carry both lethal and nonlethal weapons when we get involved in a dangerous case."

"That's impressive, Debbie. Now be honest and tell me how many dangerous cases requiring weapons you have had up to this point."

"Actually, none, but we practice frequently. Are you about to give us a dangerous assignment?"

"I was, until you admitted that you haven't had one before. Now I'm not so sure."

"Let's say that we've had dangerous cases and encounters when we worked with a larger group including Pastor Arthur Blake and some federal agent friends. Jeremy worked for the Parkville Police Department for a while too. Whatever you have, we can handle it. We even have associates we can summon for backup if necessary. Now give me the details before I die of curiosity."

"You should have received my email to the family, stating that I've contracted with Jonathan Danforth from Bruce's family to have him serve as a project development consultant to the family foundation."

"I saw it. That move surprised me, because you had talked about keeping the fund management in Lynnette's branch of the family."

"I did, but that doesn't keep me from getting assistance from other family members. Besides, Jonathan is being harassed by organized crime people because he won't help them get their hands on our foundation money. I'll give you the rest of the details after you head back this way, bringing your weapons."

"Marie, you're making me feel like a yo-yo with all of this back-and-forth travel. Please at least tell me whether you see this as a one day trip or an extended visit."

"I'm sorry, dear; I should have mentioned that you should be prepared to stay at my place for up to two weeks."

CHAPTER 58 – BRIEFING

When Debbie and Jeremy Hadley arrived at Marie Danforth's house, they found her working on her back yard gardens. As they approached, she hoisted the arms of her wheelbarrow to move two large boulders from one end of the scalloped border garden along the back fence to the other.

Jeremy rushed forward. "Let me help you with that, Marie. It looks pretty heavy."

"There you go again, inferring that I'm old and past the age of usefulness. I was moving rocks and other landscaping stuff around the yard before you were a gleam in your mother's eye. I may soon be on Social Security, but I can still do physical work. You folks made better time than I expected. Head for the kitchen and pour some lemonade for all of us while I finish this last rearrangement. I'll be right in."

When Marie finished washing her hands, she entered the kitchen and found that Debbie had augmented the three glasses of lemonade with a tray full of assorted doughnuts, acquired at a shop in the outskirts of Madison on their way up.

"That does look good. Thanks for the pastry, Debbie. After that yard work, I might need more than one of those goodies."

"Actually, the doughnuts were Jeremy's idea. He still feels he has to try to charm you into getting on your favorite people list."

Jeremy almost choked on his chocolate covered doughnut.

Marie said, "Take it easy, Jeremy, you're already on my good list, even though I keep having an urge to tease you. Relax and wash down that doughnut with a beer if the lemonade is too tame for you. As soon as we finish up with the eats and drinks, I'll fill you in on the problems that may be in store for Jonathan."

Fifteen minutes later, they sat around the cleared and washed kitchen table with their pens and paper pads.

Marie opened the conversation. "I have to plead guilty to knowing many surface facts about the various members of our extended family, but neglecting to take enough time to know them all individually. Jonathan Danforth turned out to be a pleasant surprise for me when he showed up asking for help."

Debbie looked up from her pad. "How long ago was that?"

"Slightly over a week, but it feels more like a month. I don't know how he managed to run for Congress without realizing that he could be devoured by sharks at any time. He never checked the identities of people who gave his campaign large donations, and now he has the appearance of being either naïve or on the payroll of criminals. Three thugs who bought a car from the dealership where he works told him he had to help them raid our foundation or get smeared as unethical and a friend of drug dealers and human traffickers."

Jeremy asked, "How did he respond to their demands?"

"He told them he would find the money to refund the criminal donations." Marie slapped the table top. "That's what I like about Jonathan. When things got tough, he turned to family for support and asked me whether he could get a loan from the foundation at normal bank rates."

Debbie said, "That's an honest approach to proving he's ethical. Are you giving him the loan he wanted?"

"Nope. Instead of lending him money, I brought him into the foundation to consult on new project development, and simply gave him an advance on his consulting fees – just enough to repay those bad donations."

Debbie raised an eyebrow at her grandmother. "So, you removed the financial burden that had him looking unethical, without charging him interest or making him repay the money; and now you're asking us to protect him from gangsters. You must really like this Jonathan. I don't think I remember him from family events."

"I said earlier that I didn't really know him either, but that's the kind of person I am. I decide whether I like a person, and if I do, I support him or her against all threats."

Jeremy said, "Threat is the key word. Do you know of a definite threat against Jonathan? We can only protect him against something specific and reasonably immediate. We can't sit in our car watching his doorway forever."

Marie gathered her thoughts before responding. "Let's say that I don't have an identified threat against Jonathan, but I have a definite suspicion. I told you a while back that I was sure Pat Danforth Flynn from Daniel's family wanted to take over the foundation. Pat lives in Milwaukee in a house across the street from her ex-husband, Kevin Flynn. Kevin is a Milwaukee fireman who was discarded by Pat when she decided to become a high status real estate developer. She came right out and told him that he would have to choose between a career as a fireman and being her husband. She planned to be part of a high society crowd that would not accept a fireman as an equal. Kevin is dedicated to his career, so he agreed to a divorce, but only on his terms."

Jeremy asked, "And what were his terms?"

Kevin wanted to keep in touch with our family and his neighborhood friends. In exchange for the divorce, he made Pat buy him a house across the street from their old home, which she wanted to keep for herself. He also contacted me and asked that I include him in family gatherings, even though he would no longer be a family member by marriage. I always enjoyed Kevin's company at those events, so I agreed that he still would have family member status."

Debbie asked, "Very interesting, but does any of this answer Jeremy's question about a definite threat to Jonathan?"

"In a word, yes, but you'll have to bear with me while I construct my case like a lawyer. In the meantime, pour me some coffee and take some for yourselves if you wish. This lemonade is too weak for me when I'm talking about missions and tactics."

Debbie checked that the coffee was hot and filled her grandmother's cup, knowing that Marie was less thirsty than stalling to collect her thoughts.

After a few minutes, Marie nodded to herself and began. "This may make me appear a bit paranoid, but I'll admit to doing something underhanded. I told you earlier that I was sure Pat Danforth Flynn is looking for an opportunity to take over management of the family foundation to gain power and to find ways to get richer during the process. To keep one step ahead of her, I persuaded her ex-husband, Kevin Flynn to monitor her activities from his house across the street and report anything unusual to me. He contacted me on the day that I sent out the email about Jonathan."

Jeremy asked, "What did he tell you?"

"Around ten o'clock in the morning he heard Pat scream in anger, so loud that he could hear it through his open window. He'd had enough fights with her to know that the scream indicated anger, not pain. At just about the same time, a big red car parked in her driveway, and three men got out. Two stayed by the car, while the leader went to Pat's front door."

Debbie said, "I'll bet they were the same three who tried to get Jonathan to go after foundation management with kickbacks to their organization. The red car would be the one they bought from Jonathan in order to make him more receptive to their proposition."

Marie said, "I won't take your bet because I'd lose. Yes, these three stooges were Manny, Tony, and Sam who figured in Jonathan's story. The difference between the reaction they got from Jonathan and their results with Pat was that when Manny came out of the house after talking inside with Pat, he shook hands with her in the open doorway. That tells me they made a deal to work together."

Debbie looked up from her note-writing. "Pat was probably more open to an agreement after learning that you had offered Jonathan that consulting job. She felt she needed all available help. I wonder ..."

Jeremy interrupted. "Marie, are you saying that because Pat agreed to cooperate with the three thugs, Jonathan is in danger?"

"There's that impatience again." She smiled to indicate Jeremy's interruption was welcome. "Our three tough guys work for someone that's much more dangerous than they are. That boss will see Jonathan as a barrier to Pat's taking over the foundation, and will likely instruct these three to move against him."

Debbie asked, "Aren't they forgetting something, Marie?"

"I don't understand."

"Pat doesn't have a foundation to share. You do. We'll have to protect you as well as Jonathan."

"Don't worry, Debbie. If anything happens to me, you get the foundation management. I've already signed the paperwork."

"Thanks. I always wanted to be a target."

CHAPTER 59 - STAKEOUT

Jeremy and Debbie Hadley sat in their darkened car diagonally across the street from Jonathan's Milwaukee apartment house. With the help of Marie, they had convinced Jonathan to allow Kevin Flynn to spend the night in his living room. Kevin was an Army veteran and a registered gun owner with a Wisconsin concealed carry permit. He would provide protection if anyone tried to force entry into the apartment. His fireman's training also prepared him to shift from sleep or dozing to full alertness at any sign of alarm.

At midnight, Jonathan headed to the bedroom where he would sleep in his clothes, while Kevin relaxed in an upholstered chair with his Beretta Nano pistol on the adjacent end table.

Outside, in the Hadley's parked car, Debbie positioned her camera with its telephoto lens to cover the apartment house doorway and Jonathan's parked car in front of it, both illuminated by a nearby streetlight. Jeremy checked the readiness of his weapon and hoped he wouldn't have to use it.

The stage was set. Now they would wait to see whether any bad actors appeared on it.

Debbie and Jeremy saw no activity except for occasional passing cars until 1:40 a.m. Then they observed the front end of a car as it parked in the alley next to the apartment house with its headlights turned off. Debbie took several photos of the minimally visible grill of the car and waited to see what else would happen. Three minutes later, a man dressed in black and carrying a shoebox-sized package walked toward Jonathan's car.

Debbie took several pictures of the man as he walked, realizing that she would capture only portions of his face unless he happened to turn toward her. When he reached the car he disappeared.

Debbie said, "Did you see that, Jeremy? He was walking next to the car on the sidewalk, and then he vanished."

"Aim your camera beneath the car. He flopped down alongside the curb. I think he's either planting a bomb or using tools in that box to sabotage the car. He might be cutting the hydraulic brake lines."

As they continued to watch, the man pulled himself up by grabbing the door handle. Then he walked back to the waiting car, and it drove away. Debbie took eight photos of the car as it turned the corner and left.

Jeremy started the engine. "I'll follow them from a safe distance while you call Kevin. Tell him to request the police bomb squad to check Jonathan's car, and have him ask the police to look for fingerprints on the passenger side door handle. I don't think that guy had gloves on."

Jeremy listened to Debbie as she spoke first with Kevin and then with Jonathan on her cell phone. He received the impression that everyone was thankful they hadn't gotten involved in a gunfight. As the car he was following passed through well-lit areas, Jeremy saw it transition from the universal gray of near darkness into red and then back to gray as it passed back into shadow. Determining the color was his only achievement during the slow chase, because traffic was too sparse for him to get close to his quarry without being noticed. The result was that after the red car took a turn off the main road, it turned a second time and disappeared before Jeremy completed the first turn off the highway. Further pursuit would be impossible. It was time to return to Jonathan's apartment and check on what the police found on the car.

When Jeremy and Debbie parked in their old stakeout spot, they saw that the Milwaukee police had two cars and a box truck with flashing lights on the scene. They had cordoned off the building's sidewalk plus Jonathan's car with yellow crime scene tape. Kevin Flynn was briefing a police lieutenant friend on the events leading up to his call. As Debbie and Jeremy crossed the street, Kevin waved for them to join his conversation.

"Debbie and Jeremy Hadley, meet Lieutenant Gil Beecher. Gil, these folks run a private detective agency in Illinois. They're here assisting Debbie's grandmother from Stevens Point on family matters. One of those matters was the threat made against her cousin, Jonathan Danforth, by the thugs I mentioned."

Beecher said, "For a fireman, you do a good job of summarizing a crime scenario, Kevin. I'm pleased to meet you two. Did you catch up with the car you followed?"

Jeremy said, "I lost it because there's so little traffic at this time of night that I had to hang way back to avoid their noticing me. They took several turns before I could catch up with them. They appeared to be heading for a northern suburb."

"Could you identify the car? Did you get the plate number?"

"I'll give you a definite maybe on that. The car was red, and it looked like the Ford Expedition that Jonathan recently sold to the men we suspect. Debbie took pictures of the front of the car when it was parked in the alley, so she may have enough detail to get part of the license plate."

Debbie said, "I have clear shots of the man approaching Jonathan's car, because I had the streetlight nearby. I'll have to play on the computer with enhancing my shots of the car parked in the alley shadows to try to get its license plate or identify its occupants. Do we know yet whether that guy planted a bomb under the car or sabotaged something?"

Lieutenant Beecher looked at the two men lying on both sides of the car studying its bottom surface with flashlights. "He definitely attached something to the car's underside. We think it's an explosive device, but the bomb squad men are being slow and careful as they inspect it. They'll have us clear the area before they attempt to defuse and remove it. If you folks hadn't been on stakeout to see it planted, we might have faced a real mess in the morning when Danforth started his car. That thing might be powerful enough to take out part of the building along with the car's driver."

Jeremy asked, "Did you get any prints off the passenger side door handle?"

"We did, but they were smudged. Once we get back to the station, we'll see what we can do to enhance and identify them."

The men lying alongside the car stood and returned to their truck for the tools they would need. They moved slowly in their flak-resistant protective clothing and face shields. After they gathered their supplies, they signaled the nearest policeman that it was time to clear the area of both working personnel and the curious neighbors who stood wearing coats over bedclothes outside the crime scene's tape perimeter.

Lieutenant Beecher spoke with the bomb squad people briefly before he cleared the area along with everyone else. He approached the store doorway where Kevin and the Hadleys were continuing their conversation.

Beecher said, "I checked with the guys. It's definitely a bomb, but they're not sure whether it's set to go off when the car is started or when the driver's door is opened."

Kevin said, "If it's triggered by the driver's door opening, we could climb in from the other side and drive the car to an open field for defusing or detonation."

"That's a possibility, but they told me they're not sure whether the car would blow up when the engine was started, regardless of which door was opened. Besides, they said the device includes a timer. Even if you could safely start it, you wouldn't know how long you had before the timer set it off. They're going to have to defuse and remove the bomb right here."

Jeremy said, "In case it's useful information for them, the guy who planted the device was working under the car for only a few minutes."

Beecher relayed that information to the bomb squad people by radio.

Everyone watched as one of the explosives people wheeled a heavy-duty steel container next to the car. Once the device was disarmed, they would seal it in that container for protected detonation. The police encouraged all the bystanders to move away from the taped-off area and crouch behind parked cars or stand in shielded doorways as the two men began their work. A hush fell over the scene.

The man working on the street side of the car used a low wheeled mechanic's creeper to maneuver beneath the vehicle to the extent his flak-protective clothing would permit, but the person on the curb side had only enough room to wriggle his way between the curb and the car. They worked together with only occasional murmured comments for about ten minutes, but it seemed much longer than that to the remote witnesses. Finally, the street-side man on the creeper slowly rolled himself away from the car. He had the device in his heavily gloved hands. He lay quietly on the creeper with his burden, waiting for the curbside worker to get up and walk over to him. Then the curbside worker lifted the item from his partner's hands and placed the retrieved device into the padded steel container. After removing his heavy gloves, he took out a camera and photographed the item from several angles before clamping the top of the container shut. Then the two men wheeled the padded container up a ramp into the back of their van, gave an all-clear wave to the lieutenant, and drove away. As they did so, Lieutenant Beecher's radio came to life with a brief preliminary report.

The lieutenant approached Kevin Flynn, Jonathan Danforth, and the Hadleys, as they huddled to discuss what had happened. "Mr. Danforth, you just avoided a very nasty morning headache. The preliminaries on that device indicate that it had two triggers, vibration and timing. If your car shook when you started it, the bomb would go off right away. If the car ran too smoothly for that, the explosion would come five minutes after your right rear tire started to rotate. The explosives people defused the bomb and took pictures of it. They consider it safe enough now for them to take it to their shop and process it for fingerprints. Between fingerprints on the bomb and on the passenger door handle, plus Mrs. Hadley's photographs, we should have this guy dead to rights."

Jonathan shook the lieutenant's hand. "Thanks so much for getting rid of that thing. I wasn't sure whether tonight's stakeout would be a drill event that would have to be repeated on many evenings before anything happened, but it turned out to be the real thing. You all saved my life. If Debbie's pictures match the security camera shots I took of the three guys that bought that red Expedition from me, you'll probably be able to arrest all three of them. In addition to the bomber, there was at least one more driving the car."

Jeremy said, "I got close enough to see three heads in the car, but you'll have trouble identifying the other two if the bomb-planter doesn't talk."

Debbie agreed. "If my pictures identify their vehicle as the car Jonathan sold to those three, we'd be able to suggest that the other two were accessories, but a good lawyer would get them off for lack of evidence."

Beecher wrote something in his small notebook and then returned it to his pocket. "Let's take things one step at a time. If we can prove the bomb was planted by one of those three guys, we'll grab their car and have our crime scene crew examine it for additional evidence. I have a feeling we'll find enough to lasso all three of them."

CHAPTER 60 - ANTICIPATION

Tony drank his third cup of black coffee as he switched channels on the office television. "I don't understand it, Manny. There should have been a news report about that car exploding by now."

Manny looked bored as he checked his pocket change for collectible coins. "Maybe that Danforth guy just slept late or decided to stay home. It'll happen. Give it time. I know you didn't get much sleep, but lay off the continuous coffee. It makes you jittery."

"I'm certain I did everything right. I don't want anyone to think I don't know my business. I get good money for explosives work, and I earn it because those devices are ticklish to handle."

"You did fine, Tony. Nothing's going to go wrong. Where's Sam this morning?"

"I sent him out to get the latest newspapers. When that blow-up finally happens, I'll want newspaper articles for my scrapbook."

"If that's the case, Sam should wait until he hears about it on the radio before he buys newspapers. He's wasting money if he gets them too early."

"He'll do both, Manny. I put together a before-and-after sheet in the scrapbook for each of these jobs. I like to see what the news articles were before the explosion and then compare them with my job's effect on the news. I get a kick out of the way I can change people's comfort levels."

"You do realize that in today's news climate you're likely to be called a terrorist. Once they do that, you get federal cops and spy types coming after you. I'd rather keep things local. The Milwaukee police wouldn't know how to react to a car bombing. They'd probably say that it was due to a drug deal gone bad. That's one of their favorite lines."

"That may be their typical patter, Manny, but I don't like to take chances. I have a double ignition setup on that bomb. Danforth will disappear today, and they won't know why."

"I'll give them a big misleading hint. After we hear about the explosion, I'll feed the newspapers evidence about those unchecked contributions during Danforth's congressional campaign. That will send him off with a smeared reputation, and it'll also keep them from saying this was a terrorist act. We'll only have to outsmart the local cops."

They heard a knock on the door. Tony said, "That'll be Sam. I'll get it."

He opened the door and found himself facing three uniformed police officers with drawn guns.

"Tony Ganlio, Manny Ortega, and Sam Finch ... you're under arrest for the attempted murder of Jonathan Danforth. I see only two of you where's the third one?"

Manny said, "We're not saying anything without our lawyers present. Sam ain't here."

CHAPTER 61 – PAT DANFORTH FLYNN

Pat watched the television news story with her nervousness stopping just this side of all-out panic. Those hoods said that Jonathan might have an accident soon, and they screwed it up. If the police link them to me, I'm in big trouble. I'm the one with a motive to get my cousin out of the way.

That thought flipped her outlook. I have to get rid of my motive. I'll build a scenario that says I'm not looking to manage the family foundation. That would eliminate any reason for people to think I have ties to those mobsters. How should I go about it?

Pat checked her contact list and keyed in the telephone number for Uncle Harry Danforth. She would play her sweet and busy cards.

"Hello, Uncle Harry; it's Pat Flynn. Yes, I know I'm old enough now to call you Harry and drop the uncle. I'll try to remember that from now on. I wanted to discuss a family matter with you, if you're free to talk.... You are? That's great. I'm sure you're aware that there's a good possibility that the next family gathering could be marked by arguments that Lynnette's branch of the family should no longer manage the family foundation because Lynnette was not a blood relation to anyone else. Uncle Max did the DNA analysis that proved that. If Marie is to be replaced as manager of the fund, I'll nominate you to replace her." She listened for a few minutes while Harry talked.

"Yes, I had thought about that possibility for a while, but then I examined all the property development projects I have in the works, and I told myself that the realistic outlook was for me to stick to my work and not be so ambitious. I don't want to create sub-par buildings that hurt my reputation. You'd be more able to concentrate on foundation management. I'll back you all the way. Work out a proposal for taking over if Marie is forced to retire from the job. I'll be free to discuss it and offer suggestions in a couple of weeks."

They exchanged goodbyes and disconnected. Pat wondered whether Harry would question her sudden change of heart after he had time to think about it.

The doorbell rang, and Pat went to answer it, checking her appearance in the mirror as she passed it. She hoped it wouldn't be the police.

The shortish man on her doorstep looked familiar. "Hello, may I help you?"

"I sure hope you can. I'm Sam Finch. I was here with Manny Ortega. Manny and our other friend, Tony, have been arrested, and I need a place to hide 'cause they're looking for me too. Manny said that you two had an arrangement to work together, so I figured it would be safe for me to come here."

"Manny was misevaluating our conversation. We discussed several matters, but we didn't reach an agreement. Nevertheless, I'm in a generous mood. If you can work a construction job, my company is hiring at a Waukesha job site. If you're interested, I'll give you the address and the contact to see there. With my note and signature on my business card, they'll hire you. I doubt that anyone would look for you in a construction crew."

"That's great. I did work as a carpenter's assistant at one time."

Pat wrote a note on her card and gave it to Sam. "Remember to tell anyone who asks that there was no agreement between me and Manny. You came here today looking for a construction job, not for any other reason. Do you understand?"

Sam shook her hand vigorously. “Absolutely, Mrs. Flynn. Thanks for the recommendation. I need both a change of scene and a new occupation. This is perfect.”

After Sam left, Pat poured a generous amount of white wine into a glass and sat with her legs up on the couch to both relax and plan her next move. She was still a bit jittery over the fact that Manny and his boys had tried to blow up Jonathan’s car. *That’s not an accident, that’s terrorism. I may be short on ethics, but I’m not in the same league as these guys.*

After a few minutes, she took her thinking further. *Those strong-arm guys are only tools used to reach an objective. I should be asking myself who is wielding those tools. Whether Marie continues to manage the foundation or if control passes to Jonathan, Harry, or me, someone completely outside the family is trying to rob us of our heritage and treasure. That’s a threat to all of us. How can I identify that person? That will have to be my next high priority project.*

CHAPTER 62 – MANNY AND TONY

Lieutenant Gil Beecher appreciated the unofficial assistance he had received from the Illinois private detectives. From Jeremy Hadley, he had the direction of flight of the criminals after planting the bomb, plus attention to fingerprints on the passenger door handle, and the red color of the getaway car. Jeremy's wife, Debbie, had photographs of the perpetrator as he approached and left the car, plus some dark images of the front end of the criminals' parked vehicle with the explosives man leaving it carrying a parcel. As a reward for their contributions, he would allow the Hadleys to view the interrogations of the two suspects in custody on a television monitor. In the old days, witnesses would stand behind a one-way glass window, but culprits were always conscious of those windows and less willing to talk. Nowadays, criminals assumed the video cameras were their friends, protecting them from overzealous cops, without realizing that they also opened up the interrogations to observation by remote witnesses.

Gil decided to interview the bomber suspect first. He had Tony Ganlio brought to the interrogation room and left him there, seated and handcuffed to a chair bolted to the floor. About ten minutes passed before Gil entered with his paperwork. Tony's chair faced a gray table embellished only with a styrofoam cup full of water. Gil freed Tony's right hand from its handcuff so that he could drink water. Then Beecher spent several minutes sorting his papers into neat piles on the table before he said anything.

"Hello, Tony; your little bomb turned out to be a dud. You don't know as much about explosives as you thought you did."

"I don't know what you're talking about officer. I was at home with my friend when police came and arrested us."

"Is that your home, Tony, or is it some kind of office?"

"It's actually more of an apartment where we have meetings. We sleep there when we don't want to go home."

"And you were there yesterday morning because you were out very late the night before and had to grab a short nap in the apartment."

"We were out late until our favorite bar closed."

"What bar is that, Tony?"

"I forget the name. It's a half mile from Sprecher's Brewery."

"You say it's your favorite bar, but you can't remember its name?"

"It's actually Manny's favorite bar. I don't look at names very much."

"I guess that makes you a follower. Is that right, Tony? Manny's the leader, and you're the follower."

"We're equals. Manny talks to customers more than I do."

"Customers, huh? What kind of business are you in?"

"We're consultants."

"And you're the technical consultant?"

"You might say that."

"Well, Tony, where did you get your technical training in explosives?"

Tony drank from the cup of water before replying. "I learned a bunch of things in the Army, but I'm no expert in explosives."

"That's obvious. Your bomb didn't go off."

"A bomb is a big thing contained in a metal shell of some sort."

"Then this wasn't a bomb because it didn't have a metal container?"

"That's right."

"How do you know what the device looked like if you didn't plant it under that car?"

"I want a lawyer before I say anything else."

"That's your right, Tony. This interview is terminated at 10:50 a.m."

Gil Beecher called in the officer posted outside the interview room door.

"Joe, it's time to return Tony to his cell. After he's locked up again, please get Manny from his cell on the other side of the building and bring him here to be interviewed. Be sure they don't talk to each other."

While Joe was exchanging prisoners, Gil visited Jeremy and Debbie in the monitoring room. "I think that went pretty well for a first session. What were your impressions?"

Debbie said, "You did that perfectly, Gil. By saying the bomb was a dud instead of a difficult device to defuse, you made him doubt his skills. He's obviously proud of his reputation as an explosives expert, and he wouldn't want his cohorts to think he's an amateur. Keep up that approach, and he'll probably talk even if his lawyer forbids it."

Gil asked, "What do you think, Jeremy?"

"I agree with Debbie. You might continue to talk about the bomb as a dud with Manny, implying that his men have deficient skills. Maybe you can get them at odds with each other. Next time, tell Tony that Manny thinks he screwed up, and that's why they're here."

Debbie asked, "What about the third man, Sam? Any sign of him?"

Gil shrugged. "He's done a good disappearing act. We have the leader and the explosives guy, so I'm not that concerned about Sam. We'll question these guys about

Sam, but I get the impression that he was the errand boy of the outfit, not very important."

Debbie said, "What is important is the person who assigned them this job. Manny is the leader of these three, but he's not the boss. There's someone much smarter behind these guys. He or she will find new troops to replace these foot soldiers."

CHAPTER 63 – LIBRARY

Marie drove her Saturn coupe along Main Street, enjoying the fact that even though her car was a teenager, it wasn't rusty due to its body being plastic. She wasn't sure whether other models, built since Saturn was dropped as a brand by General Motors, still had plastic shells. She remembered how, when she was younger, people looked forward to buying a new car every two years. That was another way to avoid rust, but the frequent purchase of cars went out with huge price increases, and now that she was a touch more senior, she wanted a car for reliable transportation ... not for newness or sexiness. She wondered whether that made her *over the hill*, and then answered herself affirmatively due to her destination being the Portage County Library for her research project rather than her computer search engine. Local libraries held archived public documents that were not likely to be found online, especially if you were looking for something relatively ancient.

Marie's outing today had two goals. One was to get dirt to use against Pat Danforth Flynn in case Pat contested the argument that Lynnette's non-family parentage, was known to Barbara and Cyrus when they appointed their daughter to control the family's secret fund and justified her descendants continuing to run the fund. Marie would search for documents confirming old rumors of Pat's run-ins with the police when she was younger. One juicy bit of gossip suggested that she had partially funded her first industrial building project by blackmailing a banker who didn't want his wife to know about his affair with Pat. If Marie could identify that banker, he might become cooperative in exchange for the deposit of some of the foundation's money in his bank. She was not above using the huge foundation treasury for leverage, as she had many times in the past to secure preferred investment opportunities. She had no doubt that this would be a successful effort. She would also refresh her memories surrounding the battle at Gettysburg that had led to their family's secret mission.

Two hours later, Marie dwelled on her optimism as she strolled from the library door toward her parking space. She failed to see the black car move forward out of its outlined space, turn left, and accelerate toward her from the rear of the parking lot. She heard its engine just before the black blur struck her on the left side. The impact lifted her off the ground, and bounced her off a pair of parked vehicles before she hit the pavement. As she faded into blackness, the last things she heard were tires screeching as the car turned out of the lot onto Third Street, a woman screaming, and a man yelling, "Call 911."

CHAPTER 64 – WAITING

By the time Debbie and Jeremy Hadley arrived at Ministry St. Michael's Hospital in Stevens Point, Marie had been in surgery for three hours. When Debbie identified herself as Marie's granddaughter and emergency contact, a nurse led them to an office and asked them to wait while she found a doctor who had information about Marie's condition. After about ten minutes, a tall man in surgical scrubs joined them.

"Good evening; I'm Dr. Pasqua, and I always feel slightly awkward when I greet relatives of injured patients with that word 'good.' Marie Danforth has been in surgery for several hours, and it will be a while longer before she comes out. I was involved in the early part of our effort to save her, but other specialists are working on her now. The important news is that we expect her to survive. A weaker person her age might not, but she's a fighter."

Debbie reached to shake his hand. "Thank you, Doctor. We're Debbie and Jeremy Hadley. I'm Marie's granddaughter. What injuries did she suffer? I understand it was a hit-and-run."

"The police will have the details of the incident. We restrict our concerns to saving victims following their trauma. Marie had severe injuries to her head and torso. She also had major bruising to her arms and legs, but no fractures there. We think that she'll survive, but it is much too early to predict her future quality of life. We're working on several broken ribs plus some spine and head injuries that may or may not permanently affect her capabilities. The good news is that we have not yet discovered any significant damage to her internal body organs."

Jeremy asked, "Was she conscious upon arrival at the hospital?"

"She was conscious but a bit incoherent. One of the nurses told me that she kept repeating something about going back to Gettysburg. She lost consciousness while we were preparing her for the operations. You should understand that we faced several different surgical challenges in there, involving both staff surgeons and outside specialists who are on call to us. We found her health insurance card, but there will be some costs that go beyond that coverage."

Debbie said, "Don't worry about payments. Just bring her back to us in good shape. We have resources."

Dr. Pasqua excused himself to return to his other duties, but told them that he would look for them in the waiting area as soon as he had additional status reports to pass along to them. After he left, Jeremy and Debbie debated their next moves.

Jeremy said, "Pasqua indicated that it will be several more hours before Marie comes out of the operating room. What do you think about my leaving you here to wait for her, while I contact the local police to get what I can on the person who tried to kill her?"

"Before you leave, contact the library where it happened by telephone to see whether anyone there has a good description of the car and whether they had surveillance cameras working. You might learn something by direct contact that the police missed."

Jeremy consulted his smart phone to get the library telephone number. While he was searching, he asked, "What did you get out of Marie's incoherent comments about Gettysburg when she first arrived here?"

"I wondered about that. I haven't figured it out yet, but it has to be important. When you're in danger of losing your life, you don't repeatedly say trivial things. Hopefully, Marie will get through her operations and wake up to explain those words to us. I won't mind those comments turning out to be nonsense, so long as she pulls through and talks to us again." Debbie started to pace back and forth to ease the tension.

Jeremy realized that Debbie was more shaken by Marie's injuries than he had initially thought. "Maybe I shouldn't leave you alone here. We can check with the library and police later."

Debbie exhaled forcefully to relieve some pent-up emotions and nodded her agreement. Then they left the consulting office hand-in-hand, bound for the softer chairs and couches of the surgical waiting room. It was late, and they welcomed the discovery that they would have that room to themselves, at least for a while.

Two hours later, Dr. Pasqua reappeared to announce that Marie was out of surgery, but that they had put her into a medically induced coma. She would be in a deep stage of unconsciousness for several days to reduce her brain's metabolism and allow swelling in her brain to decrease. They would monitor her brain waves to determine when to arouse her in order to minimize the likelihood of permanent brain damage. Dr. Pasqua gave them the preliminary information that the surgeons didn't expect Marie to have any paralysis when she awoke.

CHAPTER 65 – LAWYERS

Manny Ortega woke up from his nap after the fifth time the guard called his name.

"What's all the commotion? It ain't comfortable here, but at least I fell asleep."

"Rise and shine, Manny; you have company. Your lawyers are here."

"Lawyers? How come I have more than one?"

"I'm sure they'll tell you. Whoever's paying them must think a lot of you. Anyway, I'm escorting you to the private conference room reserved for legal visits."

The guard escorted Manny through several corridors to a windowless room where two men in suits were waiting. Then the guard left and locked the door behind him.

The taller of the two men stepped forward and shook Manny's hand. "Hello, Manny; I'm Robbie Conklin, and this is Larry Malcolm. We'll be defending you and Tony Ganlio. We're working together, but I'll be the lead attorney for your case and Larry will take the lead for Tony's case."

Larry shook hands with Manny but let Robbie Conklin do all the talking.

"Who sent you here, and who's paying for two lawyers?"

"Don't worry about the costs. You won't be expected to pay anything, no matter how things turn out. Our employer shall remain nameless. You're free to speculate, but we won't respond to any guesses, so let's move this conversation along."

“That’s fine with me, but I still don’t understand why there are two of you.”

Conklin said, “There are two of us because we want to separate your case from Tony’s. He’s facing a felony charge for planting a bomb, and the police think they have strong evidence. You’re charged as an accessory to Tony’s act, but they have very little proof against you. They observed shadowy heads in a car that you purchased, but they don’t have strong evidence that you were in that car. We want you tried separately, and we will work to convince the jury that you weren’t there, and that if they decide you were there, your participation and crime were minimal.”

“I love this lawyer talk. You guys talk out of both sides of your mouths at the same time. I wasn’t there, but if I was, I didn’t do anything. That sounds like nonsense.”

“It may be nonsense in normal conversation, but not in a courtroom. It’s a fallback tactic. We try to get you completely off, but if we can’t, we try to get you convicted of the least important charge possible.”

Manny stared at Conklin. “You’re going to have me face a minimal charge by throwing Tony under the bus. You’re going to say I was only along for the ride, while he stopped the car and did something terrible. Do you expect me to go along with that? Tony’s my friend.”

“We’ll try to get Tony to face a reduced charge too, because the device didn’t explode. Manny, you have to realize that if you don’t cooperate with our approach you’ll be facing the same charges and penalties as Tony. You could be sent away for a very long time. We’re good at what we do, but if you won’t follow our tactics and instructions, we may have to change our minds about representing you and hand you over to the skill set of a public defender.”

“If you put it that way ...”

"We know what we're doing, and we'll represent you well. This was our getting-to-know-you meeting. You've been denied bond and bound over to the Circuit Court, but we'll do what we can to get that decision modified. We'll soon be back to ask for specific details of that night and to tell you how to answer questions about that incident when they question you in the courtroom."

CHAPTER 66 – MARIE

What a weird feeling. I know I'm battered and bruised, but I have no pain. I try to open my eyes and move, but I can't. Am I dead? I doubt it unless I'm a ghost, because I have thoughts. Besides, I think I'm on a bed and not in a coffin. Still, I haven't moved or been awake for a long time. I suppose I could be dead, even though I haven't experienced the bright lights or out-of-body experiences that others describe when they almost die. What happened? That black shape coming at me and hitting me... It must have been a car, but it was aimed at me. I have no memory of a driver. It must have happened when I wasn't looking. My mother taught me to always look right and left before crossing streets, but she never said much about parking lot driveways.

I think I hear some sounds. Someone must be checking on me. Now it's quiet again. If I can hear sounds, I must be alive. I hope that's right. I'm not ready to leave everyone. My family needs me, especially now. I want to wake up, but I can't. I'll try again when I hear more sounds ... I'll rest for now.

CHAPTER 67 – SAM FINCH

Sam looked down from his ladder perch where he had been strapping dangling wires together as Mike Cage, the foreman, approached.

"Hey, Monahan, do you sometimes use Finch for a last name?"

He shrugged. "I have been known to vary my name. Monahan feels better suited to a construction job. Why?"

"I don't care what you call yourself as long as you keep up with your work assignments, but the boss, Mrs. Flynn is on the telephone for you, and she called you Sam Finch. I knew she had to mean you when she described you as the last guy she sent here for a job. Anyway, get over to the office and take the call. Mrs. Flynn doesn't like to be kept waiting."

Sam hustled through a newly framed wall as a shortcut to the office. It hadn't taken long for him to blow his cover. Who knew Pat Flynn would want to talk to him again? He lifted the telephone receiver and prepared himself for the unexpected. "Hello, Mrs. Flynn."

"Hello, Sam. I need to ask you a couple of questions. I'll expect you to be completely honest with me. After all, I did set up that job for you."

"No problem; what do you want to know?"

"First, why did you become Sam Monahan without informing me?"

"I figured the cops might be looking for Sam Finch, so I used my mother's maiden name. I didn't tell you, because I thought you would be too busy to contact me again. I guess I was wrong on that one."

"Fair enough. Second question; who do you, Manny, and Tony work for? Manny keeps referring to an investment group that you represent. I need to contact those people."

Sam said, "I'd like to help you, but I don't know the answer to that question. Manny never told Tony or me where our money comes from. We do what we're told, and we get paid on a fairly regular basis. I'm the low man on the totem pole. Nobody tells me anything."

"Have you ever seen unexpected visitors talking with Manny – anyone you could describe to me?"

"Sorry, Mrs. Flynn; I just mind my own business and do what I'm told."

Pat pleasantly thanked Sam for his candor, and then slammed down the telephone receiver onto its cradle, missing her target on the first attempt. Sam smiled after hearing the loud impact in his earpiece.

CHAPTER 68 – INQUIRIES

Marie's condition was stable within her induced coma, so Debbie and Jeremy felt free to investigate the circumstances of the hit-and-run murder attempt. Debbie assigned herself to the library end of the inquiry because of her research librarian background, while Jeremy opted to examine the findings of the Stevens Point Police Department.

Upon arriving at the Portage County Public Library, Debbie asked to see the library director. She expected that person to be a middle-aged woman, but was soon introduced to a man in his thirties, Austin Carmichael. His name sounded formal, but his flannel shirt and blue jeans were quite the opposite.

Debbie shook his hand. "Mr. Carmichael, I'm Debbie Hadley. My grandmother, Marie Danforth, was the woman who was struck by an automobile as she left the library."

"That was a tragedy, Miss Hadley. I believe it was the only time we've had an accident with injuries here. By the way, call me Austin."

"Fine, Austin, and I'm Mrs. Hadley, but please call me Debbie."

"Now that we have the preliminaries behind us, what may I do for you today?"

"First, you should stop referring to that event as an accident. It was deliberate attempted murder. In addition to being Marie Danforth's granddaughter, I'm a private detective, so I would like to know whether you had functioning video cameras when Marie was struck, and if so, do you have the footage, or did you give it to the police."

"Debbie, you're much more straightforward than our local police. They spoke with me only briefly and never even hinted that this might be a case of attempted murder. As a small-town library, we can't afford fancy security systems, but we do have one camera covering the entrance and a portion of the parking lot. That camera records to a memory card when it detects motion. I told the police about it, and one officer looked at the recording, but he said it didn't show enough for them to track the car. He added that I should change to a new memory card and keep the one from when Mrs. Danforth was struck in a safe place in case they wanted it later."

Debbie realized that the Stevens Point police hadn't mentioned attempted murder because they didn't know the background facts of the case. To them it was a nasty but routine accident.

"Austin, I'd like to borrow your memory card for detailed analysis."

"No problem, Debbie, but if you don't mind I'll copy it onto a flash drive for you while I keep the original here. I don't want to get into trouble with our local cops for breaking their chain of evidence."

"You're more tuned into police procedures than I expected."

"Oddly enough, I thought I would be a cop at one time. I even took a few courses at the police academy before I bailed out in favor of this career. I'm too sedentary to keep up with the pace and athleticism required for police work. I know some cops do desk work, but if I had stuck to policing, I would have wanted to be in the field responding to people's problems."

"I like your attitude. You can still help solve cases, though. I was a research librarian at the University of Wisconsin before I got into detective work, and I use my library search techniques all the time."

"That's great to know. I'll keep it in mind in case I get a chance to help the police."

"You could help me right now if you have any way of documenting what Marie Danforth studied when she was in the library that day. The summary we had earlier from the police said that she wasn't carrying any books when the car hit her. She must have been here to study reference materials."

"I can ask the reference librarian, but we wouldn't have a record of what she specifically studied unless it was something that had to be retrieved from our restricted access collection."

Austin picked up a desk phone and keyed in the reference desk extension. He inquired about Marie's activities to the person on the other end and then waited for a response after the reference librarian checked the records. A few minutes later, he listened to the other librarian's summary and said, "Thank you. That's helpful."

Austin penciled a few notes on a file card he found on the desk. Then he turned to Debbie. "Marie Danforth consulted the Civil War Military Records and the Wisconsin Genealogies collections. We know that because both of those are restricted collections of miscellaneous documents, some of which are bound and some of which are loose in file folders. We allow access only to people we consider reliable because loose documents in the wrong hands have a way of disappearing."

"Thank you for considering my grandmother to be reliable."

"She's well known to the reference people. She studies their files frequently."

Debbie thanked Austin for his assistance and especially for that unexpected last bit of documentation of Marie's library habits. Then she left to compare her findings with whatever Jeremy learned from the police.

Jeremy Hadley's initial reception at the Stevens Point Police Department had been frigid. Small town Wisconsin police are not impressed by Illinois private detective credentials. After several conversations Jeremy caught a break when he learned that the stone-faced desk sergeant had served on the Milwaukee force for eleven years. Once Jeremy mentioned that he was working with Milwaukee Lieutenant Gil Beecher on a related case, Sergeant Erik Greuner, opened up and told him that Beecher was an old friend. He said they had worked on several cases together when Beecher was a novice detective and he was a uniformed patrolman.

After sharing two cups of coffee with Jeremy, Greuner asked, "What information are you looking for?"

"Marie Danforth, the victim of the hit-and-run attack at the Portage County Library is my wife's grandmother. Can you tell me if there were any witnesses, and if so, did they see whether the driver was male or female? Do you have any details on the driver or the car?"

"Hold it, Jeremy. I'll tell you what we know, but you have to do the same. You used the word *attack*. We're still treating this as a reckless accident. What do you know that we don't?"

"Marie Danforth manages a charitable family foundation with a high level of assets. Several other people have been trying to force her out of that position and take over the foundation. One of the competing candidates had a bomb planted under his car in Milwaukee. That's the case I'm working on with Gil Beecher. If someone is trying to kill off new management candidates, it's quite likely they also want to get rid of the current manager to be sure there's a job opening for someone else."

"I see your point. I'll pass that info to our people handling our investigation. Per your earlier question, we have a witness, a female high school junior named Leah Hanks who had been at the library to get college information. She walked out a few steps behind Marie and barely avoided being hit by the same car. She's still pretty much in shock and hasn't been able to give us significant info on the car or the driver. She called it a big black blur that almost killed her."

"Do you have any other evidence?"

"We're working on getting the car identified. After it turned left onto Third Street, it sideswiped a car that was going straight down Third. We have paint scraping samples from that accident and the first two characters of the license plate, YK. If we can identify the make and model of the car from the paint, we'll search registrations for a plate starting with YK. Then we'll search out those vehicles and check for front end damage. It's good old step-by-step police work – not fast, but thorough."

"That sounds like a good lead. I'll leave you my contact information. If you get any breakthroughs on identifying the car or learning more from the witness, please send me an email."

"I'll be sure to do that, but don't get your hopes up too much. If the hit-and-run was a deliberate attack, I'll bet the driver used a stolen car."

CHAPTER 69 – FINANCIAL ANALYST

Debbie and Jeremy Hadley sat by Marie's bed keeping her company even though they knew she would remain in her barbiturate-induced coma until the doctors deliberately awakened her. Marie looked peaceful, but more than a little robotic because of her oxygen breathing mask plus the tubes and cables connecting her to various machines and monitors. Debbie and Jeremy intended to compare and discuss their findings from the library and police station visits so as to plan a direction for further inquiries, but they also hoped that if they talked about the case in her room, Marie would somehow be able to hear their discussion.

As they were about to begin, Debbie's cell phone vibrated. She had turned off the ringer, but left the phone active in case she received an important call.

"Hello, you've reached Debbie Hadley's phone."

"Hi; I'm glad you're reachable. This is Tom Tucker, the Danforth Foundation's Financial Analyst. I learned that Marie has been injured and is in the hospital. Do you know her condition?"

"I'm in her room along with my husband Jeremy right now. Marie is sleeping peacefully within an induced coma while the doctors wait for the swelling of her brain to go down. Is there anything I can do for you?"

"That's exactly why I called. There are some disturbing market trends for several of our investments, and we need to take action to minimize our losses. The size of these investments is beyond my discretion level. I normally advise Marie, and she tells me whether or not to follow my instinct and proceed. She's out of the picture, at least for a while, and I have a copy on my desk of her instructions that you are to manage the fund if and when she is unable to do so. We haven't done the formal paperwork, but would you be willing to let me proceed per my analysis?"

"Three questions, Tom. First, how long have you been providing financial evaluation guidance to Marie?"

"We've worked together for seven years."

"Second, what percentage of the time has Marie relied on your guidance?"

"I'd like to say one hundred percent, but she did overrule me three times during those seven years. Our investment results have been quite positive during that period."

"Good. Third question, how tall are you?"

"I don't see what that has to do with making a decision."

"Please answer the question promptly if we're going to work together."

"I'm six feet four inches tall."

"Then this isn't a case of Little Tommy Tucker singing for his supper as in the nursery rhyme....Sorry about that; your name just reminded me of the rhyme. I'll look forward to meeting you soon. In the meantime follow your instincts to minimize our losses. I'm hoping that Marie will be back on board with you soon, but if not, I'll complete the paperwork and pitch in to keep things going as smoothly as possible."

"Thanks, Debbie. Be advised that I've only heard that Little Tommy Tucker business a few thousand times along the way. Hopefully, it's behind us now."

CHAPTER 70 – COMPARING NOTES

Jeremy raised an eyebrow as he stared at Debbie. "What was that Little Tommy Tucker nursery rhyme comment about? I didn't quite follow your side of the phone conversation."

"I couldn't resist trying for a comical moment. Things have been so tense lately since that car struck Grandma. Sometimes you need comic relief, and when the foundation's financial analyst said his name was Tom Tucker, I seized the opportunity to be silly. That part felt good. I'm not so sure I like the fact that I'll have to make financial decisions while Marie is sidelined."

"Don't worry; you'll handle it with your usual grace and wisdom. It is good to know that we have a professional financial analyst on board. Marie didn't give us details about the fund's operations."

"Thanks for the grace and wisdom compliment. Feel free to be more generous with your praises of me any time you want. While I'm in my wise mode, I'll tell you what I learned at the library."

"Good. I'll have some contributions from talking with my new friend at the police department."

"We both make friends well. My new amigo is the library director, Austin Carmichael. He's young and informal, despite his upper crust name. I learned from him that Marie is a frequent patron of the library's reference section and that on the day she was attacked, she examined their restricted collections of Civil War military records and Wisconsin genealogical documents."

"Is that unexpected? She runs a fund dedicated to charitable support of Civil War veterans of the 2nd

Regiment Wisconsin Volunteer Infantry and their descendants. She may have been trying to identify additional families to assist."

"You could look at her interests as being entirely normal, but shouldn't she already have that information after all these years? I think she was searching for something new and unusual."

"That's a definite possibility. I learned that there was a witness, Leah Hanks, a teenage girl who was walking behind Marie and who barely avoided being struck by that car. She was so badly shaken that the police haven't interviewed her yet. They think she'll need more time to remember anything clearly."

"Make a note to contact her in about two weeks. Maybe Marie will be talking with us too by then. I'll hold tight to that thought. Can you hear us, Marie? It's your duty to come back with us soon to help us find the bastard who hit you."

"That attacker probably wasn't from this area. I learned that when the car raced out of the parking lot and turned left onto Third Street, it sideswiped another car traveling past the driveway because the driver didn't realize how narrow Third Street is."

"Was the other driver hurt?"

"No, and he may help solve the case, because he saw the first two characters on the attacker's license plate, YK. The police think that partial plate information plus paint scrapings from the collision will help them find the car. The only problem will come if it was stolen before it was used to hit Marie."

"Hold that thought for a moment, Jeremy. If the car turned out to have been stolen, I'd speculate that the culprit would be a hardened criminal or a gang member of some sort. I doubt that a relative trying to control the foundation's operations would steal a car."

"Then you think it may have been someone in your extended family?"

"What other motive would there be, except for wanting access to that huge pile of cash?"

CHAPTER 71 – DANFORTH FOUNDATION

For Marie's convenience, the Danforth Foundation operated out of a rented office suite in Stevens Point, Wisconsin rather than in a larger city like Milwaukee or Chicago. Thanks to the internet and wireless communication, it could have been located anywhere.

One day after her telephone conversation with Tom Tucker from Marie's hospital room, Debbie decided that she had better meet Tom and learn more about the operational procedures of the foundation. She left Jeremy at Ministry St. Michael's Hospital to monitor Marie's condition while she turned her attention to the foundation.

The Danforth Foundation office was located northwest of the hospital, in an office building near the University of Wisconsin – Stevens Point. Marie had selected that location for the college environs and because she had recently extended the fund's scholarship programs to Stevens Point and all the other branch campuses of the state university, expanding the original Madison program.

When Debbie arrived at the office she found the door locked and a security doorbell to request access. She pushed the button and waited. The door was opened by a tall man she knew had to be Tom.

"Hello, Mr. Tucker; I'm Debbie Hadley. I thought I'd better come over to see the operation since I now appear to be involved in it."

"Come on in, Debbie, and call me Tom. You're my boss now, at least for a while. Is there any news about Marie's condition?"

"Marie is stable and still in the induced coma. We won't know any more for several days. By the way, I apologize for that nursery rhyme silliness about your name. It has been a stressful few days, and I needed to say or do something that would trigger a laugh."

He smiled to show he understood. "I'm immune to getting upset about those jokes. They've been with me all my life. Sometimes I think my parents called me Tommy Tucker as a device to trigger informal social contacts. It works as an adult, but there were times during my early school years when I was teased and bullied because of my name. That stopped when I grew faster than my classmates and towered over most of them."

"Are you the only one normally in the office?"

"Not all the time. We have a part-time secretary, Virginia, who works irregular hours, and we have conferences with representatives of groups requesting charitable support. We also use the conference room to discuss investment opportunities. Recently, we added Jonathan Danforth as a consultant to help us select new projects to fund, so he has been here occasionally."

"I heard about Jonathan getting involved. How has he been to work with?"

"So far, it's worked out well. He has some good ideas, but we haven't yet financed any of them. Each new possible project requires detailed research and analysis before we invest the fund's money in it.

"That sounds conservative and makes good sense."

"By the way, before I forget, I'll give you a key to the office." He took a key and a notebook out of the secretary's desk. He then wrote the identifying number of the key into the notebook at the top of the next blank page and asked Debbie to sign her name alongside it. After she signed he said, "You're now officially part of the group, although we'll need a few more forms completed before you become the manager. Hopefully, Marie will soon be able to sign those forms also."

"What happens if she doesn't regain her capabilities sufficiently to sign off on my functions here?"

"She already documented her intent to have you take over, so we would just get the lawyers involved and file a few documents with the state to make the transition officially recorded."

"That sounds reasonable. Tell me how you operate and interface with Marie."

"My job is to monitor market conditions and the comments of specialized analysts regarding the probable market behavior for our existing investments and to generate analyses for proposed new investments."

"Do you work directly with the stockbrokers and bankers, or does Marie?"

"When Marie wants to handle those communications, she does. When she is busy and wants me to take over those functions, I step in. The manager can delegate or operate as she sees fit."

"That's good, because I'll be a part-time manager for so long as I have the responsibility."

"I document everything I do in the manager's absence, so there should be no problem."

"That works for me, Tom. Be sure to let me know when a market move needs to be taken. In each case, we'll discuss it and decide which of us should handle the details of the transaction."

CHAPTER 72 – TEST RESULTS

When Debbie and Jeremy arrived at Ministry St. Michael's Hospital the next day, the nurse told them that Marie could not have visitors and directed them to the office where they had met with the doctor during the earlier operations. A short while later, Dr. Pasqua joined them and greeted them warmly.

"I have the pleasure of giving you good news. Marie's electroencephalography or brain wave readings have returned to near normal, and her intracranial pressure has lessened. These measurements are what we have been waiting for, so we are in the process of bringing her out of her coma."

Jeremy felt they needed more details. "How do you bring her out of it, and what effects will it have on body functions other than brain activity?"

"We put her into the coma using a cocktail of anesthetic drugs, primarily pentobarbital. She has been on a continuing dose of these drugs during the coma. Now we will gradually withdraw the drugs, and she should begin to recover awareness and physical capabilities. The fact that we have reached this point is quite promising. The greatest dangers come from complications during the coma from lower blood pressure and potential heart failure, reducing circulation. Infections can also be a problem."

Debbie said. "You're indicating that she didn't have any of those problems up to this time."

"None at all. She has come through the drug-induced coma stage in quite good shape. There will be a lengthy recovery period, during which she will slowly recover her functions and skills, but we believe that she will eventually return to a normal or near-normal status."

Debbie raised her eyebrow at that statement. "You're hedging, Doctor. What does near-normal mean?"

"It means that there are no guarantees and that we won't know the extent of her recovery until it happens. We can predict the future based on results from other cases, but each patient is different. There could be setbacks, but we're cautiously optimistic that there won't be any. That's the most I can say until she actually wakes up and communicates with us." Dr. Pasqua shrugged his shoulders and left the office.

Debbie turned to Jeremy. "I hate it when someone says 'cautiously optimistic'."

CHAPTER 73 – HARRY AND JONATHAN

With Marie in the hospital, Jonathan saw no purpose in taking the two and a half hour drive to Stevens Point just to hang around the office with Tom Tucker. The analyst would be capable of keeping the foundation's investment positions on an even keel while he concentrated on selling automobiles in Milwaukee. His consulting job was aimed at developing new investment projects for the future, and nothing would be done in that direction until Marie recovered. Marie had bailed him out of trouble by giving him the consulting position and advance payments. He had known few people willing to give so much support to a nearly unknown relative, and he certainly hoped she would recover fully.

When the telephone rang, he looked at the caller identification screen and thought, *speaking of nearly unknown relatives...* He answered the call. "Hello, Harry Danforth, I haven't spoken with you since that big barbecue party two years ago. What may I do for you today?"

"I heard about that awful attempt to bomb your car, and I wanted to tell you how glad I was that they didn't succeed in injuring you."

"Thanks, Harry, your empathy is appreciated, but why are you calling me now? Would it possibly have something to do with the fact that Marie is in the hospital and temporarily out of business as far as managing the family foundation?"

"I called the hospital, and they didn't want to give me any information, but I finally managed to learn that she's in a coma. Marie isn't going to manage the foundation any more. Since you already worked a deal to be a consultant over there, I'm assuming that you're my main competition for taking over from Marie. I hoped we could make a deal to share the benefits of the job."

Jonathan had trouble believing what he heard. "Harry, you win the prize as the biggest bastard and vulture in the family. You're trying to pick the meat off of Marie's bones while she's still very much alive. Your intelligence from the hospital is wrong. Marie is in a coma, but it's a drug-induced coma to protect her brain while she recovers. She likely will be back to managing the fund, and if she can't handle that job, she has already designated Debbie Hadley as her successor. Your ambition is screwed, buddy. What do you think of that?"

There was a long pause before Harry spoke. "It sounds as though the person who ran her down was no more successful than the guy who planted a bomb under your car. What a bunch of misfits!" The phone line went dead as Harry slammed the receiver down.

Jonathan thought, I'm working like mad to preserve my reputation as a good guy, and that tumor on our family's body enjoys being a vicious S.O.B. I wonder whether he was the driver of that car.

CHAPTER 74 – PAT DANFORTH FLYNN

The ringing doorbell interrupted Pat's construction proposal preparation. *How can I meet deadlines with interruptions all the time? I should be doing this at the office.* She placed a letter opener on her paper to mark the disruption point for her return. Then she went to the door as the bell rang a second time.

She found two men in suits on her doorstep. One held up an open leather card case displaying an identification card and a badge.

"Patricia Flynn? I'm Detective Lieutenant Gil Beecher, and this is Detective Dave Peschki. We'd like to talk to you about a current case. May we come in?"

"Certainly, but I don't know anything about criminal matters." She escorted them to the front room that she used for meetings with potential construction clients.

"Would you like some coffee or a cold drink?"

"I don't expect we'll be here that long. We have information that three men visited you a while ago. Their names were Tony Ganlio, Manny Ortega, and Sam Finch. Do you recall their visit?" Gil watched her face for any changes in expression.

Pat remained calm. She had anticipated a possible police visit after she read about the unsuccessful bombing attempt. "Mr. Ortega came here once to discuss a possible construction project. I noticed that he had two associates standing near his car, but I never met them."

"Are you sure you never met the others? We have information that Sam Finch visited you at a later date." Gil received an unexpected reaction this time.

"What you're saying is that my ex-husband, Kevin, who lives across the street, spies on me. I guess firemen and cops are, if you'll pardon the old expression, thick as thieves."

"Please answer my question."

"Yes, Sam Finch came here on another day. He was looking for a job, so I directed him to the construction foreman on one of my projects."

"We'll need that contact information. Finch is the subject of an investigation."

Pat wrote it on the back of one of her business cards and gave it to Beecher. "Leave me one of your cards. I may want to file a stalking complaint against my ex-husband."

"I'm afraid that looking out your window is not considered stalking, but we'll be happy to discuss any complaint you file. Thank you for your cooperation, Mrs. Flynn."

The two detectives left. Five minutes later a construction site foreman in Waukesha, Wisconsin received instructions to transfer one of his workers, Sam Monahan, to a job site in Minnesota.

CHAPTER 75 – LIAISON

Jeremy walked into the police station and asked for Detective Lieutenant Gil Beecher. He had left Debbie at the hospital in Stevens Point to monitor signs of Marie's awakening while he responded to Gil's summons for a liaison meeting. That call came when Jeremy was thinking that he should call Gil for the same purpose, so he figured that today's meeting would yield either a breakthrough or complete frustration. When Gil came out to get him, Jeremy realized he was angry.

"Jeremy, thanks for coming on such short notice. I hope that by comparing notes we can make progress on this case. Your wife's cousin, Pat Flynn is doing her best to screw things up for me, and I may decide to throw a charge at her for interfering with a police investigation."

"Not that they're close or anything, but I'm glad I didn't bring Debbie with me to hear that. What did Pat Flynn do or fail to do?"

"I've been trying to round up Sam Finch. He's the third member of the bomb-planting squad, along with Tony and Manny. I had intel that Sam visited Pat Flynn. When we followed up on that lead at her house, she told us that Sam asked her for a job, and she sent him to one of her construction sites. We went to that site, and they had no record of a Sam Finch applying there. Pat sent us on a wild goose chase."

"Maybe he changed his mind about going there. I've never met Pat, and I won't make excuses for her because I think she's trying to take over a business that Debbie's grandmother runs. I hear that she manipulates people and doesn't do a favor unless there's money in it for her."

"What have you been up to, Jeremy? I haven't talked with you since the attempt to bomb Jonathan Danforth's car."

"Then you don't know what happened to Debbie's grandmother? I thought Debbie had talked to you. She probably thought that I had. I'm sorry; we dropped the ball. Here's the scoop. Jonathan Danforth's car was bombed because he wouldn't cooperate with those thugs. They wanted him to take over the charitable foundation that Debbie's grandmother Marie runs and share the proceeds with them. After that didn't succeed, someone tried to kill Marie in a hit-and-run car attack outside the public library in Stevens Point. Debbie's at the hospital there, waiting for Marie to come out of a drug-induced coma. The doctors say she'll live, but we don't know whether she'll recover all of her capabilities."

Gil wrote down Jeremy's comments as fast as he could. "This foundation must have plenty of money for it to draw takeover attacks."

"Couple large assets with family control by one or a few individuals, and you have an attractive target for jealous family members and assorted villains."

"What do you know about the car and driver?" Gil started making notes on a second sheet of paper to indicate that this might be a separate case."

"I've been working with an old friend of yours, Erik Greuner. He's a sergeant with the Stevens Point Police now."

"I wondered what happened to him. We worked on a bunch of cases together when we were younger. What did the two of you come up with?"

"We have some clues but no breakthrough. We have a video of the car that doesn't show the driver or the make. That car sideswiped another vehicle in traffic, so we have paint samples plus the first two characters on the plate from the second driver, YK. If the car turns out to have been stolen, I'll suggest that it might have been a paid hit job. I don't think a hostile family member would steal a car."

Gil thought about that one. "Then you think Marie's family would have people in it who might try to kill her?"

"There's a lot of money in this foundation."

Gil picked up his stapler and clipped his two sheets of notes together. "Jeremy, I think I'm convinced that we're working on a single case, not two different ones. That foundation is the golden apple that both the hoods and the family members are after. The next steps will be to see whether they're working together and who's paying the thugs and their fancy lawyers."

CHAPTER 76 – AWAKENING

Debbie had expected Marie to come out of her induced coma as soon as the doctors cut back on the anesthetic cocktail. She was surprised when she saw no visible change in her grandmother's condition, but Dr. Pasqua told her she had to be patient. Marie would begin to stir whenever she was ready. That conversation had taken place at three o'clock yesterday afternoon, and here it was ten o'clock in the morning. At least the medical staff had removed most of Marie's cables and tubes so that she looked more normal. *Oh, well ... time to go down for coffee and a roll.*

Debbie closed her crossword puzzle book and set it on the window sill. She stretched to get her leg muscles working again and bent over to touch her toes. On the third toe touch she straightened up and went to full alert status. Had she seen Marie's left hand move? She stiffened and concentrated on that hand ... two fingers were definitely moving. Debbie pressed the staff call button.

The speaker in the wall activated. "May I help you?"

"Marie's moving. She's starting to come out of her coma."

"Someone will be right there."

A nurse entered the room almost immediately, followed by two doctors a minute later. One doctor looked at his watch and made a notation on Marie's clipboard chart. The other turned to Debbie. "What did you observe?"

"She moved two fingers on her left hand three times before I pressed the call button. Since then she hasn't repeated it."

The doctor lifted Marie's left hand, held it for a few seconds, and then brushed her fingertips with the back end of his pen. Marie's fingers moved in response to the stimulus. "She's beginning to awaken. We'll monitor her vital signs closely now for internal changes. The process may take a while, and it's too early to predict the degree to which she'll be her old self."

Debbie said, "I'll stay by her side and talk to her. Maybe that will speed the process. At least, it will make me feel as though I'm doing something to help."

The doctor agreed and said that a nurse would stay in the room to monitor Marie's progress and make notes on her tablet computer. Then the doctors left. A few minutes later, a different nurse entered and relieved the nurse who had arrived in response to the call button.

Debbie moved her chair closer to the bed. She decided that she would talk to her grandmother without touching her to avoid any possible trauma that might result from waking up in someone's grasp. "Hello, Marie, this is Debbie, your granddaughter speaking. We're very pleased that you're starting to wake up and come back to us. I've seen your left hand moving. I'd like to see more signs of your awakening. If you can hear me, move your left hand once."

Debbie stared at Marie's left hand. A short while later, it slowly moved. Debbie continued to watch the hand. It didn't move again. "Nurse, my grandmother indicates she can hear me. Not only that, but she knows what I mean by the terms left hand and once. Those have to be good signs of her progress."

"Absolutely, Mrs. Hadley. I've noted your findings in my progress log. Please keep talking to her."

"Come back to us, Marie. We're waiting for you. See whether you can move your right hand."

Debbie paused and watched Marie's right hand. "That's it. Your right hand definitely moved." She nodded to the nurse, who recorded the movement. "It's a beautiful sunny day in Stevens Point. Come back with us and enjoy it."

Marie moaned and then tried to speak, but Debbie couldn't understand her.

"Say that again, Grandma. I didn't get your words."

"I ... don't ... need ... a ... weather ... forecast."

Debbie applauded and shouted to the nurse, "She's coming out of it!"

Marie muttered, "Not so loud. You'll wake the almost dead." She moved her right hand so that her forearm was upright.

The nurse paged the doctors to return to Marie's room.

Thirty minutes later, Debbie's grandmother was reasonably alert and sitting against the sharply tilted head section of the bed. She had sipped water through a straw and answered simple questions from the doctors. After obtaining permission from Dr. Pasqua, Debbie decided to test Marie's memory.

"I'm going to ask you a few simple questions, Grandma. If you can't answer them yet, don't worry. It will all come back to you soon."

"Do you know my name?"

"Debbie."

"Very good ... and my married name?"

"Hadley."

You're doing well. What town do you live in?"

"Stevens Point."

"Excellent. Dr. Pasqua says that you were talking about going back to Gettysburg when you arrived at the hospital. Do you remember that?"

"No."

"Even if you don't remember saying that, what would 'going back to Gettysburg' mean to you now?"

"I don't know. One for you – why do I hurt so much?"

“To wake you up, the doctors cut off your anesthetic. Do you remember a car hitting you as you left the library?”

“I remember everything going black as I left. That was a car?”

“Yes, it was. Do you remember anything else from that time?”

“I heard screaming, but it wasn’t me.”

“That would have been the teenage girl walking behind you who almost was hit.”

“How is she?”

“She’s fine but still scared by what happened.”

“Me too. Was it deliberate?”

“We think so, and so do the police.”

Dr. Pasqua interrupted. “That will be enough questions for now, Debbie. It’s time for us to examine Marie thoroughly to evaluate her stage of recovery. You can visit with her again after we’ve completed our assessment.”

CHAPTER 77 - WITNESS

Leah Hanks hadn't felt safe riding in a car since that black whatever-it-was hit that older woman and almost hit her too as they left the library. The worst part was that Leah had passed her driving test two weeks earlier, and now she was a licensed driver who was afraid to ride in a car, let alone drive one. Today, she would have to overcome at least some of her fears. The police had called her mother and asked whether she would be willing to bring Leah to the police station so that they could ask her a few questions about the incident. They had promised to avoid upsetting Leah, and good old Mom had agreed to drive her daughter over there.

The ride didn't turn out to be as bad as Leah expected, but she did cheat on normalcy by closing her eyes whenever they were in close traffic. Perhaps she would dare to drive again after a half dozen more rides as a passenger.

At the police station, they were escorted into an interview room. A few minutes later, Sergeant Erik Greuner joined them.

"Good morning. Thank you for coming in. I have just a few questions for you, Leah, and if you don't mind, we'll record your answers so that we'll remember them just as you gave them."

"Is this the room where you question criminals and murderers?"

"It is, but we haven't had any murderers to question for quite a while. If you feel uncomfortable here, Leah, I'm sure I could borrow an office for our chat."

"No, this will be better because I'll be able to tell my friends I was in the room where the scumbags get questioned."

"Let's get started. This is an interview with Leah Hanks, who witnessed a hit-and-run incident near the exit of the Portage County Public Library in Stevens Point, Wisconsin. Today's date and that of the incident have been entered during the setup of this data file. My first question for you, Leah, concerns your health. Do you feel that your recovery from the shock of nearly being hit by a car is sufficient for you to talk about what happened?"

"Yes, I can talk about it."

"Fine; what do you remember about the car that hit Marie Danforth and almost hit you?"

"It was black, but it all happened too fast for me to see much more. I think it had four doors."

"Did you see the driver?"

"Very briefly."

"Was the driver a man or a woman?"

"A woman."

"Was she young, middle-aged, or old?"

"I'd call her middle-aged."

"What age in years do you consider the start of middle age?"

"Thirty."

"Can you describe the woman in any way?"

"It happened very quickly, but I have an impression that she wasn't pretty. She looked angry."

"Thank you. That's useful information. Do you remember anything more that I haven't covered?"

"No, I was mostly looking at what happened to the woman in front of me. The driver didn't try to avoid hitting her at all."

"Thank you for answering my questions, Leah. That's all I have for now. If we find and arrest the driver, would you be willing to testify as a witness and repeat your recollections in a courtroom?”

“Sure, but would I have to be dressed up for that?”

Leah’s mother and the sergeant both smiled.

CHAPTER 78 – ERIK GREUNER

Detective Lieutenant Gil Beecher grabbed the phone on the third ring. “Beecher here.”

“How are things in Milwaukee, old-timer? You must be the most senior guy on the force by now.”

“Who is this?”

“Erik Greuner at your service. I hear from Jeremy Hadley that we’re pursuing two different aspects of the same case. It’s good to be working side-by-side with you again, Gil.”

“Either you’re drinking too much of that Point Beer in Stevens Point, or you’ve mellowed since our younger days. You used to be a gruff bastard.”

“I still am to strangers, but even though you’re more than a bit strange, you’re an old friend.”

“What can I do for you, Erik?”

“Today, the subject is what I can do for you. I have some new information that may give us a break in our mutual case.”

“I’m all ears. Go ahead.”

“As I recall, your ears were kind of flappy, but on to the serious stuff. I have a witness to the deliberate hit-and-run assault on Marie Danforth. She’s a high school girl who followed Marie out of the library and almost got hit by the same car. It took a while for this girl, Leah Hanks, to get over the shock, but she’s thinking clearly now.”

“Good. What’s her new evidence?”

“She says the driver of the car was a woman. Do you have any female suspects involved in your investigation?”

"I do indeed have one, and she's been throwing curve balls at us instead of cooperating. I'll email a photo of her to you. See if your witness can identify her as the driver. I'd like nothing better than to be able to put her out of business."

"She's a career type?"

"She runs a construction company that develops industrial and office properties. She's too rich and ambitious for her own good."

"I'll question my witness about your picture when I get it, but be careful in dealing with that woman. She sounds like someone who may have high-level political connections. Be sure the evidence will stand up before you pounce on her."

"I know the drill. Politicians complain if cops don't get results, and they blow their stacks when they don't like the results that the police do get. It's hard to win in this line of work."

"I guess you haven't changed that much after all, Gil. I can remember similar rants when we were much younger. Let's hope we get this case solved soon."

CHAPTER 79 – TRANSITION

After discussing Marie's condition with Jeremy, Debbie decided that she would have to officially take over the management of the Danforth Family Foundation. Jeremy agreed that without active leadership the fund would likely have major losses in a volatile market. Marie had an incomplete set of memories; it was time for Debbie to take control. Before she did so, Jeremy convinced her that she should take a precautionary step before officially taking the reins of the fund.

The next morning, Debbie Hadley arrived punctually for an appointment at the Ernst & Young office on East Wisconsin Avenue in Milwaukee. Ernst & Young was one of the Big Four accounting firms, although they currently aimed at broadening their market appeal by calling themselves business management consultants. To make a good first impression on staffers at this British-headquartered accounting house, Debbie wore a navy blue business suit she had purchase the previous afternoon. It wasn't her most comfortable outfit, but it allowed her to feel professional and better-prepared for her new side-career.

Upon arriving at Ernst & Young, Debbie told the receptionist she had an appointment with Louise Santanos. Then she sat and glanced at company brochures while she waited for Louise to come to the lobby. Five minutes later, she heard her name called, and Debbie rose to be greeted by a woman and a man. They introduced themselves as Louise Santanos and Herbert Greene. Louise was obviously the senior of the two, because she dominated the conversation. Following the introductions, Louise led them into a conference room adjacent to the lobby.

Once settled, Louise invited Debbie to summarize the purpose of her visit.

"I'm here because the Danforth family has a charitable foundation. Danforth was my maiden name. My grandmother has managed the foundation for many years, but at least for a while she won't be able to continue running it because of injuries suffered when a car hit her. She earlier designated me as her successor, and I'm about to take over. In order to be prudent, before I sit in the manager's chair I want to ask you to audit the Danforth Family Foundation to make sure that everything is in order and to determine where we need to improve investment and distribution operations."

Louise said, "Mrs. Hadley, I appreciate your desire to determine whether the foundation is being run properly, but Ernst & Young is a very large and respected organization ..."

"Yes, I understand you're one of the so-called Big Four. That's very impressive, and it's why I came to you."

"As I was saying, because we're so large, we hardly ever get involved with small businesses or family foundations. We generally leave work with such small entities to local CPA firms. However, I'm willing to make an exception in your case, and I'll assign Herbert Greene to work with you."

Debbie stood. "You're implying that we're not sufficiently interesting for you to work with us, and you're also indicating that Mr. Greene has a junior ranking on the staff."

"I didn't say that."

"You implied that. Tell me, Mr. Greene whether you are qualified to work with us?"

"Mrs. Hadley, I'd very much like to be in charge of your account. I ran my own CPA firm in Chicago for fifteen years and then I worked for a major bank in commercial loans for another ten years. However, I am a junior associate at Ernst & Young, having been here only two years."

"That resume is good enough for me. I'd be pleased to have you conduct our audit. If that process helps me to operate the foundation more efficiently, I might look to hire you away from Ernst & Young to be a staff employee."

Louise Santanos stood and glared at Debbie. "I'm not sure we want to work with you. We expect our associates to be loyal employees, and as I said we don't look for small accounts. How big is your family foundation anyway?"

"Large enough for this office to thrive on our business; we're on the plus side of two billion dollars in assets."

Louise sat back down. "That's much larger than I expected. I will be able to justify assigning a more senior associate to work on your account."

Herbert started to walk toward the conference room door.

Debbie said, "Come back here, Mr. Greene. Ms. Santanos, I said earlier that I approved of Mr. Greene's background. He is the one I want to handle our account. Do you agree with that assignment?"

Louise said, "Certainly, and I apologize for looking down on your foundation. How long has it been in operation?"

"In one form or another, it has been serving the needs of Wisconsin Civil War veterans and their descendants for more than one hundred and fifty years. Mr. Greene, I'll be back at three o'clock this afternoon to explain the details of our foundation and the audit project."

"I'll be prepared, Mrs. Hadley. Call me Herb."

"Fine, Herb. Call me Debbie."

CHAPTER 80 - SURVEILLANCE

Gil Beecher felt sure that Pat Danforth Flynn was behind both ends of the current case with its violent aspects, a bomb planted under a car in Milwaukee and a hit-and-run assault in Stevens Point. She had admitted being visited by Sam Finch, one of the bombing suspects, and her story about recommending him for a job sounded fishy. When detectives had gone to question him at his supposed construction job, they couldn't find him. His supervisor's tale of an out-of-town assignment hadn't checked out either. Pat Flynn was certainly rich enough to pick up the bill for those fancy lawyers. He had no proof of this, because those lawyers were hiding behind attorney-client privilege, but he gave his theory a high probability of being correct. He hadn't been surprised when Stevens Point Sergeant Erik Greuner told him the driver of the hit-and-run car had been a woman. He could visualize Pat Flynn taking such aggressive action. Now he would have to use traditional police investigation techniques to back up his suspicions.

He assigned two detectives, one male and one female, to watch Pat Flynn's house for questionable comings and goings and to follow her whenever she went out. He would take care of obtaining a court order to check her telephone and email records on the grounds that they are *relevant to an ongoing criminal investigation.* That was the language approved in a 1979 Supreme Court ruling and the 1986 Electronic Communications Privacy Act. This wouldn't exactly be a fishing expedition because he had good reason to believe she was involved in one or more crimes, but he couldn't exactly specify her crime either. Obviously, a witness saying that the hit-and-run driver was a woman was insufficient to pin that crime on Pat....It would make his job a lot easier if that witness stated that the photo of Pat he sent to Erik Greuner matched her memory of the driver.

Jeremy Hadley had told him about the big family foundation that Pat Flynn and other family members were trying to take over. It would make sense that any of her calls and other contacts with family members might be linked to the attempt to change who controls that foundation. Those calls might also be connected to the hit-and-run attempted murder of Marie Danforth.

Beecher wondered whether they would be able to scare Sam Finch out of his hiding place. He could have left the state, but Gil suspected that he was not too far away, just staying out of sight for a while. Sam would probably contact Manny and Tony if they were released on bail. So far, the prosecutor had successfully argued that they were too dangerous to release because of the attempted car bombing. Gil thought the high-priced defense lawyers would eventually convince the judge to grant bail. He felt sure that Sam Finch would show his face after that point.

All the surveillance and communication record checking would take a good deal of time, but Gil considered himself patient enough to wait until those efforts paid off.

CHAPTER 81 – AUSTIN CARMICHAEL

Debbie sat in her car, still fuming over the way she had been considered insignificant by Louise Santanos at Ernst and Young, when her telephone rang. She thought: *You had better be good news.*

"Hello."

"Mrs. Hadley, this is Austin Carmichael at the Portage County Public Library. I have developments for you. We did a careful review of the items Marie Danforth studied at the library on the day she was hit by that car, and we think we've identified her subject matter."

"How did you manage that?"

"Our reference librarians are quite rigorous in their rules for arranging materials within the files of loose documents. They reviewed the batches that Mrs. Danforth studied, and they isolated the papers that had not been refiled in the proper sequence."

"I'm impressed by your efficiency over there."

Austin laughed. "I'm anything but efficient, but I have some dedicated people working for me."

Debbie's impatience was growing, but she reminded herself to be polite. "Would you like to tell me what they discovered?"

"Please forgive me. I sometimes talk too much about processes and procedures, when I should be discussing results. Marie Danforth studied a Civil War military outfit called the Wisconsin Sharpshooters. She also sifted through an assortment of municipal documents from Fox Lake, Wisconsin."

"That's interesting information, Austin. Thank you for tracking it down. Tell your staff people they're outstanding researchers."

After disconnecting with Austin, Debbie called Jeremy. "I have one more meeting in Milwaukee at three o'clock. Meet me at Marie's house at six o'clock, and we'll go out for dinner to that steak house she recommended. Wear a jacket, because your wife is in her best business attire."

CHAPTER 82 - COMINGS AND GOINGS

Detectives Sharon Yee and Phil Hawley had the early morning stakeout shift at Pat Flynn's house. They had parked under a tree halfway down the block. From that vantage point, they could see everyone approaching or leaving the Flynn house, with little chance of being observed by anyone in the building. They did hope Flynn wasn't such a social star that her neighbors might alert her. The first two hours of the shift had been nothing but boring, so Yee and Hawley added a moment of lightness by toasting each other with the last of their coffee supply.

At 8:02 a.m. a small sedan drove into Flynn's driveway and parked. The magnetic sign on the driver's door identified the vehicle as belonging to a cleaning service. A woman wearing a baseball cap, sweatshirt, and blue jeans got out and went to the trunk, where she retrieved a bucket filled with cleaning supplies, a mop, and a vacuum cleaner. Phil Hawley took a series of photographs of her as she walked to the house's kitchen entrance and rang the doorbell. The door opened, and she entered with her cleaning items. Sharon recorded the event in her notebook.

At 8:53 a.m. the garage opened and Pat Flynn's red Ford 150 pickup truck emerged and turned north on the street. The garage door closed automatically as she drove away. Sharon radioed for a new stakeout team to take over watching the house because she and Hawley were leaving to follow Flynn's truck.

Six minutes later, a woman wearing a baseball cap, sweatshirt, and blue jeans left the kitchen door of the house carrying a bundle and drove away in the cleaning service car. Six blocks and three turns later, the woman parked that car, then got out and removed the magnetic signs from the two front doors. She opened one of the rear doors, threw her cap inside, and retrieved a stylish lightweight jacket, which she put on over her sweatshirt. Then she returned to the driver's seat and headed the car northwest toward Stevens Point.

The replacement surveillance team saw nothing interesting around the Flynn house from the time of their arrival until 11:23 a.m. when an older white Dodge minivan pulled into the driveway and a middle-aged man got out. They took pictures of him as he went to the front door and rang the doorbell. After several minutes of standing and waiting for an answer, he gave up and inserted a large envelope into the mailbox. Then he drove away.

The detective in the passenger seat of the unmarked car called Lieutenant Gil Beecher to find out whether their court order allowed them to take the envelope out of Flynn's mailbox. While she was on the phone with him, she saw a man walk out of a house on the other side of the street and head directly for that mailbox. Beecher said, "That will be the ex-husband, Kevin Flynn. If he takes the envelope, arrest him for interfering with a police investigation. Bring him and the envelope here."

CHAPTER 83 – LUNCH DATE

Upon walking into Arbuckles Eatery & Pub, Tom Tucker scanned the tables for a familiar face. His scan stopped at a waving arm, and he nodded in reply. This would be the third time they had met for lunch, and he wasn't at all sure whether their relationship would develop beyond the casual. Nevertheless, Pat was fun and rich too. Not that financial analysts have to worry about affording their next meal, but he had a staff career, and her entrepreneurial vigor excited him.

He pulled a chair back from the table and folded his lengthy frame into it. "Been waiting long?"

"Nope; I parked and then walked a few blocks to get my legs working again after the ride, but came in here only five minutes ago."

"Pat, you do realize that our getting together is a bit weird. I work for your family."

"You work for the family foundation; not for the family, and at least so far, I've had nothing to do with that charitable group."

"I like that 'at least so far' comment. You'd like nothing better than to take over and run that organization."

"And you'd like nothing better than to have me in that position so that you could have a bigger say in controlling things."

"Well, at least we understand each other. Let's get our burgers under our belts and then head for my place. My new temporary boss, Debbie Hadley, wants to have an orientation meeting with me."

"Make sure it's only a business discussion."

"Honestly, Pat, your thinking is off the deep end sometimes. Debbie's married, and I wouldn't want to fight either her or her husband. They've both had martial arts training."

"After lunch you can wrestle with me, and see how well you come out of it."

"That'll make me eat faster. You grew up a farm girl. I'll bet you enjoy rolling around in the hay."

"That reminds me. I don't know where you grew up or how you got to be a financial analyst."

He drained the last of his beer. "We still have a lot to learn about each other, Pat. Time to move on to the next step."

CHAPTER 84 - WILD GEESE

Gil Beecher couldn't believe the report from Sharon Yee and Phil Hawley. "You two are supposed to be pros, and she wasn't supposed to know you were watching her."

Sharon shrugged her shoulders. "Sorry, Gil; she just outsmarted us. That so-called cleaning person switched clothes and cars with Pat Flynn. We followed Pat's Ford truck to a dealership where the woman left it for service. Then she took a cab to some other place, and we lost her. Late in the afternoon, Pat picked up her truck at the dealer's shop and drove home as though nothing unusual had happened. She probably picked up the cleaning woman at a prearranged location, and then they drove to the dealership so that Pat could get her truck."

"Can either of you professionals tell me whether the second woman really was a cleaner? She could have been an actress, an employee, or even a neighbor. She could have been the woman who drove the car that hit Marie Danforth."

Phil said, "My turn to apologize. We don't know who she was. My guess is that we'll never see her again."

"You're probably right. Pat was thumbing her nose at us. She won't pull that same stunt again."

"Can we arrest her for anything, Gil?"

"I'd like to, but as far as I know, changing your clothes and driving a different car aren't crimes."

Sharon asked, "What about the documents the other team took from Pat's ex-husband. Is there anything interesting there?"

Beecher lightened up and smiled. "It was a piece of luck that Kevin Flynn decided to take that envelope. We would have been on shaky ground, taking and opening it without a warrant. As the ex-husband, Kevin still has some equity in Pat's house and can legally look in the mailbox. We then took the documents from him with his permission as being relevant to an ongoing criminal investigation. In exchange for his permission, we dropped the interference charge and let him go home."

Phil asked, "So who was the middle-aged man who left the envelope, and what did it contain?"

"According to Kevin, that was Pat's Uncle Harry. He considers himself the best hope for his branch of the family to take over the running of the foundation from Marie Danforth. The papers were a petition he wanted Pat to sign, calling on a judge to hold a hearing on the merits of a management change for the family foundation."

Sharon said, "He may not have much of a chance, but at least he's trying to get a change to happen through the legal system."

Gil said, "I'm not so sure. According to Kevin Flynn, Harry has a reputation as an intemperate bully, so I wouldn't be surprised if he turned out to be behind some of the dirty tricks while he openly works through the courts. All I know is that we keep discovering additional suspects."

CHAPTER 85 - REHABILITATION

The therapists were still ferrying Marie between her hospital room and the Physical Therapy Department using a wheelchair, but after arrival, they had her out of the chair and walking through an array of obstacles supported only by a cane that she lifted off the ground when she felt steady. Marie felt confident that she would regain her physical strength and skills. Her concern was that she still didn't remember anything from the time she arrived at the library until the moment she woke up from her coma. She was surprised that she had lost memories from before the car's striking her, but the doctors kept saying that everyone in Marie's situation responds differently. She did remember hearing voices while she was in the coma, but she couldn't identify them or remember what they said. The doctors told her it was possible that she would eventually regain most of the missing memories, but Marie had little faith in that prospect. She assumed that there would always be a hole in her recollections, but that it would become less important as she later added new memories.

She appreciated Debbie's stepping forward to take over management of the family foundation and felt less guilty about shirked responsibilities because of that transition. She wasn't sure how long Debbie would be willing to continue that management, but at least she would be there during this critical rehabilitation period.

Marie hadn't seen the car. She had suffered its impact while her thoughts had been focused on something else, and then everything had descended into pain and darkness. She hoped that her agonies had not been caused by a relative, seeking to gain control of the foundation through violence. One would prefer to trust her relatives, no matter how many warts they displayed.

After a brief rest period, the therapists came to her room to guide her up and down a stand-alone staircase located in the hospital corridor. It had seven steps going up to a landing and seven more descending on the other side. They required her to go up and down the stairs three times and then repeat that exercise two more times each day. Including all other facets of the therapy, it was more intense physical activity than Marie had experienced at any time during the last fifteen years.

As she thought about all of her injuries and the undoubtedly huge expenses to bring her back to what would have to pass for normal condition in the future, Marie gave thanks that the foundation had purchased an outstanding health insurance package for her. She wouldn't be eligible for government Medicare for another year.

CHAPTER 86 – FIELD TRIP

While Debbie worked to understand the ins and outs of managing the Danforth Family Foundation, her husband had freedom to tackle any aspect of the mystery that struck him as worthwhile. Having learned that the Milwaukee Police had lost track of Sam Finch and blamed Pat Flynn for hiding him somewhere, Jeremy decided he'd take on the job of tracking Sam down. He would be working on his own, but he wouldn't have the jurisdictional limits of a police detective.

Lieutenant Gil Beecher was more than happy to give Jeremy copies of his notes on Sam Finch and to wish him luck with his quest. After looking through them, Jeremy decided he'd be more likely to get results if he visited the worksite to which Pat Flynn had directed Sam. Beecher's notes said that he had contacted a foreman named Mike Cage there, so Cage would be Jeremy's target too, but on an informal eyeball to eyeball basis.

Upon arriving at the construction site, Jeremy noted the *hardhat required* signs and retrieved from the rear seat a bright yellow hardhat he had purchased for this mission. He found Mike Cage in the construction office trailer arguing with someone over the telephone. As he waited, he gathered from Cage's end of the conversation that the building inspector had rejected several computer work station installations and their interconnected cabling as not being in compliance with the code. Cage was trying to get the electrical contractor to get his people to correct the problem that day, or they would have a week's delay before the building inspector made his next scheduled visit. The call ended abruptly when Cage clicked his phone off while the contractor was shouting something at him.

The foreman looked up at Jeremy standing just inside the door. "Come on in and tell me whether you're good news or more trouble."

"Hopefully, I'll be neither. I'm a private detective, and I'm trying to get a line on your former employee, Sam Finch, for a financial institution."

"You're not with the police? They called asking a bunch of questions about him."

"Nope, I'm as civilian as they come. He should want to be found, because there might be some money in it for him."

"Would there be anything in it for me if I aimed you in the right direction?"

"How does fifty dollars sound?"

"Not bad, but a hundred would sound much better."

"I'm in a hurry, and it sounded from your call as though you are too. Let's split the difference. I'll give you seventy-five dollars, but your tip has to be more than gossip. I need something useful."

Mike Cage smiled. "I see you're used to getting something done instead of just talking about it. Here's the scoop. Sam Finch isn't going by that name. He's calling himself Sam Monahan. He said it's his mother's maiden name, but I don't know whether that's the truth. I assigned him to a construction site in Minnesota. I'll give you the address, but it probably won't do you any good. He never showed up for work there. I figured he thought it was too far away, so he's probably still somewhere in the Milwaukee area. At least the Monahan name should be useful. Now I'll take my money and try to straighten out some of my construction problems."

Jeremy took seventy-five dollars out of his wallet, handed it to Cage, and shook his hand as he left.

So I should be looking for Sam Monahan, and he's probably not too far away. That's a start.

From his car, Jeremy called Gil Beecher and suggested that the police check for credit cards issued to a Sam Monahan and then determine where they had been used recently. Then he called Debbie and told her he wanted to take her back to that favorite steakhouse for dinner that evening.

CHAPTER 87 – LIBRARY RESEARCH

The following day, Debbie Hadley visited the library at The University of Wisconsin at Stevens Point and identified herself as a former staff library researcher at the UW-Madison campus. The reference librarian issued her a ResearcherID, giving her the status of a faculty researcher, assigned her a computer work station, and access credentials for restricted documents in the library's collection.

Once settled, Debbie devoted most of her attention to state and locality records for Civil War veterans and their families. She also studied University of Wisconsin records for the various campuses to obtain lists of students who had received Danforth Foundation scholarships. Her third area of initial interest involved genealogical records for several families she had tabulated as being frequently listed in the veterans and scholarship portions of her research.

As she continued her work, Debbie printed out document pages that interested her and circled names and facts on them that she thought would fit into historical and interactive patterns she started to see. By the end of the afternoon, she had developed several theories regarding both criminal and family member involvements in recent events.

Debbie thanked the Reference Librarian for his assistance and turned in her stack access credentials. The librarian told her that the ResearcherID would still be available to her on future visits.

As she left University Library, Debbie's telephone rang. She saw that the call was from her husband and answered it. "Hi, Jeremy. What's happening?"

"My credit card theory worked. I told you yesterday that Sam Finch was calling himself Sam Monahan. The Milwaukee Police found a recently issued Visa card in that name, and charges led them to his apartment address. I'm with Lieutenant Beecher now. They're about to raid the apartment and pick Sam up if he's there."

"Jeremy, tell Beecher that it may be important to get a search warrant for that place whether Sam's there or not. I suspect they'll find incriminating evidence there."

"I'll take care of that, but I have to hang up now. They're about to move in on the apartment. I'll talk with you again later."

CHAPTER 88 – AUDIT PROGRESS

When Debbie returned to the hospital to check on her grandmother's condition, she noticed she had a message on her cell phone while she was sitting in her car. She saw that it was from Herb Greene, the auditor, and decided to call him from her car before she became entangled in hospital discussions. He answered her call after the first ring.

"Hi, Debbie; thanks for returning my call so promptly."

"Good to talk with you, Herb. I assume that you called in connection with the audit."

"I did, and my purpose is to give you an early heads up that the Danforth Foundation has not been controlled efficiently. It's too early to say whether we are looking at slack management, limited understanding, or something more malicious, but I'll identify the problems before I'm through. It will take a bit longer than expected to complete the process."

"What have you done so far, Herb, and why do you suspect problems?"

"I went to the office, where I met Tom Tucker, the analyst, and I retrieved several ledgers and other documents. Your foundation has been active for so long that you have most of your older records on paper and only recent ones in computer files. Thank you for furnishing your passwords. They allowed me to access most of the current information from my office."

"What did you think of Tom Tucker?"

"He appears to be qualified for his position. I also introduced myself to Jonathan Danforth by telephone. He told me about some of the project ideas he has generated. He sounds creative."

"But you've spotted some problems."

"Let's say that the different records don't synchronize well. It will take me a while to discover the specific deficiencies. When I get further along, I'd like to sit down with you in my office and analyze each piece of the puzzle. That's all I have for now."

Debbie nodded to herself. "Thanks for the warning, Herb. By the time we get to that meeting, I may have some feedback for you too."

CHAPTER 89 – DEFENSE LAWYERS

The guard shepherded Manny into the soundproof room reserved for meetings with prisoners' legal representatives. Manny smiled when he saw the high-priced lawyers, Robbie Conklin and Larry Malcolm, waiting for him. They gestured for him to take a seat.

Manny asked, "Is this the big day when you tell me and Tony that we're getting out on bond until the trial date? I bet you guys will be able to get that trial delayed for a long time."

Robbie said, "We've already had a meeting with Tony, and now it's your turn. We're here to tell you that we're not going to be continuing as your defense team. The person who hired us has cut off our funding. Because of that, we've gone to court and moved to withdraw from your case. The court has granted our petition and will soon appoint a public defender to take your case without charge to you."

"But a public defender won't have nearly as good a chance of getting us off as you guys will."

"That's probably true."

"Can't you represent us if we promise to pay you in the future?"

Robbie said, "We'd have trouble enforcing that promise. We would have to be paid up front, and our services are not inexpensive. Do you have access to substantial funds?"

"No, we don't."

"Then you should plan on working with someone from the public defender's office. Some of them are quite good."

"And most of them aren't. At least identify the person who was paying you and dropped out."

"Sorry, Manny, that information comes under attorney-client privilege, and we can't reveal it to you or anyone else."

"Can you suggest how we should work with the public defender?"

"Your best bet is to have that person confer with the prosecutor about a plea deal. You'll have to serve time, but a plea deal would lead to a reduced sentence in exchange for eliminating the costs of a trial."

"In other words, you're advising us to give up our chances to go free. Thanks for the recommendation. Our decision will depend on the skills of the public defender they assign to us. Maybe we'll get lucky."

CHAPTER 90 – SAM MONAHAN

Lieutenant Gil Beecher told Jeremy to stay by the police cars and out of any possible line of fire as they moved in on Sam Monahan's apartment house. Beecher didn't think Sam would resist arrest, but he took the precaution of issuing Jeremy Hadley a bullet-proof vest anyway. There were two entrances, front and rear, with a connecting corridor. He led the front door team, while partners Sharon Yee and Phil Hawley entered the back door. There was no elevator, so the police figured they had all escape possibilities blocked by ascending the front and back stairways at the same time. When they reached Sam's third floor apartment, they knocked on the door and announced their presence. No response. Beecher had an officer kick the door open. They charged in, dividing to cover the various rooms. As the "Clear!" calls resounded through the apartment, Beecher realized Sam Monahan was not there.

Beecher heard a car horn repeatedly honking an SOS code. He looked out the window and saw Jeremy Hadley pointing upward. His message was clear. Sam was on the roof. Beecher would learn that Sam had reached the roof by using a staircase hidden behind a hallway door. This side of the city block consisted of six similar height apartment buildings with common walls between them. Sam could cross rooftops and descend to the street through any one of them.

Beecher radioed Yee and Hawley to go up and cover the rooftops while everyone in position by the cars down below would block the front and rear entrances of the six buildings. Once everyone was in place, he would signal them to search all the buildings at the same time.

He looked out the window and saw many officers scurrying into position at each of the buildings with their guns drawn. Beecher radioed, "We don't know that he's armed and dangerous. Don't use your weapons unless you have to defend yourself."

Then he turned away from the window and jumped in surprise. Standing behind him was Sam Monahan with his hands in the air indicating his surrender.

Beecher regained his composure, told Sam to turn around, and handcuffed him. Then Gil radioed, "Stand down everyone. I have Monahan in custody. We'll be coming down."

As they descended the stairs Sam said, "I'd much rather go quietly than take a chance on some jittery cop shooting me. I haven't committed a crime anyway."

"You were an accessory to planting that bomb under Jonathan Danforth's car."

"I'm afraid not, Lieutenant. I can prove I was out of town that night."

CHAPTER 91 – MARIE

Debbie sat in the chair facing Marie's hospital bed. She studied the expression on her grandmother's face and wondered whether everything was back to normal with her. It was time to ask some probing questions and see whether Marie's responses sounded reasonable.

"Grandma, have you remembered anything that happened since the car hit you or even in the library earlier?"

"Nope, I still have a gap in my memories."

"How are you feeling otherwise? I'll be able to take you home in a couple of hours if the doctors give you a final check and you pass muster."

"In that case, I never felt better in my life. I'm tired of this place. They did a good job of getting me going again, but it's time for me to get back to independent living at home."

"You may be going home today, but I'm not letting go of the reins on the foundation until I think you're fully capable of running it again."

Marie chuckled, giving Debbie a hint that she was her normal self. "What makes you think I want to run that monster again? It was getting to feel like more of a burden than a blessing."

"You sound like yourself. Tell me whether you sometimes stretched the foundation rules in funding people and organizations."

"I see where this conversation is going. I'll wager you have an auditor looking over our records, and he's told you that I haven't been completely businesslike in the way I distributed money."

"Is there any truth to that statement?"

"The problem with that foundation is that the assets grow much faster than we can distribute funds. Couple that with trying to identify descendants of 2nd Wisconsin Infantry Regiment veterans a hundred and fifty years later, and you'll understand why we have to get creative about the charitable support we distribute. That's why I hired Jonathan Danforth to generate some creative projects for us. I wasn't simply helping him out with his political contribution problem. I think he'll be a big help for us in the future."

Debbie relaxed and leaned back in her chair. "Fair enough, Grandma, you've passed your first test. You're thinking and sounding like yourself again. I'll take you home today, if the doctors say you're ready. Now give me an answer to a question I've wanted to ask since you finished telling us about the history of this fund."

"Go ahead."

"You have people from the other two branches of our family trying to gain control of the foundation. They obviously knew quite a bit about it. Why didn't you or my parents ever tell me that we had a family secret that involved sitting on a huge chunk of money?"

Marie motioned for Debbie to come closer to her. Then she grasped her hand. "The chunk of money, as you call it, really was supposed to be a secret, and we managed to keep it hidden for a very long time by spreading the rumor that it had been exhausted many years ago. Then your father had to decide to play with DNA analysis. Once he discovered that Lynnette had been biologically different from the rest of the family, he shared that information with members of Bruce and Daniel's families and took the unauthorized step of telling them why it might be important. Up to that point very few in the family knew about our continuing hidden fund, but your father had to brag about his DNA findings. I think he may have done it to spite me for not letting him have a foundation grant to support some of his activities and patients in developing countries. That cause was totally different from what Cyrus agreed to support many years ago."

"That explains how you and the foundation ended up suffering attacks from the other two branches of the family, but why didn't you tell me about it. I'm in your branch."

"I didn't want your upbringing tainted by knowing about all that money. You had to learn to accomplish things without any special support. I never told anyone, including your parents, that I hoped to have you take over the management at some point."

"If Dad had known that, he might have avoided encouraging a family rebellion."

CHAPTER 92 – GATHERING

When Jeremy Hadley returned from Milwaukee to Marie's house in Stevens Point, he was excited; both because of having participated in the raid on Sam Monahan's apartment house and because of subsequent information that Lieutenant Gil Beecher had given him. He wanted to share his feelings and a few of Beecher's cryptic comments with Debbie, but his enthusiasm was stifled when he discovered that Marie was alone in the house. Debbie had gone to a meeting with the auditor. Jeremy did his best to hide his disappointment and to win a few points from Debbie's grandmother while he waited for his wife's return.

He approached Marie as she sat at the kitchen table making out a shopping list.

"When you finish that list, I'll go out shopping for you. Tell me the name of your preferred store, and I'll pick it all up there."

"Thanks, Jeremy; you must have been a big help to your mother."

"Actually, I had a few complaints from that quarter. Sometimes I got absorbed in my own activities and didn't jump up on schedule to do my family chores."

"Well, you're making up for it now. You're attentive and a big help. I'm sorry for teasing you so much along the way. It's a bit of the old family thing of deciding whether you suit my image of a mate for Debbie. Don't worry; you've passed all the tests with flying colors. Now I'm the one who has to pass tests to see whether I am or will be fully recovered."

"You're doing well, Marie. You'll be back in control of everything soon."

"Thanks for your optimism, Jeremy, but I know the human body isn't built to withstand the insult of a speeding car striking it, especially at my age. I'll mend and get back into things, but there will be some activities and responsibilities that I'll have to pass along to others."

They heard noises outside the kitchen door. It opened, and Debbie walked in, trailed by Herb Greene. Once inside, Debbie introduced the Ernst & Young auditor to Marie and Jeremy.

"I invited Herb to join us because he has a few audit-related questions for Marie. I also anticipated that Jeremy would have news from Lieutenant Gil Beecher that would require Herb to be here. How about that, Jeremy?"

"I do have news from Beecher. I planned to spring it on you as soon as I arrived, but pushed it to the back of my mind when you weren't here. Gil wanted me to tell you that the search warrant produced what you expected, and that because of Marie's only recent release from the hospital and the case's events in both Milwaukee and Stevens Point, he agrees to hold the summary wrap-up session here in Marie's house. Gil spoke with Sergeant Erik Greuner of the Stevens Point Police who endorsed the arrangement. Unless you have an objection to the timing, they'll arrive here at seven o'clock this evening. Beecher has invited Pat Flynn and Jonathan Danforth to join us, and Greuner has requested that Tom Tucker and Harry Danforth be here also. Is there anyone else we should ask?"

Debbie said, "I don't suppose we should invite Manny, Tony, or Sam. They're all in jail. We'll be able to get their inputs through the police if required. The teenager who saw the driver might be helpful, but if we need it, we'll be able to get her evidence later. I'm not sure how much he'll contribute, but I'll invite Kevin Flynn, Pat's ex-husband.

His presence should keep her from exaggerating too much. I expect that it will be an interesting evening. I'll call Beecher and Greuner to confirm the schedule and exchange a few thoughts with them."

Marie said, "In the meantime, I'll find a quiet spot to discuss foundation matters with Mr. Greene. Herb, welcome to my home. Be sure to ask all the tough questions you have. Don't treat me like an invalid because of recent physical problems. I'm back from the near-dead, and I want to make my presence felt."

By seven o'clock, everyone had arrived at Marie's house except Pat Flynn. Jeremy had arranged chairs in an oval shape within the part of the enlarged kitchen that had once been the dining room. At the head of the oval was Grandma Marie's Danforth family rocking chair.

Debbie introduced everyone to each other and suggested that they each select a seat. Marie would sit in her special rocking chair even though she wouldn't be leading the discussion.

As they crisscrossed the open area to choose their seats, Kevin Flynn approached Gil Beecher. "I wouldn't worry about Pat being late. She likes to make a grand entrance, arriving slightly tardy to every affair."

Gil Beecher said. "I hope she understands that this is less of a social affair than a command performance. If she's more than a half hour late, she may end up with a police escort."

The person in question, Pat Flynn, arrived fifteen minutes late, punctuating her greetings with apologies for having taken two wrong turns along the way.

Kevin whispered to Beecher that Pat never drove anywhere without her GPS navigation operating. "She wanted to be late so that everyone would focus on her."

Jeremy took Pat's jacket and led her to the one remaining chair, which happened to be between Kevin and

Herb Greene. Pat made brief eye contact with Tom Tucker on the other side of the room, shrugged her shoulders, and sat down.

With everyone now in attendance, Lieutenant Gil Beecher stood in the center of the oval and announced the purpose of the meeting. "Greetings, everyone. You all should know that this is a combination police and civilian meeting aimed at analyzing some facts and events in order to help solve two criminal cases that appear to be interconnected. We'll also be addressing a few peripheral puzzles that deserve attention. I'm here representing the Milwaukee Police Department, while Sergeant Erik Greuner is here from the local Stevens Point Police. I'll open the meeting, but at times I'll turn over its guidance to others. We are in this home because Marie Danforth invited us and because she has not fully recovered from injuries suffered when someone tried to murder her using an automobile as a weapon."

Harry Danforth stood up. "What you're saying is all well and good, but I don't know why you asked me to come here. I've had nothing to do with anything criminal, and I don't live in either police jurisdiction represented here. Unless someone can persuade me that my presence serves a useful purpose, I'm going home."

Gil Beecher nodded. "I understand your discomfort with being in a discussion that involves criminal activities, but we asked you here to assist our two police departments with our investigations. That's phrasing more commonly used in the United Kingdom than here in the States, but it's accurate. Mr. Danforth, you've had conversations and contacts with people in this room that may be important to our cases. We would like you to have the opportunity to represent yourself as others discuss their interactions with you. I assure you that it will be in your best interest to remain here."

Harry sat down, but grumbled a few comments to indicate his continuing displeasure.

Gil walked around the oval formed by the chairs as a device to require people to focus on him and his words. “As I indicated to Mr. Harry Danforth, it helps both us and you to have your viewpoints represented. There are three other individuals, currently held in jail in Milwaukee, who are involved in our investigation, but who will not be represented. We'll mention their involvements as our discussion proceeds.

“There are two major crimes we need to solve, and perhaps some related infractions. We had an incident of a bomb being attached to the underframe of a vehicle owned by Jonathan Danforth of Milwaukee and the attempted murder of Marie Danforth outside the Portage County Library in Stevens Point using a car as a weapon. These were two cases of attempted murder. Fortunately, neither one of them was successful. I'll now invite Debbie Hadley to take over the discussion and describe some of the connecting issues involving these crimes.”

Gil sat, but before Debbie could rise and start speaking, Marie said, “Wait. I want to say something.”

Gil rose and gestured for her to speak.

“I know that Debbie is going to talk about our family's charitable foundation. Until recently, the existence of this project was a closely held family secret. Many of you in this room are not related to the Danforth family. I would appreciate your treating all comments about the foundation as being confidential. Do not repeat them to others who aren't involved in this investigation. Lieutenant Beecher, would you mind asking each person to agree to my stipulation, and ask anyone who won't agree to leave while Debbie speaks?”

“That's an unusual request, but I'll go along with it.”

Gil questioned each person, and everyone agreed to avoid gossiping about the foundation discussions.

"Everyone has agreed. May I allow Debbie to speak now, Marie?"

"Go ahead. I may not have all of my memories back, but I can't forget my family and foundation responsibilities."

Debbie stood, and Gil sat down. She walked around the oval, looking into each person's eyes before she spoke. "Thank you all for coming this evening. My husband, Jeremy, and I are private detectives. We've been working with the police to help them understand the motives that may have led to the crimes being investigated. At this point I'm convinced that all the events that have happened are interconnected.

"My grandmother, Marie Danforth has told you that our charitable family foundation is something that should not be discussed outside of this room. I agree with her. For this investigation, all you need to know is that it has a large asset value. Marie has managed the project for many years. Because of the attempt on her life and efforts by others to gain access to our funds, Marie has officially passed that management on to me."

Harry Danforth stood. "I object. If Marie isn't going to run it, I should."

Debbie said, "Please sit down, Harry. This isn't a court of law or a competition. I am the legal manager of the Danforth Family Foundation. It is not open to question. Please confirm my status, Herb."

Herb rose to his feet. "I'm Herbert Greene, an associate and auditor at Ernst & Young. Debbie Hadley has been legally certified to be the manager of the foundation we're discussing, and our firm is working with her on an official basis." He sat again.

Once again, Harry grumbled as he returned to his chair.

Debbie centered herself within the chair oval. "As I indicated earlier, the wealth contained within our foundation caused others to crave the possibility of controlling it. Some of those individuals were Danforth family members and others were outsiders, including members of criminal organizations. When Jonathan Danforth wouldn't cooperate with a group's attempt to change foundation management and install him as their puppet, three thugs attempted to kill him by attaching a bomb to the chassis of his car. Fortunately, the Milwaukee Police rendered the bomb harmless before it could be triggered. The bombers are now in jail. Any comments at this point, Jonathan or Lieutenant Beecher?"

Jonathan raised his hand. "I'll be brief and won't bother standing. I just want to say that I'm thankful to the Hadleys, Kevin Flynn, and the Milwaukee Police for saving me from that bomb under my car. I'm also thankful to Marie Danforth for giving me a work assignment within the foundation. I'll have some mission proposals completed soon, Debbie."

Gil Beecher stood and said, "I'll amend Debbie's comments slightly. We have in custody three individuals as suspects for planting that bomb: Manny Ortega, Tony Ganlio, and Sam Finch. Sam Finch also calls himself Sam Monahan. He claims that he couldn't have been part of the bomb plot in Milwaukee because on that night he was here in Stevens Point, meeting with Tom Tucker. Mr. Tucker is with us tonight. Tom, did you have any recent get-togethers with Sam Finch otherwise known as Sam Monahan?"

Tucker hesitated slightly before replying. "I did meet with Sam Monahan three weeks ago in connection with a car he wanted to sell."

Beecher asked, "Did this meeting take place in Stevens Point, and did you buy the car?"

"It did, and I did buy the five-year-old Jeep as an extra car for camping use."

Debbie asked, “How did you find out about the Jeep, Tom? Did you already know Sam Monahan?”

“Monahan had a classified ad for it posted online. The answer to your second question, Debbie, is that I met him for the first time when he came to show me the car.”

“I find that a little hard to believe, Tom. Sam’s mother and your aunt Alice are sisters.”

“Really? I didn’t know Aunt Alice well, and I doubt if I would have met her nephew.”

Debbie continued her assault. “Tom, are you forgetting that your aunt Alice is your godmother?”

“How do you know so much about my family? The truth is that I knew Sam as a child, but I didn’t know him as an adult. Monahan is a common name, so I didn’t think that the man I met regarding the Jeep was the same kid I had played with.”

Gil Beecher stood and joined the conversation. “Tom, police procedures tend to be deliberate and thorough. When Sam gave you as his alibi for the night when they planted the bomb, we checked his cell phone records. He called you several times per week during the previous three months, and you called him too.”

“Alright, Sam Monahan is my cousin, and I talked with him on the telephone. I don’t see any crime there. I did buy the Jeep from him.”

Beecher said, “Sure you did. But the check was dated earlier than the night when he might have been involved in the bomb-planting. Supporting a fake alibi is a crime.”

Tucker looked a bit deflated, but he kept his cool. “I had no intent to do anything wrong. I must have confused the dates; that’s all.”

Debbie turned away from Tom Tucker. “Herb; it’s show time.”

Herb Greene stood and pulled a small spiral notebook out of his back pocket. “Mr. Tucker, my audit isn’t complete yet, but I have found thirty-two instances when you invested foundation funds in a firm called Distributive Arrangements, Inc. Would you mind giving us details about that firm? Why was it a good place to invest foundation money?"

Tucker noticed people leaning forward in their chairs to better hear what he would say. "Mr. Greene, this isn't the place for an audit discussion, and I don't have my analysis notes and spreadsheets with me."

"I'll simplify my questions so that you won't require analytical data. Is it not true that the principal shareholder in Distributive Arrangements, Inc. is Sam Monahan? I also discovered that the principal business activity of that firm is the funding of a subsidiary, Wisconsin Corrective Ventures, Inc. Tell us what they do."

"They fund charitable projects in poorer regions of our state."

Herb Greene turned toward Jonathan Danforth. "Jonathan, I thought I saw you reacting when I mentioned Wisconsin Corrective Ventures. Why was that?"

"That was the name under which Manny Ortega and his two associates bought a car from me at the Ford dealership."

Herb nodded. "That would make sense, because Manny Ortega is listed in public records as the president of Wisconsin Corrective Ventures, Inc."

Marie waved for attention. "Herb, if I understand you correctly, Tom Tucker got me to agree to invest foundation funds in a company run by Sam Monahan that bankrolled Manny Ortega, Tony Ganlio, and himself in his guise as Sam Finch. Those three used that money to influence my relatives to try to take control of our family foundation."

Herb said, "Marie, your logic is perfect. In my auditor capacity, I'll certify that you are rehabilitated to the point of being capable of running the foundation again, should you wish to do so."

"We'll discuss that later. Right now, I want to know why I was funding efforts to wrest control of the foundation from me."

Gil Beecher said, "Not to mention the bombing of Jonathan's car and an attempt to murder you. It's all tied together."

Tom Tucker dropped into his chair. "I knew nothing about any plans for violence. I'm an easy-going staff support guy. I only made a questionable investment in a relative's company. Pat Flynn will vouch for my character."

Pat rose to her feet as soon as she heard her name. "Hold it right there, Buster. I made a play for you as a back-door way to get influence on the way the family money was spent. You weren't bad in bed, but I'm not hooking my wagon to the illegal things you did. You wanted to push my candidacy for management so that you'd have even more control over the money."

Tom could be at least as angry as this witch. "Flip that logic, Flynn. You seduced me to get me to invest in your construction projects and to push for you to get the management position if it opened up. You couldn't move into Marie's office through a normal route, so you tried to finesse your way in through my bedroom. I wouldn't put it past you to have been driving that car that hit Marie."

These back-and-forth rants had a refreshing effect on Sergeant Erik Greuner. He thought of that old adage about *when thieves fall out.* He decided to contribute to the rising level of anxiety in the room. "As a matter of fact, the Stevens Point Police are considering the possibility that the driver of that car was a woman. Were you that driver, Mrs. Flynn?"

"Are you crazy? I'd never do anything like that. I certainly wouldn't attack a relative."

Tom Tucker said, "You've certainly attacked Marie verbally. How much more would it take for you to go after her physically?"

"You bastard. Some lover you turned out to be. Mr. Greene, don't limit your audit to Tom's investments in Sam Monahan's company. He told me about some other special projects, and I'll be more than happy to share that information with you."

Gil Beecher stepped into the center of the oval space. "I think we've had enough name-calling for now. Debbie, please escort Pat Flynn to a seat at the kitchen table, where she will tell Herb Greene about those other questionable investments she mentioned. Jeremy, please take Tom Tucker over to where Sergeant Greuner is standing. I expect they'll be leaving together."

Tom looked shocked. "Are you arresting me? I had nothing to do with any of the crimes you mentioned."

Greuner stepped toward Tom and grasped his arm.

Beecher said, "We will be placing you under arrest. We have several potential charges including embezzling, funding of a criminal enterprise, and possibly being an accessory to attempted murder."

"Are you referring to that bomb under Jonathan's car? I had no knowledge of that or anything else that Sam and his friends did."

"We'll give you a pass on that one, but we executed a search warrant at Sam's apartment per Debbie Hadley's suggestion. We found a woman's wig there, and when we took a picture of Sam wearing the wig, our witness to the attack on Marie identified Sam as the driver who hit her."

Tom Tucker decided to brazen it out. "It's a shock to learn that Sam tried to kill Marie, but that has nothing to do with me."

"Sorry, Tom, that bird won't fly. You're the one who told Sam when Marie would go to the Portage County Public Library. Sam told us that and said that it was your idea to get rid of Marie so that someone else could run the foundation. Marie suspected that you were frosting the investment cake with self-serving speculations, and you wanted her out of the way. That makes you an accessory to attempted murder. Sergeant Greuner will read you your rights. You're about to invest some of your time in a stay at the Stevens Point jail.

CHAPTER 93 – DEBBIE HADLEY

After the guests had left, Marie made coffee and sat down at the kitchen table to rehash the evening's events with Debbie and Jeremy.

Jeremy kicked off the discussion by expressing amusement. "I thought the funniest discovery of that group session was that Sam Monahan was funding the threesome of Manny, Tony and himself as Sam Finch. Sam Finch was the junior member of that trio. The others treated him as a gofer, and he was the one telling Manny what to do and supplying the money. Gil Beecher told me unofficially that Sam admitted to paying the fancy lawyers and then changing his mind when he decided they wouldn't be able to get his buddies off without jail time. Sam must have enjoyed keeping Manny and Tony in the dark about what was really going on."

Marie chuckled at that thought and then asked, "Debbie, how did you know so much about the family relationships of Tom Tucker and Sam Monahan?"

"You told me where to look, Marie."

"I did? I don't remember that conversation."

"That's because it didn't actually happen. After the car hit you, you said a few things during the time when you first entered the emergency room at the hospital. You don't remember what you said, but Dr. Pasqua told me you mumbled something about going back to Gettysburg and repeated it several times. Later, Austin Carmichael, the chief librarian, told me that their staff researchers had discovered that during your library visit you studied papers concerning the Wisconsin Sharpshooters and municipal papers from Fox Lake, Wisconsin."

Marie said, "I don't remember studying those papers or talking about Gettysburg, Debbie."

"Don't worry. Dr. Pasqua said that you may always have that doughnut hole in your memories. He said it's normal in trauma cases like yours. Anyway, I took your three research ingredients, Gettysburg, Wisconsin Sharpshooters, and Fox Lake, and decided that you were studying the family of Lieutenant Colonel George Stevens' brother Charlie."

"That sounds vaguely familiar and possible."

"I remembered your telling us that George Stevens gave Cyrus Danforth a promissory note to give to Charlie to get funds for traveling to Australia. Charlie provided the money, but presumably kept the promissory note as a remembrance of his brother or an accounting record. I realized that if someone in Charlie's family traced their genealogy as I did for our family, he or she would find the promissory note and want to learn more about Cyrus Danforth and the reason for Charlie giving him money."

Jeremy said, "That's logical, but wouldn't George Stevens' family already have something on Cyrus in their archives? Cyrus promised George he would look in on the baby who had not yet arrived at the time of George's death. That turned out to be his daughter, Lucy."

Debbie said, "I'm sure Cyrus did follow up on that godfathering promise, but he wouldn't have said anything about his work to aid veterans of the 2nd Wisconsin Regiment because of his promise to keep George's backing of that work invisible. George's family wouldn't have any reason to check on Cyrus Danforth's project, but Charlie's family might suspect that they'd lost out on a deserved inheritance. If they found out about Cyrus's charitable project, they would feel that they had earned a slice of it because of Charlie's funding of the voyage to Australia to claim the gold deposits there."

Jeremy said, "So you traced the family tree for Charlie Stevens' family and found both Sam Monahan and Tom Tucker."

Debbie said, "Marie, I'm beginning to understand your comments and teases about Jeremy. It took a hell of a lot of work for me to unearth those family relationships, and he makes it sound trivial. Thanks a lot, Jeremy."

"I'm sorry, Debbie. I know that I wouldn't have been able to trace those family connections. Who do you suppose was the first one in the Charlie Stevens' family to envy our foundation?"

"I suspect it was Aunt Alice. She was Tom Tucker's godmother, and her sister was Sam Monahan's mother. She had links to both of our culprits. She probably discovered our project before Tom went to work for the foundation seven years ago."

Marie asked, "Is Alice still living, Debbie? Do you think she might be the mastermind behind everything?"

"Alice is still living, but quite old and in a retirement home. I think we can give her a pass on any possible involvement. It wouldn't serve anyone to go after her."

CHAPTER 94 – PLANNING SESSION

Herb Greene completed his detailed audit presentation to an audience consisting of Marie Danforth, Debbie and Jeremy Hadley, and Jonathan Danforth in the Stevens Point office of the Danforth Family Foundation.

"In summary, the foundation suffered some minor losses over the last several years due to Tom Tucker having inserted several of his self-serving projects into his investment list. Dollarwise, these losses were appreciable, but they were negligible as a percentage of total assets. Marie, I have to point out that your easy-going management style and tendency to overly trust people facilitated Tucker's deceptions. On your side of the operation, there were more than a few charitable donations that did not fit within the foundation's charter of supporting descendant families of veterans of the 2nd Regiment Wisconsin Volunteer Infantry. Those would have been justifiable contributions if the charter's restraints did not exist."

Debbie looked over her printed version of Herb's presentation. "Thank you for your diligent efforts, Herb. I agree with everything you've said, and I'll sign your documents indicating my approval. I'd now like to present a few thoughts of my own."

Herb sat down. "The stage is yours, Debbie."

"Before I insert my own viewpoints into this discussion, I want to invite Herb to temporarily assume the responsibilities of acting as our investment analyst. Tom Tucker's arrest leaves an expertise void that must be filled. Will you accept that temporary assignment, Herb?"

"Certainly, Debbie; I was going to suggest the same step later in the meeting."

"Good. Now it's time for me to introduce a touch of heresy into the goals of this hallowed institution that's more than a century and a half old. My first observation is that I can see very little justification for keeping the charter of any organization unchanged for more than one hundred and fifty years. It is also getting increasingly difficult to identify the descendants of 2nd Wisconsin veterans who qualify for our support. My third observation is that all of the crimes, jealousy, and avarice we have recently suffered have stemmed from the large assets of our foundation."

Marie said, "True, but what are you suggesting as a cure for that?"

"I recommend that our planning for the future should be of the sunset variety. We should develop a plan for either distributing all of our assets over an appropriate period of time, or we should merge with a larger compatible foundation and then let them run the surviving organization. We have far outgrown the goals initially set by George H. Stevens and Cyrus Danforth. Whichever path we choose will require new broader definitions of our charitable funding goals. I recommend that we discuss my comments and then call upon Jonathan Danforth to present the long-term projects that he has developed or at least considered."

Marie stared at Debbie. "After all my years managing the foundation, you want to put it out of business?"

"I'm afraid so, Marie. It has grown to be a monster that will devour us all if we continue to run it as a family operation. You and Jonathan almost died from criminal assaults by people who wanted to control our piggy bank. There will be similar attacks in the future if we don't make the money target disappear or put it into the hands of a major organization with secure procedures. I'm also serving notice that I'm willing to manage the foundation on a temporary basis, but I will not commit my career to it. Herb, you're the professional among us. How do you react to my viewpoints?"

"I find them logical and persuasive. This foundation has essentially outgrown family operation. We can define new funding guidelines that let us use up our assets; we can continue as we are and pay a group of high-priced professionals to run the organization for us; or we can find a larger foundation with similar outlook and goals to be a merger partner. In any event, the personal aspect of foundation operation is obsolete and dangerous. If attacks from relatives and criminals don't cause trouble, government regulations and lawsuits will. Proper management of large asset pools requires rigid safeguard procedures and documentation, which you will never tolerate as individuals."

Debbie said, "Marie, Grandma, this is your baby. Tell us how you feel about the future."

"I'll tell you one thing. I don't want any Danforth family member, especially you, to go through the physical ordeal that I've suffered. Let's hold up on further discussions until we've heard from Jonathan. I suspect he's come up with some interesting project ideas."

Jonathan bowed slightly to the others and then walked over to the chalkboard. "When Debbie took center stage, I was apprehensive that her advance thinking would negate the ideas I've considered to date. Instead, her views turned out to be well aligned with mine. My first project suggestion is that we open up our distributions to descendants of all Civil War veterans from both sides. There are approximately eighteen million living descendants of those veterans. If we distributed our entire pool of assets, we would give each living descendant a check for slightly less than two hundred dollars. My second project suggestion is that we go beyond scholarships and assist 2nd Wisconsin Regiment descendants with college and mortgage loan repayments. My third project ..."

Marie interrupted. "I expected major conflicts during these discussions. We're too compatible. How about you Jeremy? You've been silent so far. What do you see wrong with the direction the conversation has taken?"

"The only thing that bothers me is that you, Marie, end up on the sidelines without a major responsibility. If the foundation is taken over or disappears due to distribution of all of its assets, what will you do? You need a new long-term project."

"I knew I loved this boy. I have a project all picked out that requires cooperation from you and your wife. Jeremy, you and Debbie are due to start a family. If you two have babies, I'll put on my great-grandmother hat and help you take care of them, even if that requires that I move away from Stevens Point. That's a long-term project I would definitely enjoy more than managing the Danforth Family Foundation."

- END -

ACKNOWLEDGEMENTS

I recently wrote a longer version of Chapter 5 under the title “I Will Not Be a Number” in the anthology *Gettysburg Inspirations*, published earlier in 2017 by Red Engine Press. Both versions were drawn from my experiences during a 2016 writers’ retreat in Gettysburg, sponsored by the Military Writers Society of America. I read the name of Lietenant Colonel George H. Stevens on his gravestone in the Wisconsin section of Soldiers National Cemetery in Gettysburg, and I decided to find out as much as I could about his life. Everything about George Stevens contained in this book resulted from that research. He did spend three years in Australia, but I don’t know whether he prospected for gold while he was there. At that point the fictional version of his life kicks in.

The post Civil War outlaw material is based on a variety of online sources plus Cole Younger’s 1903 memoir. I found it refreshing to draw upon the recollections of someone who took part in those events, even though Cole wrote his book partially to justify his actions.

The orphan trains and the need to find homes for many children orphaned by the Civil War are topics which readers may want to study further. All wars leave shattered lives and bodies in their wakes. The American Civil War was one of the worst, especially because modern medical techniques and equipment had not yet arrived on the scene.

Richard Davidson

ABOUT THE AUTHOR

Richard Davidson is the author of the self-help guidebook: *DECISION TIME! Better Decisions for a Better Life*. He has written the five-novel Lord's Prayer Mystery Series: *Lead Us Not into Temptation*, *Give Us this Day our Daily Bread*, *Forgive Us Our Trespasses*, *Thy Will Be Done*, and *Deliver Us from Evil.* He has edited an anthology, *Overcoming: An Anthology by the Writers of* OCWW. His latest four novels, *Implications, Impulses, Impostor*, and Impending, from his current series, the Imp Mysteries, continue to chronicle the exploits of Arthur Blake and the investigative associates who aided him in the earlier mystery series, taking their interests in new directions. Mr. Davidson is Past President of Off-Campus Writers' Workshop, the oldest ongoing group of its kind in the U.S. and is the founder of the ReadWorthy Books Book Review Blog. He is also the founder of the Independent Mystery Publishing Society (IMPS). Mr. Davidson is a Certified Lay Servant Speaker and a former Lay Leader in the United Methodist Church. He is an aeronautical & astronautical engineer.

WORKS BY THIS AUTHOR

NONFICTION:

DECISION TIME! Better Decisions for a Better Life,

RADMAR Publishing

ISBN 978-0-9829160-7-0 (2nd edition paperback)

ISBN 978-1-4581-8395-8 (Smashwords eBook)

ASIN B014QFZP68 (Kindle Edition eBook)

Where you are in life today is the result of all of the past decisions you have made or which have been made for you in response to the various situations and events that have impacted your life. The decisions that you will make from this point forward will determine the degree to which your future will be positive or negative. *DECISION TIME!* gives you insight into the subjective decision-making process as applied to both small and large choices you will face. It includes dynamic aspects, cultural effects, and morality as applied to decision-making for individuals, teams, corporations, and societies. *DECISION TIME!* prepares you to face continuous decisions confidently and without hesitation.

FICTION:

Lead Us Not into Temptation (The Lord's Prayer Mystery Series, Volume I),

RADMAR Publishing

ISBN 978-0-9976381-0-3 (2nd edition paperback)

ASIN B01GEK7ZZ2 (Kindle Edition eBook)

Arthur Blake, former NASA engineer turned minister, receives an emergency appointment to be pastor of the United Methodist Church in Parkville, a distant suburb of Chicago, following the bizarre sudden death of the church's unusual former pastor. Pastor Blake's attempts to unravel the mystery that shrouds his predecessor become involved with tracking the child of a possibly bigamous soldier in World War II England; art and jewelry treasures plundered by the Nazis and their sympathizers; and the eventual results of childhood sibling conflicts in combined families. Arthur's allies in his investigation include Parkville Police Chief Bobby Andrews, County Medical Examiner Irma Custis, and the married team of Penny and Joe Gonzalez who work for a clandestine government agency. During the course of *Lead Us Not into Temptation,* the reader discovers how seemingly minor historical events lead to major present-day dislocations in church, village, and family relationships.

Give Us this Day Our Daily Bread (The Lord's Prayer Mystery Series, Volume II)

RADMAR Publishing

ISBN 978-0-9829160-5-6 (2nd edition paperback)

ASIN B01H7M47M0 (Kindle Edition eBook)

Arthur Blake, Pastor of Parkville United Methodist Church, has to deal with the aftereffects of a traumatic communion incident. He works to assist the authorities in investigating the cause while doing his best to convince members of his congregation that it is safe to return to church. Working with the police and federal agencies, he discovers that the terror of the initial event is minor compared with the potential chaotic impact of future disasters being planned by the perpetrator. The investigation is interwoven with several relationship situations that affect the final outcome.

Forgive Us Our Trespasses (The Lord's Prayer Mystery Series, Volume III)

RADMAR Publishing

ISBN 978-0-9976381-1-0 (2nd edition paperback)

ASIN B01IQ1TJXS (Kindle Edition eBook)

Arthur Blake, Pastor of Parkville United Methodist Church, tries to assist his father to resolve his trauma after learning that his best friend, recently killed in a car accident, may have been an imposter with a heinous background. The investigation reveals that the presumed accident was but one link in a chain of murders. Blake works to determine the true identity of his father's friend, while also discovering the man's past activities and affiliations. Arthur works to solve the murders in conjunction with his colleagues at ABC Consultants. He also draws on assistance from associates at a covert government agency with which he has worked before. The coordinated effort to solve the puzzle examines incidents that span the period between World War II and the present in order to defuse the personal, national, and international dangers resulting from them.

Thy Will Be Done (The Lord's Prayer Mystery Series, Volume IV)

RADMAR Publishing

ISBN 978-0-9829160-2-5 (paperback)

ASIN B009JU6EZM (Kindle Edition eBook)

The sudden death of a young woman attending Parkville United Methodist Church infuriates her brother and leads to congregational outrage over his outburst and subsequent murder. The investigation of that slaying by Pastor Arthur Blake and his associates leads to revelations of a previously undetected criminal organization operating in the area. Unraveling the mystery and scope of this group entangles Arthur and his associated investigators in a web of conspiracies extending from Illinois to both U.S. coasts and through Mexico to Guatemala.

Deliver Us from Evil (The Lord's Prayer Mystery Series, Volume V)

RADMAR Publishing

ISBN 978-0-9829160-3-2 (paperback)

ASIN B00EBDUXFY (Kindle Edition eBook)

Arthur and Irma's wedding day has finally arrived, but an unexpected interruption leads to their need to investigate a possible murder committed by someone close to them. With the aid of friends and federal agents Penny and Joe Gonzalez, they follow a series of clues, crisscrossing the United States to learn more about the murder, related subsequent events, and the significance of a rare object brought home by a veteran of the Iraq War. A second murder close to Pastor Arthur Blake's church involves them in a new investigation, assisting Parkville Police Chief Bobby Andrews. Are these murders and the tracking of that strange object connected? Will marriage deteriorate or improve the relationship between Arthur and Irma? Character flaws in many relationships color the outcome.

Overcoming: An Anthology by the Writers of OCWW

Edited and with an Introduction by Richard Davidson

RADMAR Publishing

ISBN 978-9829160-4-9 (paperback)

ASIN B00E80NN4I (Kindle Edition eBook)

This anthology covers many aspects of overcoming life's problems, obstacles, and challenging developments. The contributing writers have used fiction, non-fiction, memoir, poetry, historical chronicle, and drama to highlight our continuing need to overcome our problems, rather than dwell on them. The reader will learn from many talented writers the skills needed to respond constructively, energetically, and sometimes humorously to whatever obstacle bars one's path. Apply their lessons to your own needs and to those of others you cherish.

Implications: An Arthur Blake Mystery Novel (Imp Mysteries, Volume 1)

RADMAR Publishing

ISBN 978-0-9829160-6-3 (paperback)

ASIN B00LY9IBWK (Kindle Edition eBook)

Bishop Howard Chandler has assigned Pastor Arthur Blake to investigate the burning of a church in the small city of Amboy, Illinois. He learns from that church's pastor that she had to overcome past improprieties by former members. During the investigation of the fire's cause, Arthur and the other state fire investigators uncover disturbing aspects of the ninety-year-old church's design and history. Arthur calls on his federal associates for assistance, as the investigation of a local church fire expands to seeking solutions to related crimes occurring from the present to recent years and back to the Prohibition Era. Progress in the investigation intertwines with new developments in Arthur's family life.

Impulses: An Arthur Blake Mystery Novel (Imp Mysteries, Volume 2)

RADMAR Publishing

ISBN 978-0-9829160-8-7 (paperback)

ASIN B012LFQXYI (Kindle Edition eBook)

Several disturbing dreams cause Arthur Blake to wonder whether he is trying to do too much for the many people who seek his services. These qualms are complicated by Bishop Howard Chandler's suggestion that Arthur temporarily set aside his official duties and take an extended sabbatical leave. His resulting internal debates about career moves are set aside when the pastor who replaced him at the Parkville church dies in an apparent suicide possibly linked to several deaths at the Parkville Rehabilitation Home. The bishop assigns Arthur to determine the circumstances behind the new pastor's death, while Arthur and Irma, his wife and constant investigative partner, also study a mysterious shipment at his father's antiques shop. The sudden disappearance of a young associate provides another mystery and leads to questions of life after death and reincarnation. Events that initially appear simple become increasingly complex as the true natures of many people come into question.

Impostor: A Genealogical Mystery (Imp Mysteries, Volume 3)

RADMAR Publishing

ISBN 978-0-9829160-9-4 (paperback)

ASIN B01FZQZEK4 (Kindle Edition eBook)

When Debbie Danforth discovers a flaw in the genealogy of her live-in boyfriend, Jeremy Hadley, he and his family try to discredit her findings, but eventually admit they must be true. Jeremy and Debbie run a private detective business, the Sandley Agency and commit their skills and resources to learning about the impostor Debbie has discovered in the Hadley ancestry. They are assisted in this effort by Penny and Joe Gonzalez, principals in a covert federal agency, with whom Jeremy has previously worked as a consultant. Their joint investigation uncovers both unique details concerning the mysterious Hadley impostor and little-known facts about events leading up to World War II in both Britain and the United States. Was the person who masqueraded as a Hadley a villain or a hero? Did other Hadleys know he was a fraudulent member of their family? Did his actions assist or impede the British and the Americans as they faced the growing menace in prewar Europe?

Impending: A Genealogical Mystery (Imp Mysteries, Volume 4)

RADMAR Publishing

ISBN 978-0-9976381-2-7 (paperback)

Young married private detectives, Debbie and Jeremy Hadley, discover that Debbie's family, the Danforths, have a family secret. Grandma Marie Danforth summons them because she fears that alienated family members and underworld characters will attempt to wrest control of the secret from her. The history of the secret begins at the American Civil War Battle of Gettysburg and develops through a century and a half of Danforth family twists and intrigues. Although written as a continuous story, *Impending* actually is two novels in one: the saga of how the secret developed from its inception to the present day, and the mystery of how to counter multiple attempts to hijack it. *Impending* is history and mystery all-in-one. Debbie and Jeremy team with police from two cities to unravel the mystery and reach its surprising conclusion.

Learn more about the writings, humor, and random thoughts of Richard Davidson at: radmarinc.com davidsonbookshelf.com betterlifedecisions.blogspot.com and at the Independent Mystery Publishing Society (IMPS) https://www.mysteryimps.com

Richard Davidson's author page on Amazon is located at https://www.amazon.com/author/richarddavidson
Follow and *Like* Richard Davidson, Author on Facebook at https://www.facebook.com/richarddavidsonauthor?ref=hl
Follow him on Twitter @mysteryimp

www.ingramcontent.com/pod-product-compliance
Lightning Source LLC
Chambersburg PA
CBHW051236260626
47162CB00002B/453

* 9 7 8 0 9 9 7 6 3 8 1 2 7 *